Barry Wardle was born and raised in South Shields. He served a five year apprenticeship as a Marine Fitter and then joined the Merchant Navy visiting Japan, Singapore. Hong Kong and Australia.

After he married, he and his wife emigrated to South Africa, and then moved to Rhodesia where he volunteered for the Police Reserve and then the Police Anti Terrorist Unit. The author's two children were both born in Rhodesia.

When independence was granted in Rhodesia, the family moved back to the UK. However Barry found it hard to settle. He went to Angola with his second wife, Maureen, and worked in the Diamond Mines as a mechanical foreman. He then worked in Guinea, again on the Diamond Mines, as a Plant Maintenance Superintendent. Maureen travelled with him on both occasions.

Barry now lives in Cleveland with his second wife of 22 years, Maureen.

OPERATION
HURRICANE

Barry Wardle

Operation Hurricane

Vanguard Press

A CIP catalogue record for this title is
available from the British Library
ISBN 1 84386 192 5

Vanguard Press is an imprint of
Pegasus Elliot MacKenzie Publishers Ltd.
www.pegasuspublishers.com

First Published in 2005

Vanguard Press
Sheraton House Castle Park
Cambridge England

Printed & Bound in Great Britain

Dedication

Since the late 1950's, Communist trained black Rhodesians were crossing back into Rhodesia to wage a war of intimidation, mutilation and terror against their fellow tribesmen, and the isolated white farming communities. Their sole purpose was to bring down the white government and to impose self rule, regardless of the suffering or loss of human life. This book is dedicated to those who paid the ultimate sacrifice, and to those who lived through those years and can recall the horrors of OPERATION HURRICANE.

And to my wife, Maureen, who has given me total support and encouraged me to write this novel.

Also to Ian, my son, and Sharon, my daughter, who were born in Rhodesia during the "Operation Hurricane" conflict.

I love you all.

The most valuable thing that everyone has is worth nothing until you give it away.

A Smile.

Acknowledgements

Karen Spowart, our neighbour and trusted friend of many years, for her hard work and advice during the proof reading of this book.

OPERATION HURRICANE

As darkness filled the evening sky, taking away the security of daylight, three figures emerged from the undergrowth, they were dirty, aching, and hungry. They had been hidden in the thick African bush for three days, watching every movement, looking for a soft target, waiting for the right moment to strike, their biggest worry was the Rhodesian security forces who were in the area. If they were spotted they would very quickly be killed. They knew that they must strike tonight, and start their campaign of terror to drive the white farmers from the land, then and only then could they move to the towns and cities, and ultimately take control of the country.

Joshua Matabu was like many other black Rhodesians, who believed that Rhodesia would be a better place to live in if it were governed by a black government. He had left Rhodesia to undergo training in Mozambique and Zambia, Joshua had been a very willing recruit, and soon caught the attention of his communist masters. After spending two years of intensive training he was sent back to Rhodesia with three other freedom fighters, their orders were to disrupt the farming community, hit isolated farmhouses, then disappear into the night, always strike at dusk, and under no circumstances were they to engage the security forces. Hit and run, blend in with the locals, trust no one, not even your own tribesmen, not even your own family, not even your own shadow.

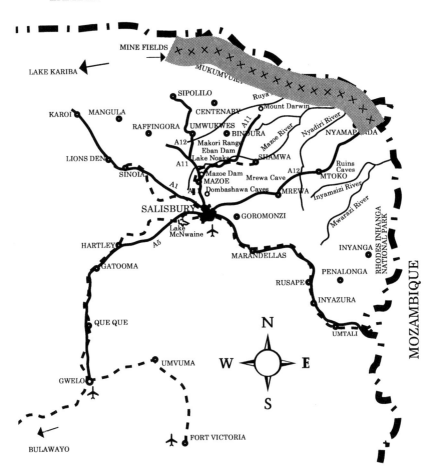

Chapter One

Tony and Joyce Marshal had been farming for the last ten years; it had always been his wish to follow in the footsteps of his parents and grandparents. His grandparents Raymond and Grace had emigrated from Scotland, when Rhodesia was just virgin bush, there were no houses, no roads, no hospitals, and no means of communication, they had to start from scratch. Life had been very hard, full of sweat, blood and tears, but through sheer determination they had carved out a life for themselves, that was forty- two years ago. As they grew older their son Hammond took over the running of the farm, enabling them to retire.

Eventually, Hammond married and their first grandchild was born. He was called Anthony, life was perfect, it had never been better, the farm was doing very well, there was no debt, but soon this would change forever.

Hammond and his wife Susan decided to visit Kenya, he asked his parents if they would look after their son while they were away, they said it would be a pleasure and not to worry, just go and have a good holiday. Hammond and Susan drove to Kenya and spent an unforgettable time, sightseeing, going on safari, and in general having a good time and relaxing without a care in the world. On their way home disaster struck, as they were driving through the night, eager to see their son, they were both killed instantly in a car crash. The news devastated his parents but life had to go on. They now had the added responsibility not only of running the farm once again, but to bring up their little grandson. The years soon passed, and Tony was now in his final year at University, but once again disaster struck the family, with the sudden death of his grandfather. Tony was thrown in at the deep end, and had to make all the decisions and run the farm on his own.

Tony was now married to his childhood sweet heart Joyce, and they had their own little bundle of joy, Benji. He was two years old, and what a hand full. Tony was often glad to go to work in the early morning to get some peace; he was working from first light until bedtime. He enjoyed working on the farm, it was tiring work, the sun was blistering hot, the work was heavy and sweaty, but it was the only life he knew, and he loved it, he was determined to make a go of it, he owed it to his parents and grandparents, and to be honest he knew nothing else but farming. Tony was now twenty six years old, six foot tall, with not an ounce of fat on his body, his hair was bleached blonde, and his skin was a golden brown from working in the sun all day.

Joyce was a year younger, she was five foot six, slim build, with raven black hair and a healthy sun tan, she was determined to do her fair share on the farm as well as bringing up their son. She loved swimming and horse riding, and was a member of the local Bisley rifle club. Tony on the other hand liked a few beers with the other farmers, either at their local pub the Dungeon, about twenty miles away in Bindura, or at the occasional barbeques that the farmers took in turns to have at their farms. Tony was sports mad, enjoying rugby, and swimming, but due to the turning tide of events, he was heavily involved in PATU, the Police Anti -Terrorist Unit.

Tony drove fast through the farm gates, reddish brown dust rose in thick swirls behind his Landrover. He stopped the engine, jumped out, and walked briskly onto the veranda. "I'm home" he shouted as he dropped into the chair. "I could kill a cold beer love", he called out.

"I saw you coming, long before I heard you", said Joyce, as she walked onto the veranda. "Here's your beer love, you look shattered, get it down your neck, dinner won't be long.

Tony took a long slow mouth full of the cold lager, "It's like bloody nectar. He shouted through to Joyce, who had gone back to the kitchen. "Do me a favour darling, bring me another one." Tony eased his back off the chair; his shirt was sticking to him with the sweat. He lifted his left arm, and lowered his head to his armpit.

"Bloody hell I smell."

At that moment Benji toddled into the room.

"Now my little tiger." he said, as he lifted him up. "and what have you been up to today". he said, as he bounced him on his knee. "Here before your Mam comes in".

Tony held the can of lager up to Benji's mouth; he grabbed it with both hands and took a mouth full. Tony moved the can to his own mouth, just as Joyce walked onto the veranda. "I'm watching you, you must think I'm daft, he will end up a real boozer just like his father".

"It will do him no harm," replied Tony, "I'm making sure that he grows up to be a true Rhodesian."

Tony showered and sat down to have his dinner.

"It's been a hard one today love," he said, "Every thing has gone wrong: I got a puncture, the tractor has a fuel leak, and half the workers didn't show up for work...."

"Before I forget," interrupted Joyce, "I looked on the calendar, and next week end it is our turn to have a barbeque."

" No problem love, can you ring round? Better still I will do it tonight, before I forget all about it, and the last one at Robin and Sara's was a great night. You know I really enjoy the crack, yes, let's go for it, next weekend it is then."

The remainder of the week seemed to drag. Tony drove to Bindura to pick up the extra meat and vegetables, but most important, the booze. It would be an overkill as usual, far too much wine, but it would come in useful for the next time. As for the beer and the lager, well you can never have too much of that can you thought Tony.

Sunday afternoon was soon upon them, and everything was almost ready. Tony kept looking at his watch, he was itching to open a beer, but he knew it was more than his life was worth. 'You just can't wait can you,' Joyce would say, 'you have always had to be the first to start on the beer.' Tony turned and looked into the darkening sky. He could have sworn he could hear the sound of an approaching vehicle. His hand reached towards the cans of lager, he quickly pulled his hand away as he looked to where Joyce was standing. He closed his eyes and looked up to the sky, it's a landi he thought to himself, our guests have started to arrive. He walked over to the side of the farm house, and there in the distance he could see the headlights of an approaching vehicle. He turned quickly and walked towards the braai, and gave it a good poke. Glowing sparks rose in a shower, the charcoal was glowing red. He picked up some more logs from the pile, and placed them on the embers. 'Give it another hour and we will be ready to party.'

Alan Crompton was the first to arrive he was Tony's nearest neighbour who farmed, no more than three miles north of Tony's farm, Camburo.

As the Land rover pulled to a halt, Tony walked over and held out his hand, "now my mate, and how the hell are you?"

Alan shook his hand, We are fine Tony just fine, and how is Joyce?"

"Oh she is just the same as the last time that you saw her, and how are you Karen?" asked Tony, as he kissed her on the cheek. Karen did not answer, she was off into the farm house to see Joyce, they really were the best of friends. Tony walked over to the table near to the braai, and pulled the rings on two cans of lager. "Are we the first to arrive?" asked Alan.

"You are the first to arrive", replied Tony. "You're never the bloody last when there is booze and food on the go. Come on lets get stuck into the lager." He handed a can of Lion Lager to Alan, "Good health mate."

Just then two more vehicles arrived. Tony walked over to greet his guests, Richard and Mandy who were from Shamva, which is a small mining town about twenty miles away as the crow flies. The couple lived on the outskirts of the town and had a tobacco and cotton farm. They were both Rhodesians and were in their early thirties. Richard and Mandy had been farming for about five years and they took it very seriously indeed, as they knew the rewards from their hard work would be worthwhile if they stuck at it. They also liked to enjoy themselves though, and always jumped at the chance for a party.

"Hi", said Tony "nice to see you both again, Alan is here with Karen. Just go through and help yourself to a drink, I will be with you in a moment".

Robin and Sarah were laughing their heads off as they approached Tony, Sarah gave Tony a big hug and a kiss, "I'm really looking forward to this," said Sarah and "I'm in the mood to party all night."

Robin just shook his head and said, "I don't know where she gets all the energy from, I get exhausted just watching her."

"You just enjoy yourself," said Tony, "I think we are in for a good night."

Nigel and Debbie were the last to arrive as they lived the farthest away at Mount Darwin, and would be staying a few days if at all possible, it all depended on the weather. It had been a very dry year, with intense heat, and no one could afford to be away from their farms too long, but everyone needed a break. They had been farming for as long as anyone could remember, their two children had grown up, and much to their disappointment had decided to work in the city rather than go into farming. This had blown a great big hole in Nigel's plans as they thought that they would automatically hand everything over to their son and daughter and then retire.

As usual, the men sat outside drinking, while the women sat inside, catching up on all the gossip. Roars of laughter drifted into the living room, the beer and lager were going down a treat. "What a life," said Alan, "You know this is Gods own country, can you believe the lifestyle that we have got? I know we have to work hard, but bloody hell man, I couldn't imagine living any where else in the whole bloody world. Hey Robin, don't hog all the booze; pass me another one, before I die of thirst."

Tony was showing off the shotgun that he had just bought, Nigel had it in his hands, "It's a beaut. And how much did you say you paid for it?"

"One hundred dollars, this guy is going back to the UK, and wanted a quick sale, so I took it off his hands," replied Tony. It was getting really dark now and the wood embers were glowing, "I think it is time that we got the meat on." said Tony. Just as he spoke Joyce walked over carrying a large tray of meat that she had prepared followed by the other woman with laden trays.

"Well as you're here," said Tony, "don't let me stop you from doing the honours, and show us how to cook on an open fire."

"You should be so lucky," replied Joyce, "Get to it, while the charcoal is just right, if you get stuck just shout."

Roars of laughter erupted,

"That's you put in your place, good one Joyce!" chuckled Nigel.

"Bloody hell," said Tony, "I get no support from you lot."

Stop your whinging and get cooking, your guests are getting hungry," said Richard. More meat was cooked, and an awful lot more beer was drank, the conversation was, as usual, sport and more sport. Eventually the women went indoors, and the conversation changed to jokes, then onto more topical subjects; the price of tobacco, cotton, and farming in general. Everyone had their own views, but one thing they all agreed on was the political situation.

For months now there had been a lot of sabre rattling amongst the black African countries, pushing for independence in Rhodesia. Ever since Northern Rhodesia was granted independence and became known as Zambia, black extremists had been waging a war of words, and threats, towards the white government of Rhodesia.

"Let the bastards come and try and take the country from us, then we will see how tough they are, bunch of bloody cowards." snarled Alan, "I bloody hate them, if it wasn't for us they would starve to death."

"You are totally prejudiced," said Tony, "You must give and take with these people, let's be honest, where would our farms be with out them. We could not survive without them, and you know it Alan."

"Absolute crap," said Alan, "I need them like a hole in the head." "You will possibly get one the way you treat your labour force." said Robin. Everyone started to laugh, it was well known throughout the farming community the total contempt, and hatred, that Alan had for the blacks. He knew deep down that he needed them to run his farm, but he would never admit it, he was a real stubborn old sod.

As the evening drew on it started to come in a bit chilly, everyone retired indoors, and Tony served up the coffee and the brandy. The conversation had now turned to fire arms, then the army, and eventually to the Police Anti Terrorist Unit that they all belonged to. Tony was a stick leader, he still went on regular training to keep himself sharp, but it had been very quiet for a long time now. They used to get the occasional call out when some one reported a sighting of some armed African in the area, but for months now it had been very quiet indeed.

"Look at the time," Karen suddenly said, "It's two o'clock in the morning, Come on Alan, we must be getting home."

"Ok love just one more for the road, and I will be with you." replied Alan.

"You never know when to stop do you, it's always one for the road. I don't know where he puts it, he must have hollow legs." said Karen.

"Woman will you stop bloody moaning, I'm coming." Alan

stood up and downed half a glass of brandy, "Right everyone, we are off home. Thank you very much indeed for a lovely evening, Tony, Joyce. We have really enjoyed the company."

Alan moved slowly towards the door." You're drunk," said Karen, "You're in no fit state to drive, here give me the car keys."

"No bloody way, woman, I'm more then capable of taking you home safely." replied Alan. He walked outside and got into his Landrover.

"Come on love, let's get home" said Alan in a jovial voice.

Tony and Joyce stood on the veranda, and watched the last guests depart. They had tried to talk Nigel and Debbie in to stopping over the night as they had arranged, but at the last moment they had decided to travel back to Mount Darwin.

"It was a good evening," said Joyce "I think everyone enjoyed themselves there was plenty of food and drink, and they all seemed to have had a good time".

Tony nodded his head and yawned, "I'm shattered, just leave all the dishes until the morning, lets get some sleep."

Joshua Matabu, Robert, Isaac and Ticky had been watching the road for more than two hours; their eyes were aching, and were beginning to play tricks on them. The clouds cast shadows on the ground, and the trees and bushes seemed to move.

"We are wasting our time" said Robert, "No one will be out this time of night.

"We saw them leave earlier today didn't we?" said Joshua, "Ok, maybe they won't be back to night, so we will try tomorrow."

Just as he spoke, he saw lights on the horizon. "Wait," he said, "look, light." They all looked at the headlights in the distance, slowly they came closer.

"Come on" said Joshua, "Tonight we will strike a blow for freedom."

Alan Crompton let out a loud belch.

"You have had too much to drink." said Karen, "You never know when to stop, you always have to have one more than any one else."

"Woman," said Alan "it's been a great night, so don't spoil it with your moaning. How often do we get to unwind, we are home in one piece aren't we." He stopped the Land Rover.

"I'll get out and open the gates," said Karen, "If you have to do it in your state, we will be here all night." Karen opened the Land Rover door and stepped onto the mud road. She quickly walked over to the fence and reached for the gate, a slight sound behind her made her turn.

"I told you I will open the gates..." she started to say. As she looked over her shoulder, her mouth dropped wide open with shock. Standing in front of her was an African with a horrible smile on his face. "Who the hell are you?!" she cried. "What do you want?"

Joshua spat into her face, and opened fire.

"Die bitch." he said, as a full magazine tore into her body. Karen was dead before she hit the ground. Alan was sitting half asleep in the cab, and woke with a start; he looked through the wind screen, and peered into the night. The blood drained from his face as he saw an African looking at him. With an agonized scream Alan scrambled out of the land rover and stumbled over to the lifeless body of his wife.

"You bastard!" he yelled, as he lunged forward. His body stopped as he felt a blow to his chest, the bayonet of Joshua's AK47 sliced through the flesh, the force of the blow had broken two of Alan's ribs. He felt the warm rush of blood as it ran down his stomach, then the intense pain began to radiate through his body. With a vindictive twist Joshua withdrew the bayonet as Alan slowly slumped to his knees dead! Joshua held his AK47 above his head, "Victory" he yelled, "Burn the vehicle and let's get out of here."

Chapter Two

Tony slipped out of bed, taking care not to wake Joyce or Benji. He quickly got dressed, quietly went into the bathroom, gave his face a quick wash and made himself a strong cup of coffee. "Bloody hell, what time is it?" he thought to himself. He looked at his watch, six thirty. 'Oh shit.' he said to himself 'I'm knackered.' He took a sip of the coffee, and put the cup down, stretched his arms and yawned. 'I must be dreaming, this can't be true, I can't remember getting into bed.' Daylight was just breaking as he walked out of the house and closed the door; he climbed into the Land Rover and gunned the engine. As it roared into life, he drove through the farm gates and headed towards the tobacco sheds.

Crispen, his boss boy, was already at work, and organising the workers.

"Morning Crispen." Tony mumbled.

"Morning Mr Tony." he replied, "A late night sir?" asked Crispen.

"Don't ask." replied Tony, "I feel like shit. Thanks for getting things sorted; sometimes I just don't know what I would do without you." Tony smiled, and patted Crispen on the shoulder. He stood and looked around at the work force, rather sullen lot he thought to himself, everyone was working, but there was no singing. Usually you could not shut them up, no one was talking, very unusual he thought to himself. Tony walked over to Crispen and said "Is everything all right?"

Crispen looked up and frowned, "What does the boss mean, is every thing all right?"

"Exactly what I say, is every thing all right with the workers, I have never seen them so quiet, has someone died?"

'No,' replied Crispen, "No one has died, and nothing is wrong. Now let me do my work."

Tony stood in amazement, never before had Crispen spoken to him in that manner. Tony walked back to his Land Rover, climbed in, and started the engine.

"Surly bastard." he said to himself, "I give them the best of everything, especially him, and he talks to me as if I am the worker, and he is the boss." Before he realised, he was driving through the farmhouse gates, and had pulled up in front of the veranda.

"You're home early." said Joyce as she came out to meet him. Tony strode onto the veranda, went into the house and came out holding an open can of beer. Joyce smiled, "Hair of the dog, a little hung-over maybe?" she asked with a smile.

"No you're totally wrong" replied Tony, "No bloody hangover; I'm puzzled, angry and bloody annoyed. The workers are acting very strange, they are not singing or talking, normally I have to tell them to shut up. No one is even making eye contact with me. I spoke to Crispen, and he almost bit my bloody head off. I have never seen them like this before, but stuff them, if they want to act like children, then I will treat them like children."

Just then the telephone rang, Tony picked it up, "Now Mike," he said, "Of course you can, you know that you don't have to wait for an invite to visit us. What is so important that you can't speak over the phone? Ok then, as you wish, we will see you as soon as you arrive. I will wait here for you, bye,"

Tony frowned, "That was Mike Johnson, the Chief Inspector in charge at Bindura Police Station."

"Hell," replied Joyce, "I know who Mike Johnson is."

"Sorry love of course you do, I just don't understand. He wants to speak to me urgently, but not over the phone, he is on his way now to see us."

Tony had just sat down when one hell of a roar shook the farmhouse. They both ran onto the garden and looked up to the sky. "What the hell was that!" shouted Tony, as three military helicopters screamed over the farmhouse. "Bloody hell, they are in a hurry and flying very low."

"I wonder what is going on," said Joyce, "Maybe it's a military exercise in the area, that's what Mike is coming to see you about."

"Then why couldn't he just tell me over the phone." Tony replied.

"Maybe he wants a chat and a cup of tea, you know what Mike is like," said Joyce, "I will put the kettle on and make some sandwiches."

Tony looked at his watch as he saw Mike pull up, it was 8.45 and he had not done a thing. It would be a wasted day he was sure of it, Mike never stayed for less than two hours when he came to visit. "Now" said Mike as he shook Tony's hand.

"You're doing your rounds early today aren't you, what is the urgency, wanting to speak to me personally, and not over the phone."

Mike put his arm over Tony's shoulder, "When did you last see Alan and Karen." he asked.

"Last night," replied Tony. "We had a bit of a party here you know, a bit to eat and too much to drink. Why, what is the problem?" asked Tony, "What has he been up to now?"

"He has been up to nothing," replied Mike, "He is dead, and so is Karen. They were both murdered last night, or early this morning."

The blood drained from Tony's face, "You can't be serious, tell me that this is just a bad joke." stuttered Tony.

"Sorry mate but it is true. Think carefully, last night, did you hear gun shots? Did you hear any thing unusual at all? Did they look worried in any way?"

"No nothing at all," replied Tony, "You say they were murdered, what happened?"

"Well their boss boy found them early this morning, just outside the farm gates. Karen had been shot, and Alan, well it looks as if he had been stabbed, and whoever did it, burnt the Land Rover then disappeared into the night."

It took another hour for Tony and Mike to give Joyce the terrible news and to console her.

"It's not a pretty sight." said Mike, "There are dozens of cartridge cases at the scene, and they must have used half of them on Karen, bastards, bloody cowards. She was a darling to everyone who met her."

"So that's why the helicopters were flying about earlier this morning." sobbed Joyce.

Mike nodded, "All stops have been pulled out, the area is swarming with police, and we have trackers out looking for tracks, so expect a call at any moment. We have no idea who it could be or why, but as from this moment and until further notice, PATU are on standby. I will leave it to you to notify your stick."

Tony rubbed his chin, "It is possibly nothing, but this morning I noticed a difference in my work force. They were very sullen, no one was even talking, and Crispen, my boss boy, he was very surly and that is not like him at all. Normally he is full of chatter, and really pleased to see me. But this morning I did notice a difference. In fact that was why you caught me at home when you rang, I was so annoyed and puzzled that I came back to the house. It's probably nothing but it may fit into place later on."

"Have you spoken to Alan's workers yet?" asked Tony.

"Oh yes," replied Mike, "That was the first thing that I did after I cordoned off the area. They are all being questioned at this very moment."

"You know, Alan was always very hard with his workers, they hated him." said Tony.

"Yes I know that" said Mike, "but not enough to do this, and to Karen. No, I doubt if his workers had anything to do with it. I could be totally wrong mind, but they must have heard something."

Mike's radio crackled, he went to his Land Rover and lifted the hand set, "Bravo one, speaking over," he said, "Are they on tracks yet?" he asked, "They have lost them, blast". "Any other news?" he asked, "four people? Are they sure? What is happening with the work force? Do they know anything? Nothing. They must know something surely. They seem frightened about something. Ok I will be with you in about an hour, over."

Mike walked back to the veranda and sat down. "Nothing to go on as yet," he said, "They have picked up the tracks of four people, but have come to a dead end and lost the trail over rocky ground and cattle tracks. The workers are either afraid of something or someone, or they know nothing, which I cannot believe for a minute. They live so near to the farmhouse that they must have heard something. All those cartridge cases, the noise must have been deafening, and the burnt out Land Rover, no, they know something. I must get back to Kadyo Farm, We are going to use Alan's farm as a base for the time being. I have Special Branch setting up a working base there, I would hope that within forty-eight hours we will have this thing sorted out, and the farm cleared of all signs of a police presence.

I'm off now" said Mike "but I will call you tonight, and give you an update, but until then be on your guard."

Tony stood with his arm around Joyce as Mike drove away.

"I just can't believe it," he said, "It was only twelve hours ago that we were all sitting here having a good time, and now they are both dead."

"Don't worry about it love," said Tony, "It's an isolated incident."

Joyce cuddled into him, 'an isolated incident' thought Joyce, hoping against hope that Tony was right, 'but I'm still terrified,'

Tony hugged her tight and looked up to the sky. He was worried, was this the start of something much bigger? For years the blacks had been threatening, the 'night of the long knives', to butcher the whites as they lay in their beds at night. Once and for all rid they would rid the country of their white masters. Tony had heard his parents talking to his grandparents many years ago about it and with deep foreboding he prayed for his family and his way of life.

Mike arrived back at Kadyo Farm, and found everyone still trying to pick up the pieces of the horrendous incident. Inspector Hugh Russell of Special Branch saw Mike arrive and came straight over to speak to him.

"A bad business," he said, shaking his head, "A very bad one indeed , nothing taken from the house, at least everything of value is still there, or at least so it seems, not even the food has been touched. Alan's firearms are still locked up. It just does not make sense, it's as if the sole purpose was just to kill them both, but why? I'm still waiting for the forensic report, and the ballistic report." said Hugh, "but I'm almost certain that the cartridge casings are from an AK47 assault rifle. I hope that I am wrong, but who in this country uses such a weapon?

"I will tell you," with a vehement oath Mike said, "No one, no one except a bloody terrorist, and if I am right then the shit could be about to hit the fan."

"Well I hope that you are wrong." said Hugh, with a worried frown. "I just hope that you are wrong."

Three days later, almost everyone in the area congregated at the local church for the funeral. It was a very sombre occasion, not much was said, just the nod of the head to acknowledge. No one was in the mood to say much, every one had their own ideas and thoughts.

Once the service was over, everyone stood in little groups, and talked about the terrible events that had changed their lives. Eventually they started to make their way back to their homes in a determined effort to get on with their lives.

Tony and Joyce invited a few people who farmed near them, back to the farm for drinks. Soon the atmosphere changed, and bits of laughter were to be heard, but still the conversation had one main topic. It became obvious that the women wanted to talk about the usual things, albeit in a subdued manner, and the men wanted to talk about the recent events, and what steps they should be taking. So they all went and sat outside on the veranda. The beer started to flow; soon everyone was giving their opinion as to making their farms safer, and how to repel any attack should it ever happen.

Tony sat and listened to every thing that was being said; he said nothing until everyone had said their piece. "Right" he said, "I would like to say something if I may, I have listened with great interest to what you all have had to say, and in some aspects I agree totally, but in some ways I tend to differ."

"What I intend doing, is to do nothing different to what I have been doing before this incident. We cannot let one incident like this change our lives. Yes, by all means be more observant, come back to the farm house at different times, be alert, be on your guard, and of course carry a weapon at all times. Not only you, but your wives, and if your sons or daughters are old enough, arm them also. We cannot let our guard slip, we must be vigilant, and don't be afraid to use the telephone, call each other if you are not happy about something. If it means ringing someone in the middle of the night then do it, because if I have any doubts, I will be ringing you, make no mistake about that."

Each and everyone had their own ideas about the recent situation, who they thought was responsible, what action should be taken, and what they would be doing to protect themselves.

Tony mentioned his concern about the sudden change in attitude of his workforce, never before had he seen them like this, and he was even more concerned with the recent events, could they be linked, or was it a coincidence? He walked into the house and returned with his arms full beer cans.

"Come on you lot," he said, "Drink up, we have a lot to get through, and it will take me weeks to drink it all by myself" and as we are on the subject of security, can any one tell me if they have noticed any change in their workers, are they downbeat, surly, or in general not their usual selves?" Tony asked.

"Well now that you have mentioned it," replied Richard, "I have noticed a change in the last few days. I had five on the sick yesterday, ten came in late, and when I asked them if there was a problem it was eyes to the ground and hardly a reply. Something seems to be bothering them, maybe it's my imagination, or is there something that they are afraid of, but can't, or will not tell us. You have got to admit that after what has happened it certainly makes you wonder."

The conversation slowly changed to another subject, so Tony thought he would leave it, the last thing he wanted to do was to start everyone jumping at shadows. Soon the night started to draw in, and everyone made a move to get home to the relative safety of four walls before full dark. At the moment it seemed crazy to be moving about at night, it wouldn't do to tempt fate they thought.

As the last guest drove away, Tony locked up, drew the curtains, and poured himself a large brandy. "Well what a day," he said to Joyce, "You never know what tomorrow will bring do you." He said with trepidation.

"I just can't believe that the next farm is now deserted. Can you remember if there was any family we could contact" asked Tony.

"No" replied Joyce, "In fact, it was only recently that Karen was saying that neither of them had any living relatives, and therefore no one to leave the farm to."

"So what will happen to the farm?" asked Joyce,

"I've no idea; said Tony, "No idea at all, if they left a will of some kind, then it will be dealt with by their solicitors I would imagine. If there is no will, then possibly the courts will have to sort it out. We will just have to wait and see, but someone is going to look after the farm for them in the meantime. There is a lot of money tied up in crops and livestock. We will do what we can but any way we have our own farm to worry about as well". Tony put down his empty glass, "I'm off to bed it has been a hard day" he said.

Sitting in his office, Chief Inspector Mike Johnson turned the pages of the Coroners report, both persons had died instantly. The female, Karen Crompton had died of massive gunshot wounds to the upper body. The ballistics report showed that an AK47 had been used, only one weapon had been used in the murder, but that did not mean that only one weapon had been at the scene. Alan Crompton had also died instantly from a single deep stab wound to the chest, possibly a bayonette, or a dagger had been used inflicting massive fatal injuries to the heart and other organs.

Mike dropped the report onto the desk, took a deep sigh and ran his fingers through his hair. He sat for a few moments then got up and poured himself a cup of coffee, 'what the hell is going on' he muttered to himself. He sat back down at his desk and picked up the report from Special Branch, there was nothing in it that he did not already know, as he said at the scene of the incident, he thought that the cartridge casings were from an AK47 assault rifle, this had been confirmed. Possibly four persons were at the scene of the incident and trackers had followed their tracks for about half a mile then lost them in the vicinity of a village, amongst the cattle tracks. Mike placed the reports in his brief case, and walked out of his office. It was an hour's drive from Bindura to Salisbury and he did not want to be late for his meeting with the Commissioner of Police.

Joshua smiled as the Land Rover burst into flames, he stepped back as the heat intensified. He looked at Robert and smiled, "Ok let's get out of here." Isaac and Ticky wanted to ransack the farm house, "There must be something of value that we could take with us." said Isaac,

The men set off running in the easy loping gait of the true African. The only sound the rhythmic slap of bare feet on the stony ground. On reaching the nearest village, they stopped for a few precious moments to cover his tracks. Joshua led them in a different direction. They ran on, muscles rippling and dripping with sweat, through thick brush and over streams. No word was spoken till they reached a rocky out crop half way up the side of a hill overlooking the valley.

"We will rest here" said Joshua "We have a good vantage point and plenty of cover if we need to move quickly".

From this point they could see that the Land Rover was still burning. Silhouetted against the moonlit night, like young children they laughed and hugged each other.

"A good night's work." Said Ticky in a deeply satisfied voice.

"Yes, and this is just the beginning," laughed Joshua, "Our work has just started."

Joshua was from the Umvukwes area in the North East of Rhodesia. He had been brought up on a farm that was owned by an old white Rhodesian. Joshua's father had spent almost all of his life working on the farm. When he was too old to work any longer he retired, then spent most of his time trying desperately to make ends meet. The responsibility of the family, then fell on the mothers shoulders. As soon as he was able Joshua began to share the burden by working for a white farmer. The work proved to be very hard with long hours for little pay. Due to their harsh living conditions Joshua decided to look for better paid work in Salisbury. As with most young men his intentions were honourable in that he intended sending money each month in an attempt to help his parents. He was also very determined to start studying to improve his education and never have to do manual work again.

During the next two years, he continued his studies in the evening, and worked in a furniture shop in Salisbury during the day. One day he arrived at work to find the police waiting for him, that night the shop had been broken into and all the previous days' takings were missing. As he was responsible for cashing up at the end of the day, he was automatically under suspicion, and as he was the only black office worker in the shop everyone pointed the finger at him. He spent the next two days pleading his innocence at the police station, the police had searched his home and found nothing. Joshua was black and blue from his beatings, when he was released his boss told him that there was no longer a job for him, and to leave the premises immediately. This experience changed Joshua from a quiet hard working young man into a person full of hatred, and seeking revenge.

Soon he fell into the wrong company and found himself in trouble with the police. Within two months he was on the run. One evening as he sat drinking in a shabeen, he started talking to a stranger who said that he could help him.

Matambo told Joshua, that he was like many other black

Rhodesians who could not, and would not; get a good job until the white man was driven from the land. Joshua was eager to find out more, and spent the next two days listening to communist propaganda and the wonderful picture that unfolded in front of him. Soon he was totally under the control of his new master. A month later Joshua and a group of ten other Africans were driven across the border into Mozambique and into a small communist training camp. For the next year he would undergo hard training by Chinese instructors in all aspects of terrorism. It was during this time that he met his three comrades; Isaac, Robert and Ticky. They trained together, and became firm friends.

Joshua soon caught the eye of his communist masters, he was keen to learn and adapted quickly to what he was being taught, it was obvious that he had the ability and strength of character to become a leader.

As dawn broke, the four bodies stirred. Ticky was on watch, but was just starting to doze when he heard the others starting to move. He woke with a start and quickly got to his feet, he moved out of the undergrowth and stretched his legs, he was aching all over, it had been a cold night. He took a few steps into the open and raised his eyes, suddenly there was a terrific noise, his mouth opened and before he could say a word a helicopter came roaring overhead. The noise was deafening, he slipped on the damp grass and quickly crawled back into the undergrowth. His heart was pounding, and he was gasping for breath as if he had run a mile. Everyone was now fully awake and staring up into the sky.

"Where did that bastard come from?" croaked Robert. "Be quiet," said Joshua, "Stay still, don't bloody move." He slowly looked around then looked at his three companions, "Keep quiet." he whispered, the sound of the helicopter faded into the distance. "I don't think they saw you." Joshua said. Slowly he crawled out of the thick bush, he paused for a while then moved further into the open. Slowly he made his way into the clearing so that he could see into the distance, he looked towards the farm that they had been to last night. It was crawling with police, two helicopters were standing on the open road, one had its rotors turning and slowly rose into the air, it hovered for a few seconds then flew away in the opposite direction. Joshua scanned the immediate area in front of him, then looked towards the farm again, no sign of life, he moved back into the undergrowth, "It's all right I am certain that no one saw us, we will lie low for an hour, then we will get to a better vantage point."

Mike Johnson drove away from the police station, turned right at the junction and drove into Bindura. For a small town, the main street was fairly busy, people doing their shopping, and in general just going about their business. Mike pulled up outside the Pink Blossom flower shop, and waved to Sonia Botha, "morning," he said with a smile, "I just want to say a big thank you for the lovely flower arrangements that you made for the funeral, everyone commented about how nice they were."

Sonia smiled, she put her hand on his arm, "It was the least that I could do, we are all terribly saddened by what has happened, it still hasn't sunk in yet that we wont see them again."

"Keep your chin up." he replied, "I must be on my way or I will be late for a very important meeting."

Mike pulled away from the shop and waved to George Hammond. George was the owner of Hammond Engineering, which was situated on the outskirts of Bindura and in a perfect position to service Trojan Nickel Mine.

George had set up the business about ten years earlier with his brother. Due to the fact that the mine had massive reserves, and was the only mine of it's kind in the country, he knew that they were on a winner. With steady work and a very good income, their future was secured.

Mike drove out of town, passing the Coach House Inn on his left, and put his foot down on the gas. Half way to Salisbury he stopped at the Mazoe Citrus Estate, they sold the best pure orange juice in the world. Mike stood at the counter, and slowly sipped the cold juice. It was so nice that he could have finished off a couple of pints, but he had to go. He savoured the last drop, put down the cup, and got back into his Land Rover and roared off towards Salisbury, towards the Police Headquarters.

"Come in," was the reply to his knock on the door. Mike gripped the door handle, cleared his throat, and entered the room.

"Morning sir," he said,

"Morning" replied the Commissioner, "come on in and sit

down." Adam Ross Stapleton had been in the police for twenty-three years. His first posting had been in Gatooma near to the Golden Valley, he had spent six years there before moving to Fort Victoria. In his spare time he had spent many an hour fishing on Lake Kyle, and watching the wild life in the Zimbabwe National Park. The wonders of the Zimbabwe Ruins still mystified him, who had built it and why, what was its purpose?

He had seen rapid promotion through the ranks, and was now based in Salisbury as the Commissioner of Police. His wife Angela had been his childhood sweetheart and had given him a son Scott, who was in the Rhodesian Army and a daughter who was studying to become a nurse in Bulawayo. In his day Adam had been a very keen rugby player but due to the long hours at work and arthritis in his shoulder, due to an old injury he had hung up his boots many years ago. He was still a striking figure of a man six foot five, thirteen stone, and still not an ounce of fat on him. The only sign of his age was the full head of silver grey hair. Adam placed his pipe in the ash tray, and got up from his chair.

"Now then Mike," he said "It looks like the shit has hit the bloody fan in your neck of the woods. Let's get a cup of coffee and you can give me all the details, I have read the reports but I would like to hear it from the horse's mouth."

Mike settled in the chair, took a sip of coffee, and started to relay the events of the past forty-eight hours,

The Commissioner listened in silence, he picked up his pipe and started to fill it with tobacco, he pressed it down firmly into the bowl and picked up a box of matches. Mike stopped talking and stared at the cloud of smoke that rose into the air.

"Don't worry about me." The Commissioner said, "I'm listening to everything that you are saying." Mike continued for another half an hour then picked up his cup of coffee and took a sip, "And that's about it." he said. "I'm sure that your officers in Special Branch have given you the facts."

"Indeed they have," replied the Commissioner "but it's nice to get it from the man at the sharp end, and as I see it, we don't have a great deal to go on really. We think it's a group of possibly four persons, an AK47 assault rifle was used, absolutely no mercy was shown. Was it planned, or was it that Alan and Karen were just at the wrong place at the wrong time? No apparent motive, nothing stolen, and whoever did it, covered their tracks, and just disappeared into the night."

"Well, as I see it," replied Mike, "It was an act of pure evil, planned or not, who ever did it took great pleasure in doing it. I know that some people are saying it was just an isolated incident, but I must say I have my doubts. You have said yourself; whoever did it went to great lengths to cover their tracks. They took nothing, just killed and destroyed, the Land Rover, why? Was it because Alan was a total bastard towards his workers? Karen, well she has never said a bad word about any one, I don't think she had an enemy in the world. Why hurt her? Was it revenge? Or was it to stir up hatred, put fear into the hearts of everyone? There are a lot of questions to be answered".

The Commissioner put down his pipe, leant back in his chair and ran his fingers through his hair. "I'm afraid I don't have the answers Mike," he said, "I really wish I did, but believe me, everyone is working with you on this one, we will get a break. Whoever did it will make a mistake, they always do, let's hope it happens soon. I'm trying to put myself in their position, what would I do next?" the Commissioner stroked his chin, "I would lie low for awhile, lie low and just watch, see what the reaction is, then I would plan my next move. But I could be totally wrong, maybe it was an isolated incident, and nothing else will happen. I have been in touch with the District Commissioners who work in the North East of the country. Normally they have their fingers on the button, and know everything that is going on, but they haven't seen or heard anything. Usually they get a whisper, if something is about to happen, they have spoken to their informers but have come up with nothing.

As you know Kadyo Farm is now occupied by the police. I was going to pull them out next week, but I think I will leave that for now. I think a police presence will be good for moral for the farmers, yes, lets give it a few more days. We have five sticks on patrol in the area, I think in the next few days I will increase that. If they are in the area then let's try and flush them out."

Mike got up out of his chair, "You know Sir, the farmers are pretty well pissed off about all this. How about involving them, they are all in the P.A.T.U., they are all highly trained, and just waiting for the word to get stuck in."

"That's just the problem," said the Commissioner, "maybe emotions are too high at the moment, believe me I do know the value of these men, I have seen them in action, and when the time is right they will be used."

Mike held out his hand, and said goodbye to the Commissioner, "I must get going, as I have a few calls to make on the way home and with the current situation I don't fancy the idea of driving in the dark."

"Ok" replied the Commissioner, "Drive carefully and give my regards to everyone, and please apologise for my absence at the funeral."

Mike walked briskly down the corridor and out into the brilliant sunshine. The sudden contrast from an air conditioned building to the sudden heat of the open air made him shiver. He reached into his breast pocket and pulled out his sunglasses and slipped them on. No sooner had he sat down in the driving seat of his Land Rover than the sweat started to run down his back between his shoulder blades, down his fore head and started to drip off his nose. "I'm bloody knackered." he said to himself as he started the engine. He took off his hat, threw it onto the passenger seat, loosened his belt, made himself comfortable, and reversed out of the parking bay.

Chapter Three

Tony lay on the floor, it was playtime for Benji. Joyce had bathed and fed him, and now it was Tony's turn to keep him occupied until it was his bedtime. Tony knew how hard it was for Joyce to look after Benji all day, but by the time he got in from the farming he was often so tired, all he wanted to do was to have a few beers, get showered and to get to bed. Where does he get all the energy from, he never bloody stops, he was into everything, you couldn't take your eyes off him for a second. Tony picked him up and took him into the bathroom, "you sit there while I get a shower, OK, and don't you move" he told Benji. He quickly stripped off and stood under the shower, the hot water cascaded over his body, easing away the aches and pains of a hard days work. He quickly shaved and rinsed away the lather and stepped out of the shower. He smiled at Benji who was looking up at him with his arms raised wanting to be picked up. He wrapped a towel around his waist and lifted him off the floor and walked into the bedroom. He was just about to pull on a pair of shorts when Joyce called from the kitchen, "your dinner is on the table, come and get it."

An hour later Tony was stood washing the dinner plates while Joyce put Benji to bed for the night,. She quietly moved up behind Tony and slipped her arms around his waist. "You look worn out love." she said. "Have you had a hard day?" "Not really" replied Tony, "It's just trying to get back into the swing of things again. What with the funeral and all the additional activity in the area, and all the time I'm trying to read into the minds of the workers, heaven knows what they are thinking." Joyce gave him a kiss on the cheek and said, "Let's try and forget it just for tonight, lets just have a drink and relax."

As soon as Tony's head touched the pillow he was dead to the world. Joyce lay thinking about the recent events, and tossed and turned most of the night. It was about two thirty when she finally dozed off to sleep. No sooner was she asleep, when suddenly, she was wide awake. She lifted her head off the pillow and strained her ears, 'was she dreaming?' she thought to herself. Again she heard a faint noise outside. Slowly she slid out of the bed and tiptoed to the window. Very slowly she moved the curtain and peered out into the night, it was eerie, the moon cast long shadows through the clouds that reflected onto the garden. She felt the hair on the back of her neck prickle and her skin crawl, she stood silently hardly daring to breath, all she could hear now was her heart beating faster and faster, it sounded so loud she thought that it would wake Tony up. She turned to look at the bed and saw that Tony was sound asleep, again she peered out of the window, again she heard noises, but now she was sure that she could hear voices. She reached out to Tony and gently shook him, "Wake up" she whispered, "wake up" will you.

Tony turned over and slowly opened his eyes, "What's wrong" he said in a hoarse voice, "What time is it?"

"Be quiet." Joyce whispered, "I can hear a noise outside, I'm sure that I can hear voices."

Tony was out of bed and standing at her side, slowly he moved the curtain to one side and looked out of the window, his eyes were blurred with sleep, he rubbed his eyes and closed them for a few moments, slowly his night vision came to him. He stared out into the night but saw nothing. Joyce began to say something, "Keep quiet," he said, "don't say any thing, I'm listening." There was a slight breeze and he hoped that it would carry any sounds in his direction, he stood for a few moments then shook his head. "I can't hear anything." he said.

"I'm telling you I heard something." said Joyce, "I wasn't dreaming." Tony slid back into bed, "It's your imagination love, it's probably a jackal or bats, come on back to bed." "Bats and jackals don't talk like humans," she said, "I'm telling you I heard voices." Tony jumped out of bed, "Bloody hell woman it's nothing." He stood at her side and listened, "There," said Joyce, "Now do you believe me." Tony strained his ears, "Yes," he said, "something is out there, get away from the window and get into Benji's room and stay with him."

"Why, where are you going?" said Joyce, ""What are you going to do?"

"I have heard something, so I'm going to see what it is out there." whispered Tony.

Tony pulled on a pair of shorts and a shirt, slipped on a pair of trainers and walked to the back door then stopped and walked back into the bed room. He reached into the wardrobe and from the top shelf picked up his pump action shotgun and a walther pistol. He checked that both were fully loaded, put the pistol into his waist band and slowly opened the back door.

The warm night air hit him like a fist, the breeze had dropped and there was not even the slightest movement from the leaves on the trees. He stood and listened, nothing. His eyes were darting everywhere, the shadows were playing tricks on him, bushes appeared to be moving towards him. 'Calm down' he said to himself, 'just relax,' slowly he moved away from the doorway and crouched down. He carefully made his way along the side of the house. Tony stopped again to listen, straining his ears for any sound, again he moved forward, his heart was pounding and his lungs were bursting as he held his breath. With a determined effort 'Calm down,' he said to himself again, he started to take shallow breaths, as his breathing came back to normal his senses cleared, and again he slowly moved forward. Tony came to the corner of the farmhouse and peered around the corner. Straining his eyes as he looked into the eerie darkness. 'Nothing' he said to himself, turning to go back into the house. Then he heard it. Straining his ears and eyes towards the main gate he heard it again. Tony crouched down and slowly moved forward, now he was certain that some one or something was out there. He kept totally still, holding his breath, then he saw them, two figures bending down at the main gate. Tony was in no mind to be asking questions, he raised the shotgun, aimed it at the crouching figures and fired, then fired again. He moved forward, only to stop in his tracks as return fire came his way. Again he fired until the shotgun was empty then drew his pistol, as the roar from the gunfire died away, silence filled the air. Tony backed his way towards the backdoor slid inside and locked it, "Are you alright?" he called to Joyce, silence. Again he called to her.

"I'm in here." she whispered.

Tony moved into Benji's room, "Where are you?" he said,

"We are under the bed." Joyce replied,

"Ok stay where you are, we have had company I don't know who they were or what they were up to but they were not friendly. I'm going to ring the police station and get help."

Tony held the phone and waited, holding the phone to his ear with his shoulder he loaded the shotgun, "I know that you are on duty by yourself, and that there's not much that you can do!" Tony shouted down the telephone to the African constable, "Look put me through to the Chief's home will you, never mind you can't do that, just bloody well do it, or your arse will be in a sling, now stop pissing me about and give me his number."

Tony waited for what seemed like an hour, then heard Mike on the other end of the phone, "Bloody hell Tony, do you know what time it is?"

"Yes I do, and I am under attack. We are all right, but we have had visitors. I am back in the house now, I gave them a full mag of triple A, I've no idea if I hit anyone but I certainly put the shits up them. It's been all quiet for the last ten minutes."

"OK" shouted Mike, "Stay indoors, I will get help out to you immediately."

The phone went dead, and Tony felt all alone again. He heard Joyce calling from the bedroom, "What is happening?" she called in a nervous voice,

"It's OK," he called to her, "Just stay where you are, help is on its way."

Tony again checked his shotgun to see if it was fully loaded, he then checked his pistol, everything was OK.

Soon dawn was breaking, it's amazing how much more confident he felt now. It was as if the daylight was his friend. He felt like running outside and taking the world on. He walked into the bedroom and sat on the bed next to Joyce, "You were right love, someone was out there, I've no idea who but one thing is for sure, and they were not friends of ours."

The quietness of the early morning air was suddenly broken by a thunderous roar outside. Tony grabbed his shotgun and ran to the window, he quickly pulled the curtains to one side, the sight took his breath away. Three helicopters were landing on his front garden, and out of the helicopters, heavily armed security forces were hitting the ground and running towards the farmhouse.

Tony's heart was pounding again, but this time it was with excitement, he rushed to the back door and quickly opened it. Stepping outside into the cool morning air gave him a great adrenalin rush, he quickly made his presence known, "Stand still," a voice called to him, "We will come and see you in a moment, please go back inside." Tony opened his mouth to say something, and was told in no uncertain terms to shut up and to do as he was told.

"What is going on?" Joyce asked him in a shaking voice.

"It's OK," Tony told her, "We must stay inside until they have secured the area, and when they have done that they will come to speak to us. Are you and Benji OK?

"Yes" said Joyce. "As she put her arms around his waist, Tony put his arm around her and gave her a kiss on the cheek. "Do me a favour?" he asked.

"Of course I will." Joyce replied, "What do you want?"

"A good strong cup of coffee," replied Tony, "A good strong coffee."

It seemed hours since the security forces had arrived, and Tony was still waiting for them to come and see him. At nine o'clock Tony heard a voice shouting to him, "OK now Tony, it's OK for you to come out." a voice called.

'Thank God' Tony thought, he picked up his shotgun and went outside.

Two helicopters were in the air, either moving troops or going for reinforcements, and the third one was on the ground with its rotors spinning ready for take off. Suddenly its engine picked up speed, its rotors slicing through the air and with dust flying everywhere and a deafening roar, it took to the sky.

A member of the security force ran over to Tony and held out his hand, "Morning Tony" he said, "Sorry about the delay, but obviously we had to secure the area first. If we have people walking everywhere they could destroy vital tracks or evidence.

Well one thing's for sure, someone was out to get you last night. When you disturbed them they were planting a hand grenade with a trip wire to your front gate next to your tractor. It would have been a sure thing, if you or anyone had opened the gate it would have caused terrible injuries or death."

"But you got one of the bastards, you certainly meant business or you had a lucky shot. You blew half of his head away. We have men on tracks as we speak, and it looks as if there were about four or five of them, they were carrying AK 47 assault rifles and by the number of cartridge cases, they were not afraid to use them. We will be here for about another three or four hours at least. I am drafting more men into the area, to use as stop lines, and more trackers. I'm using the men who are left here to totally secure the area, and Special Branch are on their way to go through the area with a fine tooth comb, and to remove the body. So make yourself available, as they will want as much information from you as possible"

Tony walked quickly back to the farmhouse, "It's only me." he called, as he walked into the living room.

"We are in the bedroom" Joyce called, "I'm just dressing Benji, is every thing OK?"

"Well as good as can be expected," replied Tony, "We will have company for a while though, Special Branch are on their way, and you know what they are like, they could take days."

Joyce walked into the room carrying Benji, "Before I forget while you were out, Mike Johnson rang, he said he would be out to see you within the hour"

Joshua, Isaac, and Robert had been running for about an hour. They had been caught unawares, they knew that Ticky had been badly wounded if not killed, they were now out of breath, their lungs were bursting, their bodies were covered in sweat, but they knew that they must put a good distance between themselves and the farm. Soon Joshua called for them to stop and rest.

"OK" he said, "Be quiet and listen, it will be a while before they find our tracks and start to follow us, but they have helicopters and they are either moving troops about, or they are looking for us. So we must keep out of sight, but keep our eyes open, the last thing we want right now is for them to find us."

For the next two days Joshua stayed holed up, thinking what they should do next, he felt he had failed in this second attempt, but the next time he would strike terror into the white farming community.

On the third day they discussed what they should do next, food was low, and they were hungry. They decided to leave their hiding place and visit a village, after all they were freedom fighters and they would be greeted as heroes. At first light they moved out. In single file, they walked through the bush about five yards from the dirt road, slowly they made their way north, they pressed on, every minute they expected the sound of gun fire. As they wended their way through the thick bush they heard the sound of an approaching vehicle. It was very distant but seemed to be coming their way. Robert stood up turning his head from left to right, "Its coming this way." he said,

"Stay still" Joshua said, "It could be the security forces, we must wait until we can identify it before we make a move."

They all peered out of the bush and looked along the road towards the sound of the approaching vehicle.

"It's a bus" whispered Isaac,

"I can see, it is, it's a bloody bus." replied Joshua, "Get down, you two stay out of sight, I'll wave it down, it's obviously picking people up and taking them into town, when it stops, wait until I wave to you before you come into the open…"

Joshua stood in the middle of the road with his AK 47 held out of sight behind his back. The bus slowed down and came to a stop about four feet in front of him, clouds of dust billowed into the air almost obscuring him from sight..

Joshua stood looking through dust at the bus. On top of the bus were boxes of belongings put there by the passengers, wooden cages full of chickens, and about ten children all peering at him with wide open eyes.

Joshua slowly walked to the door of the bus, "Come on man," yelled the driver, "If you're getting on board then get on, don't just stand there."

Joshua stepped onto the bus, "Where are you going?" he asked the driver.

"I'm heading for Salisbury, do you want a lift or not? Come on man I'm in a hurry."

"Don't you talk like that to me" snarled Joshua, "While you are driving a bus for a rich white man I'm out in the bush fighting for your freedom, so shut it man." Joshua looked down the bus, "Come on you lot what are you all staring at, I am part of the revolution, I am fighting for you, soon this country will be free of the white man, we will run our country, it will be ours."

Everyone sat in silence too terrified to move.

"Look man are you getting on the bloody bus or not, if you are then take a seat if not then get off my bus".

Joshua brought up the rifle and shoved it into the drivers face," brave bastard eh, white mans lapdog, come on man give me all of your fares. I will put it to better use."

Joshua grabbed the drivers' money bag, but the driver grabbed a hold of it. "Piss off you piece of shit you ain't getting it, now get off my bus."

Joshua was in a fury now, he pulled with all his strength, and as he fell backwards he squeezed the trigger. The driver slumped into the driving seat, blood pouring from his stomach. Everyone on the bus started screaming and pushing towards the back of the bus. Chickens were flapping and feathers were flying everywhere. Joshua looked down again at the lifeless body of the driver, blood was everywhere. It was on the windows , the steering wheel and all over the drivers' seat. Flies were already starting to settle on the driver's open stomach, the stench was terrible. Joshua stood transfixed. The wailing cry of a child brought Joshua out of his trance, grabbing the money bag, he ran off the bus. In his terror Joshua ran on into the bush straight past Isaac and Robert. He only stopped when they caught up with him.

"What happened?" asked Robert.

"He attacked me" lied Joshua, "So I shot him, come on let's get out of here."

As the makeshift football shot between the goal posts, it bounced in the dust and rolled into the thick bush, as the final whistle went. Everyone cheered and all of the spectators clapped with delight as the winning team ran towards their parents.

Richard Tumbayi, who had just scored the winning goal, walked slowly off the pitch and started the long walk back to his village. No one had been there to see him play, and he had played so well. He knew that his mother was working to provide for the family and that his younger sister and brother would be at school.

He remembered the days when he had sat on his father's shoulders as they walked for miles through the bush to go fishing, he remembered the times and the laughter from his parents as they told him of the good days. But his father was gone, he had been killed while on duty by a drunken driver, the small pension his mother received from the Rhodesian Police was a help, but most certainly not enough to provide for the growing family.

Richard remembered the love that he had for his father, and the look of pride on his face, as his father got dressed in his uniform as he was about to go on duty. From a very young age Richard had only one wish and that was to join the Rhodesian Police and to follow in his father's footsteps.

Twenty years later Richard sat at the back of the bus looking on in horror as the events took place. Did anyone know that he was a police officer; he was dressed in civilian clothes as he had been on leave to attend his cousins wedding. All he had on him was his warrant card, and that was no match against an AK 47. He sat in silence, watching every movement, memorising every single detail, after a few moments it was clear that the gun man was not coming back. Everyone on the bus sat frozen in their seats, frozen with fear. Richard knew that someone had to take the lead and do something. He quickly moved from his seat and told everyone to try and stay calm. As he approached the driver's seat he could smell the warm blood and the spilled content of the dead mans stomach. He quickly dragged the dead driver from the driver's compartment and gently placed him in the aisle. Returning to the driver's seat, he could see that the seat was awash with blood. Richard took off his shirt and wiped the seat and the steering wheel as best as he could, his mind was racing as he started the engine, he selected first gear, and with a roar the bus and its terrified passengers moved away from the scene and on towards Bindura.

Richard was sweating profusely, he felt certain that if he had been in uniform he would now be dead. He was now about ten miles from the scene and would be in Bindura within the hour. He knew Bindura well as he had spent time there as part of his training. At last he saw the road sign, two miles to go. Sighing with relief he pulled up outside the Dungeon, adjacent to the police station. He stopped the engine, jumped from the bus and quickly walked into the front office.

Mike Johnson had just returned from Tony's farm when he saw the bus pull up in front of his office. 'What the bloody hell is going on?' he thought to himself as he moved from his desk towards the outer door. As he went into the next office he was met by his duty officer, "Sir, I think you had better come quickly, it looks as if there has been another attack."

Mike Johnson sat at his desk with the telephone pressed tight to his ear, "Yes sir, it happened about three hours ago in the Mtoko area close to the Nyadiri River. The bus was brought in by an African Constable who was actually a passenger on the bus at the time of the incident. He has given us a very good description of the gunman and is now on his way back to the scene of the incident with Special Branch Officers.

I have informed Crusader and they are on standby, three P.A.T.U sticks are now on their way."

"OK" replied the Commissioner, "Keep me informed. One other thing before you hang up, I want you in my office at ten o'clock on Wednesday morning, and don't be late Mike, it doesn't pay to keep the Prime Minister waiting."

Looking around the room, Mike took particular notice of everyone who was present; he was putting names to faces. Names that he had heard mentioned with utmost respect in many conversations, he was looking at the faces of the men who would be responsible for the survival of Rhodesia as it fought for it's very existence.

To his left was General Willis, Commander in Chief of the Army [Crusader], next was Air Marshal Raymond Vesting [Cyclone], Minister of Internal Affairs Vincent Morley, Chief Inspector Hugh Russel Special Branch, Minister of Defence Arthur Higgins, and from Mount Darwin Police Chief Inspector Tim Osby, from Centenary Police Chief Inspector Alan Cross, from Umvukwes Police Chief Inspector Brian Tomby. To his right was the Commissioner of the Police Adam Ross Stapleton. At the head of the table the chair was empty, as was the small desk and chair to one side of the main table.

Everyone was discussing the situation when the door opened and in walked a man, but no ordinary man. Slim with very broad shoulders, a very determined face that was topped with a full head of white hair his back was straight and upright. It was obvious that in his younger days he had been a very fit and athletic man. Behind him was his private secretary. Everyone stood up in respect but were quickly asked to sit and make themselves comfortable. As the Prime Minister sat down he looked around the table and smiled, "Good morning gentlemen, thank you all for coming. I know this meeting was unexpected, but due to the events that have taken place over the last week or so, I thought that a meeting of all those who are in the front line was very important. Please don't feel afraid to speak up and say your piece, needless to say everything that is discussed here today is confidential. My secretary will be taking notes of the meeting and you will all be given a copy in due course."

Mike was staring at the man as he spoke, 'So this was the Prime Minister of Rhodesia, what a charming man.' He thought to himself, 'no airs or graces, just an ordinary man who was prepared to lead his country against the onslaught of what was possibly the beginning of a terrorist war.'

The Prime Minister took a sip of water and looked up, "Gentlemen over the past few weeks there has been a number of incidents, some minor and some very serious."

At this point he rose from his chair and walked over to a map on the wall, "All of the incidents have taken place in the North East of the country. At this exact moment in time we do not know if the perpetrators have just arrived in the country." He pointed to the areas that were marked with coloured pins. "I did say that some of the incidents were minor and that some were serious, well let me correct myself, every incident is a serious one, and must be dealt with accordingly. Most of the attacks have taken place in the Matepatepa area, which is predominantly your area Mike. No one is pointing a finger at you; it just happens that your patch has taken the brunt of the attacks. Other area's that have been hit are Mount Darwin, that's yours Tim, don't worry gentlemen, I have done my home work, I know exactly who is in charge of what area, and what is being done. Tim you have had two farms hit, no one killed thank goodness, but two farmers wounded, and one African worker badly beaten up. Centenary, your baby Alan, three incidents, one white farmer wounded, and one outhouse set on fire." He turned to Brian, "And you have your share of trouble up in Umvukwes haven't you? One Land Rover set on fire, one landmine found, and two farmers shot at."

The Prime Minister sat down in his chair, "Need I say more, gentlemen this is going to escalate, I have no doubt about it at all. I have been well informed by the District Commissioners in the south of the country that reports are coming in from their informers that there is a change in attitude amongst the local tribesmen. People are frightened to talk; people are not turning up for work. As you can see from the map on the wall I, along with the Joint Operational Command [J.O.C.] who you see sitting at the table today, have divided the country into four sections, North East, North West, South East, and South West. Here in the North East, as we are the only area to be presently targeted, will be known as OPERATION HURRICANE.

"Let me make it very clear to you all, for years now our neighbouring countries have been sabre rattling, making threats to us and demanding one man one rule. It will never happen, not in a thousand years, but if we have to fight then so be it. The gloves will come off; we will fight fire with fire. We will cross any border to defend our sovereignty. If we are attacked we will hit back hard, very hard. If any country harbours terrorists then they will do so at their peril. If they assist terrorism, then they are the enemy of this wonderful country of ours. We will not be threatened; we will not tolerate terrorism of any kind.

"Now gentlemen let's get down to business, I want your views, it is an open discussion. I have my own ideas, but as your Prime Minister, I am now asking for your help and advice."

Chapter Four

Tony sat on the veranda and looked into the distant hills. His thoughts were not on farming, but on the immediate future. He knew that soon he would be called up to do his bit and had no wish to leave his family alone during his absence. It could be for a week, may be two, but who knows, it could be for much longer. If you are in the thick of it they don't call a halt just so that you can go home to your family. He had been the stick leader, call sign Trojan 4, for two years. They were a close group of men, all very good friends. Young, fit, and totally dedicated, they had all done their army training, and then joined P.A.T.U. They trained together on a regular basis, and were a compliment of eight men, but only five would go out on patrol at any one time, as a helicopter would only lift five fully equipped men.

Joyce sat down opposite him, "Here I've brought you a beer." Tony smiled, "Thanks love I could do with it."

"You seem miles away." she said as she touched his hand. "I'm Ok love honestly, I'm just thinking about you and Benji."

"We are Ok." said Joyce with a reassuring smile.

"Yes at the moment your Ok… but what will happen when I get a call to go on patrol. I don't like the idea of you two being on your own, what if the farm is hit again. How would you cope out here all on your own? I would prefer it if the two of you went and spent time with Mark and Susie in Mabelreign. They have been asking us to go and spend some time with them for ages and we always put it off. Well I think it would be a good idea to take them up on their offer and for you both to go."

"I'm not going to leave you on your own out here." said Joyce, "No way, lets all go."

"Don't be stupid" replied Tony, "The way things are at the moment, and some one has to run the farm. I could get a phone call at any time, and be told to report with my stick within the hour, and you would be on your own, so don't act brave. You don't want it and neither do I, think of Benji. I have no doubt of your ability to give anyone who came to the farm a good fight, but think of our little boy."

Joyce sat in silence, she looked up with tears in her eyes, "But this is our home" she said.

"I know it is" replied Tony, "But it's only a home. Its no bloody good if you're dead, I'm not saying that we should give it up, all I am saying is while I am away, I think it would be better if you were not here on your own." Tony held her hand, "You know that I am right, you know that it makes sense, don't you?"

Joyce nodded, "I don't want to go, but I will if you insist." Tony felt as if a great weight had been lifted of his shoulders. It was not the fact that he could be called up at any moment that worried him, it was the fact that at any time night or day, the farm could be hit again. What if it was a sustained attack, What would happen if it was attacked when he was out in the fields? Would he be able to get back in time? All of these questions, he had asked himself over and over again, and he knew that if his family were not on the farm, then he had only himself to think about.

Tony stood up and looked at Joyce, "Come here," he said to her. She stood up and put her arms around him. "You and Benji are more important than the farm, if I don't have you two then I have nothing."

They stood on the veranda kissing and cuddling like two newly weds, Tony knew that tomorrow he would have to phone Mark and Susie.

The sun was so strong that he could feel it burning through his shirt and the top of his bush hat. No matter where he moved the wind seemed to blow the smoke in his direction. His eyes were constantly running and stinging, but the smell of the meat on the braai made it all worthwhile. Tony opened another cold beer, he felt a hand on his shoulder, "How's it going my old mate, no burn't meat I hope?"

"It's great to be here Mark; I don't know what I would do without you and Susie." said Tony.

"Well your visit is long overdue, we have been asking you both to come and spend some time with us for well over a year now. You know that you are always welcome and that you don't need an invitation. But fill me in, on what is going on at your end of the world."

As the evening light started to fade and the embers turned to ash, Joyce and Susie were clearing up, washing the dishes and still catching up on all the news and gossip. Tony and Mark were doing a very good job of killing a case of Lion Lager; they didn't even notice that the night air was now getting a bit chilly.

"How do you farmers live in a situation like that? I'm bloody sure that we couldn't do with it." said Mark

"That's exactly it." replied Tony, "We are farmers, it's our living, it is all that we know, what else can we do? I am certainly not running away from the troubles. It's our farm, I was bloody well born there, no bastard is going to take it from us. If they try, then they will die trying, but I will tell you this, it will get a lot worse before it gets any better, that's why I want Joyce and Benji out of the way for a few weeks. I don't think Joyce realises how bad it is, or how bad it will possibly get, so please don't say too much to her or to Susie."

Mark threw the empty can over his shoulder, "Don't you worry, not a word I promise you, and don't worry about Joyce and the little one, they can stay with us as long as it takes As you said, it's less for you to worry about. Now come on how about another can of the amber nectar, and then we'll open a bottle of KWV Brandy. The night is young and there is no way that you are going back to the farm tonight. Anyway we have not been on the piss like this, hell it must be at least two years. Come on mate relax, you must be like a coiled spring, and it's time to unwind."

Tony woke up with daylight shining through the bedroom curtains. 'Where am I?' he thought. It was strange getting a full night's sleep and then waking up to see daylight. He lifted his head off the pillow and very quickly realised that he had one hell of a hangover. After a quick shower and a shave he felt slightly better and went down for breakfast. He looked at Mark and smiled, "Shit mate, you look like I feel."

"And so you should," said Joyce, "Have you two seen the amount of booze you put away last night, a full case of beer and a full bottle of brandy. We have no sympathy for either of you and when you have finished your breakfast you two can wash the dishes, it's our turn to relax."

Mark knew that he would take most of the flack as Tony was heading back to the farm within a few hours. But knowing what he was going back to, it was possibly better staying at home and facing the fury of two women. Soon, Tony was loading up the Land Rover and was all set to go, "Thanks again mate, it's been great seeing you both again."

"Take care," said Mark, "And ring us when you get back, and don't worry about Joyce and Benji they will be OK I promise you." Tony put his arms around Joyce and gave her a kiss, "I'll be OK, so don't worry about me OK?"

He picked up Benji and ruffled his hair. "Look after your mam and be a good boy, it won't be long before we are all back together again." Tony closed the Land Rover door and gunned the engine. Slowly he reversed down the drive and onto the road, he waved to them all, slipped the gear stick into first gear and drove back to Bindura and home.

Mike Johnson sat at his desk with a concerned look on his face. He was drawing up a list of men who would be called up within the next few days to go out on patrol. Nearly all of the P.A.T.U. were farmers, and he knew how difficult it was for them to be away from their crops and the everyday running of the farms for any length of time. It was a twenty-four hour job and it certainly did not run itself, but the problems facing them all at the moment could not be ignored and they certainly would not go away, if anything they would get worse. The most obvious choice for the area he was thinking of at the moment was Tony's stick, they knew the area better than anyone else, and they were the most experienced. He had no other option, 'yes,' he said to himself, 'Tony and four of his men,' he knew that Tony was due back today from Salisbury, he would speak to him when he called in on his way to the farm.

Tony slowly led his men through the thick bush, his call up came as no surprise, he had been expecting it, in fact he had been hoping for it. He wanted to be involved in the operation; it was his country as well as anyone's. He had trained hard for years, and now the time had come for him to do his bit. All the men in his stick were also eager to go and it had been a hard decision for him to choose four men out of the total of eight, but a stick was made up of five men and he had made his choice. They had been deployed into the Matepatepa Tribal Trust Land. Their objective was to seek and destroy, sightings had been reported by reliable sources but as yet no contact had been made with any terrorists. Tony knew that from previous experience a patrol could last from two or three days up to two or three weeks, it all depended on results. If they came under fire from the enemy, or if they saw the enemy first, he knew the chances of taking prisoners was very remote, they usually went down fighting, or ran into the bush and disappeared.

Tony and his call sign, Trojan 4 were slowly making their way towards Eben Dam. No matter how good you were, there is one thing that every living thing needed in the bush to survive, and that was water, and that is where the latest sighting had been made. Tony stopped his men, and checked a map reference. They were now about half an hour from their destination, "Let's get to high ground so that we can view the area ahead." said Tony.

His men agreed and slowly they moved off again looking for a vantage point that would give them a good view of the dam and the two rivers that fed into it.

Tony patiently scanned the area through his binoculars, looking for any sign of life, or anything that was out of place, anything that would give him a clue. Then he saw movement, his heart seemed to skip a beat, 'could this be it?' he thought. From out of the thick bush he saw two young women walking towards a small water fall, they disappeared once again into the thick bush. He scanned the area to the right and saw in the distance a small village. Tony quickly looked back to where he had last seen the two young girls. There they were, they were walking out in the open again. On their heads they were carrying large tin dishes, the contents were covered with a large white cloth. As soon as they appeared, they were out of sight again, Tony slowly moved his binoculars from left to right, nothing. Slowly he scanned the area again, he had lost them. 'Shit,' he said to himself. He kept looking, then thought to himself, 'Maybe they were just taking washing down to the river, maybe I'm being paranoid, after all there is a village nearby. He was just about to start looking elsewhere when he saw movement again; it was the two young girls. They were walking back the way that they had come but this time they were not carrying the dishes on their heads they were carrying them in their hands by their sides and they were empty. He watched them for a while, 'strange' he thought, 'they would never leave washing by the river, and the time that they had spent down by the river they could never have washed all those clothes.' Then he thought maybe the dishes didn't contain washing, what if they were carrying food to feed someone. Tony called his 2nd in command over, he told Colin what he had just seen. "I think we should go down and take a look. It could be totally innocent but I have a feeling that we could be on to something, let's brief everyone."

Everyone agreed to go for it, so as quietly as possible they made their way down towards the waterfall. They had about six hours of daylight left, more than enough to get to grips with the situation. Alec took point, then Colin, followed by Tony then Ken with Buz bringing up the rear. They were now within striking distance. Very slowly, and totally alert, they moved into the area where Tony had seen the two girls disappear. Without warning Alec opened fire with a double tap, right in front of him a large African had stepped out of the thick undergrowth, and was taking a leak against a tree; over his shoulder were three RPG rockets. With two shots to the head he hit the ground, then all hell let loose. Return fire came fast and furious, but it was wild, they had been taken by surprise. In went two hand grenades, then rapid fire. Colin was on the radio "Contact Contact Contact!" He yelled down the hand set. This is Trojan 4 do you read me, this is Trojan 4 we have a Contact, one Terr down size of group unknown, we are under heavy fire."

"Trojan 4 Trojan 4, read you strength five, give me your loc, repeat give me your loc, we have Cyclone standing by over." Colin read off the loc.

"Ok Trojan 4 Cyclone is airborne, I repeat Cyclone is airborne, one Lynx, and four choppers are on there way, e.t.a. 1210."

Colin quickly looked at his watch, it was 1200, 'shit' he said to himself, 'this is going to be a big one,' he quickly advised Tony of the pending air strike, Tony gave the order to pull back from the immediate area. They all lay low in the thick grass putting down fire. Colin's radio crackled into life "Trojan 4 this is Cyclone do you read me over."

"Yes Cyclone, this is Trojan 4, we read you loud and clear."

"Ok Trojan 4 I will be over you in about one minute, indicate your position with flot."

Colin discharged a canister of orange flot over to his right, at the same time Buz discharged one to his left.

"I have you visible Trojan 4," called Cyclone, "Indicate the enemies position with a pencil flare."

Colin fired the pencil flare. As the small crimson ball rose into the air towards the enemy position, "Enemies position indicated" he called into the radio, "It's about twenty yards short."

"I see your marker." replied the pilot, "I'm coming in now, put down rapid fire."

The noise was deafening, everyone was firing into the enemy position and the Lynx came screaming through the air with both cannons blazing. 'Surely nothing could survive that' thought Tony, 'It must be total hell in the enemy camp.' The radio crackled into life again "I'm coming in for another run, hold your positions, one more run and I will be going back to base. Four choppers are waiting to come in."

Once again the Lynx screamed into action, this time it dropped two canisters of phosphorus. They hit the ground and exploded, sending an agonising death into the area. "Trojan 4, this is Cyclone, I will give the choppers some air space, I will stick around for a few minutes, good hunting, over and out."

The air was thick with smoke, and the smell of cordite was overpowering. Tony was aware of fire coming his way, 'tough lot of bastards.' he thought to himself. He could now hear the screams of agony coming from the thick bush, his thoughts were quickly interrupted by the sound of the incoming helicopters. Three Alouette 111 helicopters were hovering about three foot off the ground, the gunner was raking the area as troops jumped out, and gave covering fire. High in the sky was a K car; it was pounding the bush with an awesome fire power from its cannon. Soon the area was full of security forces, five from each chopper. The helicopters pulled back and gave air cover.

Tony signalled to his men to form an extended line, and slowly advanced into the target area. His heart was pounding, and knew that it was far from over. How many terrs were in the bush? How many had survived the onslaught? Were they hard core? No time for pissing about. Every man knew what he had to do, if you saw an injured terr, you gave him a double tap in the head, even a badly injured terr could still put up a fight. You may think he is dead, it's not until you have passed him and he sees your back that he will make his move. One thing is for sure, dead terrs don't fight back, kill the bastards, it's the only way. Slowly he made his way forward, small fires were burning from the air attack, the smell was sickening, it was like burnt pork. Parts of bodies were hanging from the branches, like Christmas decorations. Tony moved his eyes and his FN rifle in the same direction, finger on the trigger, waiting for the slightest sign of movement, and there it was. He fired twice into the head of a terr who was lying against a tree with his AK47 in his hands. Tony's bullets tore into the body and lifted it away from the tree and sprawled it on to the ground. He moved over to see the body, it was a total mess. He slowly moved forward, his eyes moving from left to right, then up and down, taking in the total field of fire that lay before him. He flinched as shots sounded near to him, slowly he made his way forward, he was aware of every footstep he made, he could hear his every breath. Against a rock lay a figure; his face was the size of a football. Tony froze, he fired two shots into the body, it didn't move, slowly he approached. The face was a mess, it was bloated out of all proportion, the skin was all peeled away from the skull, the hands that held the AH47 were just bones. 'Phospherous,' he thought to himself, 'shit what a weapon, who could possibly survive it.' He wiped the sweat from his stinging eyes, as he moved past the body, he gave it one last look, fuck you, he thought. You came here for a war, you found it, you met your match, rot in hell. Tony slowly moved on, he missed nothing, every blade of grass, every twig on every tree, every rock..

Still shots could be heard, he looked to his right and he saw Colin, and to his left, he could see Ken, they were also intent on the job that they were doing. Total professionals, nothing was missed in their field of vision, his men were a dedicated killing team, eager to get the job over and done with, and get back to their families and to farming.

They had now moved through the killing ground, their feet were burning with the heat from the hot embers, the ground was still smouldering, burning grass and branches, set alight from the explosions of the phosphorous bombs. The air was full of death, the smell of burnt pork hung as a reminder of the recent contact.

'No time for pity,' thought Tony, 'It's either them or us.' Suddenly he stopped and listened, the silence was eerie, nothing, not a sound, it seemed as if everyone else had stopped. He looked over at Colin; he was also standing still, waiting to catch the slightest indication that could mean danger. Tony turned to look over to see Ken; he was also motionless, crouched down, his rifle pointing into the thick bush, looking for the slightest movement. Tony looked past Ken and saw Buz , he was slowly moving through the bush towards Ken, and not far away he saw Alec. Tony signalled to his stick to move forward. As they moved out of the bush and into a small clearing, Tony could see other members of the security forces who had come in by chopper, slowly moving ahead of him. He beckoned to Colin to make contact with their leader, it was time to talk and to discuss the situation.

Tony shook hands with Brian Cooper, Brian had been in the Rhodesian Light Infantry for six years, and during this time he had seen his share of action. He had been a very popular trooper, and for the last two years had held the rank of sergeant.

"Were you ambushed?" he asked,

"No, luckily we saw them first and initiated the contact." replied Tony, "We had a feeling that something wasn't right, and I decided to go in and take a closer look. Luckily we did, we slotted one of them straight away, and the rest, well you know."

Sergeant Cooper ran his hand over the stubble on his chin and said, "I feel that we could still have a fight on our hands. There is no way of knowing at this moment in time how many terrs there were. As yet, we don't have a head count of the dead, so we must presume that either some got away, or they are out there waiting to see what we do next. We have cleared the initial contact area, and I am happy that there is no danger in that area at all. If anyone got away, then I feel that the only direction that they could of gone is to the west of us. And that leads to that large rocky outcrop over in that direction." Sergeant Cooper looked over and pointed to an area about twenty yards away, "I have called for a tracker unit to be brought in by chopper, and they are sending a four man stick of Rhodesian African Rifles, they should be with us any time now."

"What the hell for?" asked Tony, "I am a tracker; I am as good as anyone that they can send to help us."

"Sorry mate I had no idea, but at the moment the more men on the ground the better."

Twenty men in extended line slowly moved towards the new target area. If anyone was up there, then they had the advantage, both the element of surprise and very good cover. Tony looked up and thought, 'Bloody hell we are sitting targets, totally out in the open, and not a lot of cover if the shit hits the fan.' He looked over his shoulder towards the sound of an incoming chopper, 'Bloody hell mate you are coming in close, pull back and drop your men.' he said to himself. For some reason he quickly looked back towards the rocky outcrop, and saw it, the dark trail of an RPG rocket as it left it's launcher. "Rocket!" he yelled, and turned towards the chopper. The pilot had also seen it and was revving the engines to take evasive action and get out of the line of fire. There was a look of horror on Tony's face as the rocket streaked towards it's target, Tony was about to shout again when there was a terrific explosion and a blinding flash. Everyone hit the deck as flames, burning fuel, and bits of wreckage flew through the air. As the helicopter hit the ground there was another massive explosion that shook the whole area. Tony hugged the ground; his back was burning from the intense heat. Then came the automatic fire from the rocks, short bursts of RPD then what seemed like two other bursts of AK47 fire. 'Shit' he thought, 'they have us pinned down.' Tony was lying near to Colin, and he could hear the radio crackle into life, "This is Crusader Zero Echo, put down fire and move back, I repeat move back. All call signs acknowledge, are you there Trojan 4?" Sergeant Cooper yelled into the radio.

"We hear you," yelled Tony, "moving back now."

"Ok" yelled Sergeant Cooper, "Keep your heads down and prepare for Cyclone to pound the area, two Hunters on their way, over." Tony grabbed the hand set and shouted, "Zero one, this is Trojan 4, I read you, we are pulling back now, over."

All eyes were now on Tony, "Ok," he shouted, "Watch your backs and pull back now, if you don't do it quickly, you will wish you had when the Hunters get here."

'The shit had really hit the fan now,' thought Tony, 'Bloody hell what more could happen to them today?' The air was full of men shouting, and automatic fire, again the radio came into life, "This is Cyclone, this is Cyclone, do you read me?"

Before Tony could answer, Brian was on the air, "Cyclone, Cyclone this is Crusader, I read you loud and clear, I can now see you, turn left, I repeat turn left, that's it come on in straight, we are putting down flot now."

"Crusader I see you, on my next pass indicate enemy position."

The two hunters roared over head, everyone cheered, the adrenaline was flowing fast now.

"Crusader, Crusader, put down rapid fire as I come in, I am targeting the rocky outcrop, confirm target,"

"Confirmed" replied Sergeant Cooper, "Give them hell, over."

The two hunters screamed into the target with rapid cannon fire, then they dropped their bombs. The earth literally moved, everyone held their breaths and hugged the ground. The noise was deafening, pieces of stone and earth rained down on them. 'No one could survive that,' thought Tony. "Crusader this is Cyclone, we will give it another pass."

Again the two hunters came in screaming at the target, cannons roaring again.

"Ok Crusader this is Cyclone, we are going back to base, we will leave you to clean up the mess."

Chapter Five

In Salisbury the street lights cast long shadows over the rain soaked roads and buildings. A constant stream of cars were heading down First Street and into Jameson Avenue, all looking for that one precious parking place, before hitting the pubs and clubs. It was a bank holiday, which meant a long weekend, four days off, time to relax and enjoy the break.

Joshua walked past the Jameson Hotel, then on towards the prestigious Monomatapa Hotel with it's now famous, enormous crystal chandelier hanging in the reception area. It looked a hive of activity, people booking in and booking out, porters carrying suitcases to and from the lifts. 'Enjoy it while it lasts' thought Joshua, 'soon you will not know what has hit you.'

Robert and Isaac followed in the shadows, they watched Joshua as he crossed the road, and made their way into a dark side street which led them to the Queens Hotel. Joshua knew that it would be safe here, as it was one of only two hotels in Salisbury where very few of the white population would wish to be seen in. The only whites that used the place came for one reason, and that was to pick up a black woman.

After the recent events, he knew that they would have to lie low for a while and what better than to get out of the area completely. It also suited his needs perfectly as he needed to be re-supplied with ammunition and anything else that he could get his hands on.

During his training in Mozambique, Joshua had been supplied with information regarding a contact, who he could reach through the Queens Hotel. It had been stressed that this contact should only be used in a dire emergency and then only with the utmost caution..

Joshua walked into the smoke-filled room, and gently pushed his way to the bar. He caught the barman's eye and ordered three cold bottles of Lion Lager. As he waited to be served he opened a packet of cigarettes and placed one between his lips, 'now' he thought, 'I look the part.' The barman placed the drinks on the bar and took the money.

"Got a light man?" Joshua asked,

"Sure," replied the barman, and handed over a box of matches. Joshua passed the two bottles to Robert, then turned to the barman, "Are you always as busy as this?" he asked,

"It's the start of the long weekend, and you had better believe me, we are going to be very busy." replied the barman.

"I'm looking for a friend of mine," said Joshua, "I was told that I would possibly find him here, his name is Dick, Elliot Dick. You may know him."

"I know him." replied the barman, "I know him well, but you are out of luck, he worked here for about three years, as the head barman, but he left about three months ago. Just upped and left, said he had other things to do."

"Is he in town?" asked Joshua, "Do you know where I could find him?"

"He sure ain't in town that's for sure, he went back to his village." replied the barman, "His family come from the Mazoe area, he was always talking about the Domboshawa caves, I think his village is just north of the caves."

"You don't know the name of the village, do you?" asked Joshua,

The barman smiled, "What do you want that for, just ask for Elliot Dick, everyone knows him."

An hour later, Joshua stood outside the Queens hotel. "Bloody hell," said Joshua, "We have come all this way to see him, and he is living almost where we started from."

They stepped out into the rain, Joshua knew that there was no chance of getting a bus at this time of night, and he had no wish to travel during daylight. He knew that to try and walk it was out of the question, it was a good hour by bus, and that was just to Mazoe. From there he had no idea where to look. He looked at Robert, "We will go by car, there are plenty to choose from, just take your pick. "Go on," he said, "Get us a car, but nothing too flash."

Within half an hour they were on their way in an old Ford Anglia. They drove through Avondale and onto the Mazoe road, not a car in sight. Robert drove with his face right up to the wind screen.

"Relax will you," snapped Joshua, "It will be morning before anyone notices that the car is missing, and by then we will be well out of it."

As they approached the Mazoe dam they left the main road and made their way along a dirt track. They drove for about twenty minutes then decided to abandon the car and headed off into the bush at a brisk trot.

As the morning sun lit the sky, they made their way through the thick bush.

"Look and listen for any signs of life." said Joshua. They kept close to the banks of the dam, as he knew any village would be within easy walking distance of water. Soon they heard the sound of voices in the distance, a dog barked, and children laughing. Within minutes they were standing at the very edge of a village.

"Come on," said Robert, "Let's just walk in, I'm starving, surely they will give us food and water."

"OK let's go." agreed Joshua. As they walked into the clearing they could see five mud huts. They approached the largest of the huts, and everyone stopped what they were doing. The children stood and stared; the women who were pounding maize stopped what they were doing and covered their faces. Two little scrawny dogs came running and barking at them, snarling and showing their teeth. "Stand still, and don't look at them." said Joshua, "They will soon lose interest in us."

In the distance a voice barked an order, the dogs turned and ran with their tails between their legs.

"Welcome to our village." Walking towards them was an old man. He had a big smile on his face, "welcome, welcome," He held out both of his thin arms, and shook hands with everyone. "Come," he pointed to one of the huts, "Come into the shade, it's not very often that we get visitors to our village. Have you been travelling long you must be thirsty." Cautiously they followed the old man into the darkness of the cool mud hut. "Sit," he said. As they sat down two children appeared in the door way. One brought in a bowl of water and lay it at the feet of the old man. The other child carefully skirted round the three visitors to place another bowl containing ground maize beside the water.

"Please" he said, as he indicated with his outstretched arms, "Help yourselves, food and water, it's not very much but we are a very poor village, but you are most welcome."

They all sat in silence as they finished off all the food and water.

"You are most kind." said Isaac,

"Thank you very much indeed, are you just passing through?" asked the old man. Before any one could answer and possibly say the wrong thing, Joshua quickly spoke, "Actually we are looking for a friend that we have not seen for some time, his name is Dick, Elliot Dick. Do you know where we can find him?" The old man tossed his head back, opened his mouth, revealing three stumps of rotting teeth, saliva trickled down his chin as he roared in great bursts of laughter, "Do I know Elliot Dick? do I know where to find him? Everyone knows him, everyone knows Elliot Dick."

That evening, in a small room lit only by a single candle, the three of them sat in silence.

"And who sent you?" Elliot asked, "Why do you want to meet me, who are you, and who gave you my name?"

"No one sent us," replied Joshua, "Your name was given to me by a person called Matambo."

At this Elliot's eyes opened wide, "And how do you know Matambo?" Elliot asked,

"I met him in Mozambique when I was training with ZAPU." said Joshua with great pride.

"Describe him to me." Elliot said,

"He is a very big man, with enormous strength. He is an Albino, and has a large scar across his face." "That is Matambo." said Elliot, "But what did he call me apart from my name?"

"He said that you are his blood brother, but that you are a..." Joshua hesitated, "You are a...", "Go on," said Elliot "Say what he called me."

Joshua licked his lips, "He said that you are a bloody rogue, but that he loves you."

Elliot clapped his hands, he grabbed Joshua and hugged him, "You are my friends, you are welcome, now what can I do for you."

The following morning Elliot led the three of them away from the village. They walked for at least an hour then entered a cave that was well hidden from view. Deep in the cave they stood in silence as Elliot opened up box after box of ammunition and weapons. "Take what you need, but never come here without me."

65

"We need landmines, and plenty of ammunition. We are going to start a war that they will never forget.

"And where are you going to start this war?" asked Elliot,

"In the Matepatepa area," replied Joshua, "North of Bindura."

"We will come back tonight when it's dark so you can pick up your weapons. I want you to meet another freedom fighter called Magumbo, said Elliot. He commands a group of ten men. He is planning on going to Mtoko to fight."

That evening, just as the sun was going down, they sat together eating what was possibly their last properly cooked meal. With them was this man called Magumbo, he was very powerfully built, but short and squat. His reputation was fearsome according to Elliot Dick, who seemed to know him well.

In whispered tones Elliott told Joshua how this was the man who cut off peoples lips, ears and their noses, made their families cook them, and then eat them. He would do this on the slightest suspicion that they were collaborating with the security forces. If he was certain then he would hack the whole family to pieces, or lock them into their mud hut and then set fire to it, he was totally evil.

"So where are you and your men heading?" Magumbo asked Joshua.

"We are going back to the Matepatepa area, there are plenty of white farmers there, and we have a score to settle. We hit a farm there recently, and one of my men was killed by the farmer. "Yes," Joshua said slowly, "Ticky was a good man and an old friend of mine. And where are you heading for, Mtoko I believe, is that correct?" asked Joshua,

"Yes," replied Magumbo, "It's an area that has very few white farmers, but a massive population of people, who I'm sure would come and join our cause and fight for their freedom. It's an area that the security forces have kept away from, why, I have no idea. Maybe they regard it as of no importance, as there are no white farmers there. So for me it is a good area to operate from. We can use it as a base to return to after attacking white farms on the outlying areas. Anyway enough talking, let's go and collect our arms and get on our way while we have the cover of darkness."

Magumbo led his men into the dark cave to collect their

weapons, as they returned to the entrance of the cave he stood before Joshua and his men.

"Good luck brother and a safe journey, soon this land will be ours, and the white man will either be kicked out, or killed. The choice is theirs."

Within the hour Joshua was again standing at the entrance of the cave, he shook hands with Elliot, "Thank you brother, one day we will meet again when this country is ours."

They all shook hands again and disappeared into the night, carrying their new supply of weapons of war.

Chapter Six

Shamva was a small mining town, east of Bindura surrounded by white farmland, farming maize, tobacco, cotton, and cattle. A very friendly community, where everyone was always ready to help his fellow man. The central point of the small village was the church, where on a Sunday, nearly everyone would try and attend the morning service, possibly more to gossip and catch up on the latest news than anything else.

George Hastings had been farming there all his life, he had been born on the farm when it had been virgin land. He had grown up seeing his mother and father turn it from a wilderness into a very successful business.

The farm had been passed onto George when his parents had passed away, then at the age of sixty-two and not in good health he had handed the everyday running of the farm to their only son Peter.

Two years ago tragedy struck. Peter had been killed in a freak accident on the farm, leaving his wife Gwen and two children, Wendy aged eleven and Robin aged eight. Unable to run the farm himself, George had taken on a manager. Martin had a lot to learn, but getting a manager was not easy, and Martin was very keen and seemed the right person for the job.

Gwen's parents had been living in Salisbury, in the suburb of Avondale. Both had been teachers, and when Gwen's father had died, her mother had decided to return to Scotland. Gwen was very upset to see her go, but knew that it was the best thing for her to do as politically the country was not as stable as it had been, and Gwen did not like the idea of her mother living alone.

Three day's ago Gwen had received a phone call from her younger brother in Scotland, telling her that her mother was in hospital and in very poor health, and it would be wise to fly home to see her.

It had been such unsettling news that Gwen had left the next day, calling in to see her children at their private school in Salisbury. They had been very upset and had wanted to go with her, but she had persuaded them that it was for the better if they stayed behind and looked after their grandparents in Shamva.

"I won't be long," she said, "Grandad is coming to collect you on Thursday, it's a bank holiday, you're off for four days and you will be spending it on the farm. Just look what you will be missing."

After a lot of tears, Gwen headed for the airport.

George finished his plate of eggs and bacon, wiped the plate with a piece of bread and pushed it away from him, "That was lovely my dear." he said to his wife in a deeply satisfied voice.

He picked up his pot of tea, rose from the table and sat down in his favourite moth-eaten armchair, "Just what a man needs to start the day," he said with a sigh, "Even if he has no work to do."

Betty was busy in the kitchen, baking chocolate cake for her grandchildren, apple crumble, and their favourite fruit biscuits.

"Don't you fall asleep, you will have to leave here about lunch time if you are going to pick up the children from school." She scolded George.

"Don't you worry," George replied, "I'm just letting my breakfast settle, then I will check the car and be on my way in good time."

It was eleven o'clock, and George was ready to go, "Will you be alright while I'm away?" he asked.

"I will be fine," Betty replied, "I will lock up as soon as you have gone. Don't you worry about me, just drive carefully."

"Remember if you want anything just ring someone as Martin is away for the weekend." George gave her a peck on the cheek and closed the door behind him.

George lit his pipe, started the car, and drove from his farm onto the A13 leading to Mermaids Pool, and then onto Salisbury.

The drive was uneventful and by the time he arrived in Salisbury he was beginning to feel the effects of the heat and the humidity. He parked outside Wendy's school, turned off the engine, and opened the drivers' door to let in some cool air. He took off his trilby and wiped his brow with the back of his hand, 'Bloody hell' he thought 'it's a hot one today.'

"Grandad, Grandad," he heard some one call out, he turned to see Wendy running towards the car and waving her arms. She ran up to the car and threw her arms around his neck and gave him a great big hug and a kiss, "Where is Nana?" she asked, as she looked into the car.

"Nana is back at the farm," George replied, "She is baking your favourite chocolate cake and cookies. Come on get in and we will pick up Robin."

"Oh Robin isn't coming." said Wendy, "He asked if it would be all right if he stayed with one of his friends from his class for the weekend, he gave me a telephone number to give to you so that you can ring his friends parents." "OK, we'll give them a call when we get back home " said George with a smile.

An hour later and they were on their way back to the farm. George felt more relaxed now that he was on his way home again, and that his little princess was with him, even though she never stopped talking until they pulled up in front of the farm. After she had hugged and kissed her Nana, she started all over again telling her the same things that she had told her Grandad on their journey from Salisbury.

George sat down heavily in his favourite chair, he reached to the fireplace and picked up his pipe and tobacco. Slowly he filled the pipe and placed it in his mouth, he sat for a while then lit the tobacco, clouds of pungent smoke filled the room. He sat back in the chair and closed his eyes.

It was now dark outside, and George woke with a start, as someone was calling his name, "Mr George," the voice called "Mr George your dinner is ready," George opened his eyes and looked around the room. Standing next to him was his house boy of thirty years. Kenneth had been working on the farm all of his life, he had started in the fields, then in the tobacco barns. He was very slightly built and not a strong child, so George had given him the job as his house boy. He was now forty-six years old but looked as if he was eighty. He had virtually grown up with George's son Peter, and treated Wendy and Robin as if they were his own.

"All right I'm coming." said George as he lifted himself out of his chair. He stood up and put his pipe on the fire place, scratched his head, turned and made his way to the dining room.

A short time later Kenneth came into the room and cleared the table. Everyone was now sitting in the living room relaxing. George was sitting in his chair with a glass of brandy in his hand, Betty was busy doing some needlework, and Wendy was playing on the floor with her dollhouse that George had made for her last Christmas. As the clock struck nine Kenneth came into the room and said "I'm all finished now, if there is nothing else for me to do then I will say good night to you all."

"Goodnight Kenneth," everyone said at the same time, he smiled and let himself out of the back door.

George poured himself another brandy, and turned on the television. "I wonder what has been happening today." he said out loud. He flicked the channel and listened to Adrian Cairns read out the news Security Forces announced today that five more terrorists were killed in the Mount Darwin area, follow up operations are continuing. We are pleased to announce that no members of the security forces were injured. Meanwhile in the Mtoko area, sightings have been reported of a large force of armed tribesmen moving north, security forces have been deployed to the area. We will give you more news as and when it comes in. George turned the television off, 'Bloody cowards' he said to himself. 'Why don't they just come out into the open and fight, why do they have to run into the shadows, and hit soft targets all of the time.'

Betty put down her sewing and took off her glasses, "Come on young lady," she said as she rubbed her eyes, "It's time that you were in your bed."

"Five more minutes please." Wendy said.

"All right but five minutes and no longer." Wendy replied indulgently.

Just then there was a sharp knock on the front door, George looked at Betty and got up from his chair. He walked to the door and in an anxious voice asked, "Who is it?"

"It's me," replied Kenneth, "I must speak to you."

George opened the door, "Come in," he said to Kenneth, "What is the problem, couldn't it have waited until the morning?" Kenneth stood there visibly shaking the whites of his eyes showing as they rolled in fear "No Mr George you must come now" replied Kenneth frantically, pulling all the time on George's arm. "You must come with me, there are men out there and they are armed!"

George moved quickly, he grabbed his shotgun, loaded it and put one into the breach. He picked up his revolver, checked that it was loaded and stuck it into his waistband.

"OK" he said "Show me.

"Be careful," Betty said, "Why don't you ring for help?"

"No time." George replied, "Lock this door, I won't be long."

The black of the night momentarily blinded George, he stood for a few moments to get his night eyes. "Which way?" he whispered to Kenneth,

"Straight ahead down towards the river." came the whispered reply.

"How many of them did you say there was?" asked George, "How many Kenneth," asked George again,

"Kenneth, where are you?" George whispered fiercely. He turned to look back and realised he was on his own. Moving forward again he peered into the darkness. Shakily George drew a shallow breath trying to draw the air into his aching chest. "Kenneth you bastard where the fuck are you?" he ground out.

Still no reply. George did not like the feeling at all, then from behind him and in the direction of the farmhouse he heard gun shots.

George's heart seemed to stop; he peered into the night, looking back the way he had come. He started to run as best as he could, his breathing was laboured and his heart was pounding in his chest. As George approached the farmhouse he could see flickering shadows through the living room window. Scrambling onto the veranda almost falling in his haste George burst into the living room. There lying on the floor lay his beautiful granddaughter-most of her head missing. In mind numbing horror his head turned to sweep the room to see his wife lying across the chair, her body almost torn in two by automatic gunfire. Movement made him turn, standing next to the dining room door was Kenneth. He was smiling and in his hands was an AK 47 assault rifle, before George could bring his shotgun up to open fire, Kenneth fired a long burst straight into his master's chest.

As dawn broke Kenneth was deep in the thick undergrowth with his new found friends. They all knew that it was only a matter of time before the alarm was raised and the security forces would come looking for them. It was at this point that Kenneth realised the mistake that he had made. He was now deep in thought, he had done a terrible thing, but it was now impossible to go back to the farm or to the village. He remembered the first moment that he had seen and spoken to Joshua, "Now my friend," Joshua had said, as he had embraced him, "I have come to help you and your friends, I have come to set you all free, what prospects do you have as a slave to your white master,"

Kenneth had listened intently.

"You have no future, your children and your children's children, think of them what will they have to look forward to. I will tell you, they will have nothing, as they do now."

It was later in the evening that Joshua handed him an AK 47, "Come and join us, and you can break the chains of your slavery forever."

Kenneth gripped the weapon and rose to his feet, "What do you want me to do?" he had said in a trembling voice.

Chapter Seven

It was noon before the news broke. All the farm workers had been woken by the sound of gunfire, but were too afraid to venture outside to see what was happening. They all knew that there were people in the area who were armed, and who were fighting for changes, but this was the first time that anyone had come to their village. They had heard stories of torture and mutilation, stories of people who had argued with them and who had been taken away, never to be seen again. No one opened their doors, they all huddled together and shook with fear.

Bob Smith was a company rep, and had been with the same company for twenty-two years, he considered many of the farmers as personal friends. He was often invited to parties, and he and his wife would often spend the weekends at various farms. Leaving early on a Monday morning to drop his wife off at work, he would go to his office, and then set off back to visit the farming community. The company that he worked for manufactured fertiliser and insecticides, Bob's specialised knowledge was of great value to every farmer in the area. The current situation in the country had made his job a very difficult one. Travelling on dirt roads in most areas was now very dangerous. Knowing that he could be attacked at any time and with the knowledge that terrorists had started laying land mines gave Bob grave cause for concern.

Bob glanced at his watch as he approached River Bend farm. '10.30,' he said to himself, 'just in time for a cup of tea and a slice of home-made apple pie.' He killed the engine and slipped from the driving seat, his shirt was sticking to his back as he stood in the thick dusty path leading up to the farmhouse. He arched his back and stretched his arms above his head. 'Bloody hell,' he said to himself, 'It's hot for this time of the day.' He looked towards the veranda and frowned. Normally, Betty was halfway down the path by now, and George, if he was not out on the farm, would be standing in the doorway, yelling 'Come on you old sod, you've only come to see us because you know that I've got cold beer in the fridge.' Bob walked up to the veranda and started to mount the four steps when the hair on the back of his neck stood up, and his skin began to crawl. He could see a pair of feet sticking out of the doorway. He hurried forward thinking someone had fallen, he stopped suddenly in his tracks and was violently sick with the sight that met his eyes. George was lying face up in a pool of blood, flies covered the gaping wound in his chest and stomach. Bob wiped his mouth and stepped over the lifeless body, he didn't want to go into the house as he was afraid of what he would find. He felt his feet sticking to the blood soaked carpet as he slowly moved into the room. His eyes saw what he did not want to see, sitting in a chair was Betty, but no big smile or a warm welcome this time. She was almost cut in half. It was then that he saw little Wendy, or was it Wendy? With the mounting horror his gaze settled on the tiny crumpled body. 'Please God' he prayed 'don't let it be Wendy' At first sight you identify a body by the face, but when just about the whole head is missing it is very difficult. Bob's eyes filled with tears as he lifted the phone and spoke to Mike Johnson and told him what he had found.

Mike was almost speechless, he had known the Hastings as if they were family.

"OK Bob," he said "Get out of the house, don't touch anything, just get out of there, I will be there with back up within the hour."

Bob sat in his car, it was very difficult stopping himself from returning to the farmhouse. He had known the Hastings for so long that he could not remember a time when he had not known them. He had been there with his wife to give them comfort when they had lost their son. Bob sat up with a start, Their grandson, he suddenly thought. Where was he? Bob ran back to the farmhouse, I must find the young boy, he kept saying to himself. He was almost at the front door when he heard an increasing noise coming towards him, suddenly the noise was deafening. He stopped in his tracks and turned and looked behind him, the noise was now hurting his ears as four helicopters roared into view. He had to turn away as the wind and dust churned around him, suddenly the noise was gone and he was surrounded by armed police. Mike grabbed his arm and led him back to his car, "I told you to stay away from the house, now get into your car and stay there."

"It's Robin, its Robin where is he, I didn't see him in the

house, but he must be in there."

Mike nodded to his men to enter the farmhouse. "Look for a young boy." he told them. Bob sat in his car waiting for news of young Robin, he felt totally frustrated that he couldn't do anything to help. It seemed like an eternity before Mike walked over to his car. Mike shook his head, "No sign of Robin," he said quietly, "There is nothing to indicate that he has been here this weekend. We need to make some calls and check if he has stayed with friends. Do you have any idea how to contact his Mother in Scotland?

Bob shook his head, "But it will possibly be in the diary next to the phone." he replied.

Mike nodded and walked over to the troop carrier that had just arrived, and shook hands with the Army Captain.

"We have plenty of daylight left, I've instructed the helicopter crew to lift off and do some ever increasing sweeps over the area. We also have a tracker team out at this very moment to the west of us, if you could deploy some of your men to give them back up if they need it. There are two P.A.T.U. sticks on their way, and should be with us any moment now." Mike told the Captain.

"Do you have any thing to go on at all?" asked the Captain,

"Not a bloody thing just three dead bodies. Special Branch will be with us soon to do what they have to do, and then the ballistics experts will get to work." said Mike.

"I heard someone mention a young boy was possibly missing." queried the Captain.

"Yes" nodded Mike, "That is a possibility but we are not sure at the moment if he was ever at the farm. Bastard cowards, old people and children, what animals would do a thing like this?"

The silence was once again interrupted as two more choppers roared over the farm, turned and landed. Tony Marshal led his four men over to the command centre which had been set up on the back of a Land Rover. Tony held out his hand to the Army Captain, "Tony Marshal P.A.T.U. Call sign Trojan Four."

He nodded to Mike, "Where do you want us?"

The other P.A.T.U. stick joined the group and introduced themselves, "OK, my name is Vince Hall." said the Captain, "Lets cut out all the bullshit and formalities, we are here to do a job. Mike and I will be working closely together, at this moment in time I have got men out with local trackers, we have men on ops, Tony can you take your stick due East, down to the river. It's about seventy yards from here, cover both sides if you have to, they may try to use it to cover their tracks."

Tony led his men slowly down to the river. Everyone was looking for the slightest sign, no matter how small that would indicate that someone had passed this way very recently. A turned stone, or a bent or broken blade of grass, anything that would not have happened naturally. Only animals or humans would leave the signs that they were now looking for. Tony stopped his men; they all crouched down, and took up defensive positions as he scanned the area in front of them and to the sides. Slowly he swept from left to right and back again, it was on his third sweep that something caught his eye; slowly he focussed the binoculars onto the river edge. He scanned first left and then to the right and then he stopped. 'Got ya' he said to himself. Lying amongst the rocks he could see a shoe. He beckoned his men forward towards the river edge. Sure enough, all around the handmade sandal and along the river bank were footprints and they were fresh. He pulled the sandal out of the mud, it was one that the locals made out of a car tyre, the tread was used for the sole, and the straps were made from the thin side wall of the tyre. It was all held together with baling wire, it must have taken sometime to make, and would have been of great value to the owner. One thing was sure, whoever it had belonged to had been in a hurry, so much of a hurry that he had left it behind.

He now knew that he was onto something, and decided to move left up river, and then moved to his right, and there it was, a bare footprint next to an imprint of a sandal exactly like the one that he had just found. Whoever they were following, they were making no effort to hide their tracks. Tony called Buz over, "How many do you think were here?" he asked,

"I would say four or five," replied Buz, "and they were in a bloody hurry. I feel sure that we are onto something, and it's my guess that they have crossed the river."

"OK," said Tony "Let's get to the other side and pick up tracks, we have plenty of daylight left."

Having crossed the river they were now again looking for tracks that would lead them in the right direction. Within minutes they were back on tracks, "It looks like four men travelling light and going like the clappers, you can see how deep the front of the footprints are." said Buz, "They are definitely running, they are trying to put as much distance as possible between themselves and the farm." "Cowardly bastards." replied Tony under his breath.

"I think it's time for a sitrep?" said Tony, "Alpha Bravo Alpha Bravo this is Trojan Four do you read me over."

"Trojan Four this is Alpha Bravo reading you loud and clear."

"We have crossed the river, and are on tracks heading north." replied Tony, "The tracks are fresh and it looks like four persons travelling light and moving fast, over."

"Message received and understood, do you need back up?"

"No back up required." replied Tony, "Over and out."

'Bollocks,' thought Tony, 'Do we need back up. This is in my back garden, no bloody way is anyone going to get the glory of this one, it's ours.' The stick pushed on, searching for more clues, well knowing that at any time they could walk into an ambush, but also knowing that the terrs were cowards, and would only fight if they were trapped. The last thing that they wanted was to make contact with the security forces.

Tony knew these people; he had virtually grown up with them, and knew that they would be hell bent on putting as much distance as possible between themselves and the farm. They would then use the cover of darkness to try and make good their escape.

During the next few hours, Tony could hear helicopters in the area and he knew that against his wishes, more security forces were being brought into the area. He could now see fixed wing aircraft circling overhead. They would be trying to spot any movement on the ground and to alert ground forces of the position, but they would also be trying to stop or slow down the movement of the terrs and hopefully prevent their escape.

Tony wiped the sweat from his brow, "Take point." he called to Ken, "I'm losing my concentration," he said, "Alex take over from Ken when he gets tired."

Tony dropped back two places, and the stick moved off again in single file. Tony knew that if they did not make contact within the next two or three hours then the pursuit would have to be called off until first light in the morning. They had gone about a mile when Ken held up his hand and beckoned to Tony; Ken pointed down to the ground, and gently kicked a sandal with his boot. "Matching pair." he said with a smile, "Too bloody true," Tony replied, "No doubt about it we are on the right tracks."

They both bent down and looked at the tracks, "Very new," said Ken, "No more than an hour old if that." Tony signalled to his men to gather round, "OK" he said in a hushed voice, "We are close, very close, so be on your toes. We think there are four in the group, but we are not sure. We also don't know what weapons they are carrying, or if they are hard core, well-trained terrorists They may run, or put up a fight, my guess is that they will run when the first shot is fired. That does not make them easy meat, they could ambush us at any time, so easy as we go, OK lets move out."

Alex now took point, he was well aware of the dangers that lay ahead and was more than ready to deal with it as and when it happened. Within twenty minutes his eyes were burning with the strain, and the sweat that was running into them didn't help. He wiped the back of his hand across his forehead. The sweat that ran down his back tickled as it made it's way down to his waist line and stopped in a soggy pool just above his belt. His underpants were soaked, soon the chafing would start and then the dreaded prickly heat rash. Alex tugged at his webbing and took a better grip of his FN rifle. As he moved his eyes from left to right he saw movement. He froze; he raised his rifle and looked along the barrel into the direction where he had seen the movement. There it was again, just the slightest movement but it was there, two Africans with their backs to him, and both of them were armed with AK47 assault rifles. Alex did not hesitate, he let rip with a burst of automatic fire.

"To my right!" he yelled, "To my right." The sound was deafening as the air was filled with the sound of automatic fire, the single line formation was now an extended line and was moving forward with speed towards the enemy position. Tony slipped a rifle grenade onto the end of his rifle, turned the gas regulator to grenade. He quickly took off the magazine, ejected the round from his rifle and slipped in a ballastite cartridge.

"Grenade" he yelled as he fired into the enemy position. .Everyone dropped to the ground as the grenade curled in the air and dropped onto the target, then came the thump as it exploded. Immediately every one was up and running into the killing area. Alex saw the first body lying face down, blood was pouring from the back of the head. He put a double tap into the head and ran on.

The next body must have taken the full impact of the grenade as there was a gaping hole in the chest, and no sign of a head at all. Within minutes the area had been overrun, but just two bodies had been accounted for. Where were the other two or three? Tony looked at the feet of the dead terrs and saw that both of them were wearing shoes, so where was the one who had lost his sandals, either lying low or he had made a run for it. He was in no doubt that the tracks showed at least four sets of footprints. Having done a three sixty and secured the area, the stick moved on, nothing of importance had been found on the bodies, Tony had decided to leave them until he either returned, or until he called in backup.

Chapter Eight

Joshua led his men away from the farm taking Kenneth with him. He had done his bit and seemed like a willing and capable person. They moved quickly away from the immediate area and soon they were hidden from view by the thick bush and heading for the river. Kenneth was at the rear of the group and was struggling to keep up with everyone else.

"Come on." shouted Robert, "You're dropping too far behind."

"I'm coming." called Kenneth, "I've lost my shoe."

"Leave it." said Robert, "You don't have time to look for it. Come on move it or we will leave you behind." Kenneth stumbled behind, still looking over his shoulder with regret for his lost shoe. For four hours they moved on without stopping, when at last they stopped Kenneth was exhausted and dropped to the ground. He sat rubbing his feet, he had now lost the other sandal, and his feet were cut and bleeding. With a rising sense of fear Kenneth began to worry about his actions and more importantly the consequences. He was now on the run, in fear of his life with no likelihood of ever seeing his family again.

Joshua felt good, he had scored a direct hit against the white farmers. He knew that they had never been hit like this before, and he knew the effect that it would have on the white farming community.

As darkness closed in they rested again, "We will rest for about two or three hours then we will move on towards the Mount Darwin area." said Joshua, "So get some rest as we will be moving fast tonight."

Joshua woke up with a start and looked around him, every one was asleep, and the night sky was now breaking into daylight. 'Shit' he said to himself, 'We should have been on the move ages ago.' He jumped to his feet and gave everyone a good kick, "Get up." he hissed, "Get up, let's get moving."

As they started to break camp they heard the sound of low flying aircraft. "Bloody spotter planes." Joshua said, "We can't move from here at the moment, not with aircraft in the area, they would be onto us in no time. We had better stay where we are, and wait until they have completed their sweep of the area. "Get undercover," he said to everyone, "But be alert, as ground troops will be in the area."

The four men moved deep into the bush, being as careful as possible not to leave any signs of their presence. As the day drew on, the spotter planes moved away from the area, and soon they could not be seen or heard. Joshua decided it was safe to break cover and to continue their journey northwards. Without stopping they moved through the bush for the next two hours. He could see that Kenneth was struggling with the harsh pace and was in need of a break; in the distance he could see a large baobab tree with a rocky outcrop around it. 'Good place to use for a resting area, a good vantage point and plenty of cover.' he thought to himself. Within half an hour they were all resting, Robert and Isaac were sitting together next to the baobab tree and Joshua and Kenneth sat away from them amongst the rocks. Joshua was telling Kenneth about the fight for freedom that was going on within the country. He told him about the recent events, including the attack on the bus and the attack on a farm where he had killed the white farmer and his wife as they had returned to the farm at night. He told him about the attack on a farm called Camburo in which his friend Ticky had been killed, "But one day I will go back to that farm," he said, "and kill every one on the farm."

Kenneth was totally enthralled by the stories, "How many more men do you have in the area?" he asked Joshua,

"Plenty." Joshua replied, "We have no shortage of men willing to fight for the cause, and plenty of weapons." he said, "We have all the weapons that we will ever need, you name it and I can get it. I have a good friend called Elliot Dick in Mazoe, he supplies everyone in the area with weapons and ammunition. One day you will meet him."

Joshua was now in full flow with his stories, so much so that he had dropped his guard, and had not noticed that nobody was keeping watch. Robert and Isaac were talking in low whispers to each other. Just as Robert stood up to stretch his legs, the air was full of automatic fire and shouting. Robert took a burst full in his chest and was dead before he hit the ground. Isaac grabbed his rifle and started to fire, but the fire was so intense that he could not see what he was firing at, he never saw or heard the rifle grenade that took off his head.

Joshua grabbed his rifle and ran into the thick bush, "Come on!" he yelled to Kenneth, "Follow me at the double, let's get out of here."

Kenneth scrambled to his feet and ran like the wind behind Joshua. Bullets were flying everywhere, branches were falling off trees, the noise was so loud that his head was buzzing. With his heart pounding and a mouth so dry he could not speak Kenneth realised he must be screaming to Joshua in his head. In total panic he tried to make himself heard above the tumult. He ran faster trying to catch up with Joshua, who was now well ahead of him and moving as if the devil was on his tail. Tears of fear ran down Kenneth's face. His whole body soaked on sweat, quivered with exhaustion. It seemed as if he had been running forever when at last he caught up with Joshua. They both stopped and gasping dragged air into their tortured lungs, both unable to speak a word. Joshua was bent double, the sweat was now pouring from his body, "Where the fuck did they come from." he asked Kenneth, "Have you seen either Robert or Isaac" he raged,

"No." replied Kenneth, "I've no idea where they are, I didn't have time to look I was just trying to keep up with you."

"OK let's go." said Joshua, "Let's get well away from here, if they are alive then they know where to make contact with me."

Joshua was now heading south; he needed to regroup, and to make contact with more fighters. He knew now that he was possibly three men down, and he couldn't rely on Kenneth. He would be more of a hindrance than a help, his plans were now to make his way back to Mazoe and visit Elliot Dick, or try and make contact with Magumbo. At the speed that Joshua was moving, it was obvious that Kenneth was not going to be able to keep up with him.

"OK," said Joshua, "You rest, wait for me here, I will come back for you. I'm going to get help, whatever you do don't move from here OK?" Joshua set off again, knowing full well that he would never see Kenneth again. He had no intention of ever coming back for him. Kenneth was now alone and feeling very vulnerable.

Tony was now sure that two more terrs were in the area and on the run. Soon they were on tracks again, 'yes two men on the run' he said to himself. Realising that daylight does not last for ever, he was pushing on as fast as he possibly could without putting every one at risk. Knowing that at any moment an ambush could be sprung. Everything was now in the favour of the terrs, normally they would move for half an hour then rest for ten minutes, but now it was just go for it. After an hour they were all feeling the strain and decided to have a break, they spread out and took up defensive positions, Taking small sips of water and adjusting their webbing they were soon ready to forge on.

Kenneth saw them before they saw him. Should he open fire, and try and kill as many as he possibly could? He knew that he would certainly be killed as he was totally outnumbered; he had no wish to die, to die for what? He would tell them that they had taken him as a hostage, and then they just left him, Kenneth could now see them more clearly as they headed straight for him. Buz saw him first, and almost opened fire, but stopped when he saw that in his sights was a man who was holding his hands up in the air and did not look as if he was armed.

"Don't move or I will blow you away." shouted Buz, Kenneth froze and watched as the other members of the patrol swept the area, it took almost an hour before Tony was happy that it was not an ambush. Slowly Buz approached Kenneth, who was now trembling with fear.

"OK Kaffir, slowly get up onto your knees, and keep your hands behind your head, move slowly, don't make any sudden moves or you're dead." Buz noticed the AK 47 half hidden in the undergrowth. "This yours?" he snapped at Kenneth,

"No" he replied, "It's not mine."

"Don't lie you bloody kafffir, it is yours, do you think I'm bloody stupid, what's your name, come on answer me, what is your bloody name."

"Kenneth, I'm called Kenneth."

"And where are you from, come on, don't tell me that you live in the middle of the bush and that you just found this assault rifle, do you think I'm fucking stupid, start talking or I'll bury you here." screamed Buz.

"Easy does it." said Tony, "I'll take over the interrogation. Now look my friend we can do this the easy way or the hard way. I'm not all that bothered, but one thing is for sure, and that is you are going to tell me what I want to know. Now let's start from the beginning, your name is Kenneth, and where are you from?"

"River Bend Farm." Kenneth replied, "I am the house boy, and these men came with guns and killed my boss. They made me leave the farm and go with them."

"And where were they taking you." asked Tony,

"They were heading for Mount Darwin, but when the shooting started everything changed." said Kenneth shakily.

"What are the names of the two dead men." "Robert and Isaac." replied Kenneth,

"And who is with you now." Tony asked,

"No one." said Kenneth, "Joshua told me to stay here and to wait until he came back with help."

"And who is this Joshua, "Is he the leader?" queried Tony.

"Yes he is the leader, and he said he was going to see someone called Elliot Dick and get some help." said Kenneth.

Tony was now in his element, all this information was of immense importance. "Tell me more about Joshua, how old is he, is he tall, short, fat, thin, what does he look like."

"He is about six foot tall." said Kenneth, "Slim build, he wears thin rimmed glasses, and he has a very long scar running from his right elbow down to his wrist, and his front teeth stick out"

"How long has he been in the area?" asked Tony.

"I don't know." replied Kenneth,

"Come on" said Tony, "I want to know everything about him."

Kenneth hesitated, "He told me that he had killed a white farmer and his wife at a farm called Kadyo."

Tony's mouth went dry, he took a sip from his water bottle and lent forward, "Continue," he said, "tell me everything that you know about this bastard."

Tony listened with great interest to everything that he was told, then Kenneth started to tell him something that made Tony's scalp crawl. When they first came into the country to fight, there were four men Joshua, Robert Isaac, and Ticky, but Ticky was killed when an attack on a farm went wrong."

"What was the name of the farm?" asked Tony,

Kenneth hesitated, "I think it was in the Bindura area, a farm called Camburo."

Tony's heart missed a beat, so these were the bastards who had attacked his farm. Before he could say anything, Kenneth said,

"Joshua has said a few times that he will destroy that farm, and kill everyone on it."

Tony had now heard all that he wanted to hear. That night they all waited for the return of Joshua, but to no avail. It was obvious that Joshua had no intention of returning and had left Kenneth to fend for himself. What a big mistake that had been thought Tony.

At first light they broke camp, Tony called in a chopper to lift the bodies and for them to take Kenneth away for more intensive interrogation. All Tony had to do now was to find Joshua, but first Elliot Dick.

Mike Johnson sat at his desk, and looked again at the mound of paper work that had accumulated on his desk within the last few days.

"Can you believe it," he said to Tony, who was sitting opposite him, "Could you imagine what my office would be like if we were at war, I mean a full scale war." He placed one pile on top of another pile then leaned back in his chair.

"Well, it's been a hectic few weeks, to say the least." Mike groaned.

"You don't have to remind me." replied Tony, "I'm just pissed off that we lost tracks when we did, and that bastard Joshua got clean away."

Mike ran his fingers through his hair, "I know what you are going through and I know how frustrating it can be, not just for you and your stick but for everyone involved. It seems as if he just vanished into thin air, I have spoken to the member in charge at Glendale police station, and he assures me that every thing that can be done is being done. There are two P.A.T.U. sticks out at the moment, and they are at present keeping a close watch on the village where Elliot Dick lives, but nothing to report at the moment. We have two African constables who went into the village in plain clothes, and very discreetly asked a few questions but they came up with nothing. Either no one knows, or they are not saying a word, maybe out of loyalty or out of fear. "

"As for your contact at Eden Dam, it's very sad, but as you know, no one survived the helicopter crash when it was brought down. Five terrs were killed, one was wounded and at this moment he is singing like a bird, seemingly the leader of the group was hurt, he lost his little finger on his right hand. This is the chap who has been causing havoc amongst the local tribesmen, cutting off lips and ears, and then making their families cook and then eat it. His name is Magumbo, he is more than likely sitting low, licking his wounds and feeling rather sorry for himself. He has been active in the Mount Darwin, and the Centenary areas, and also as far away as Nyamapanda area, but he seems only interested in hitting the local population, and keeping well away from the white farming areas."

"Says a lot," said Tony, "He is a fuckin' coward, just like the rest of the bastards. They hit isolated farmhouses, unarmed tribesmen, or some poor sod just doing his job in the field. But when it comes to take on the security forces they will only do it if they are cornered.

"Now that we are on the subject." said Tony, "What the bloody hell are the District Commissioners doing, aren't they supposed to be our eyes and ears, aren't they supposed to know exactly what is going on in the tribal trust land. Surely you can't tell me that they have nothing to report, surely they must have noticed some changes in the areas. Even I bloody well know that there has been an exodus of young African males from the tribal trust land."

"It's a very difficult job." said Mike in a conciliatory tone.

"Come on Mike, don't give me that crap." said Tony, "They get bloody well paid, and for doing what, attending cocktail parties and sipping pink gins. They should be out there and doing the job that we pay them to do." Tony said in an aggrieved voice. "That's a bit harsh, you must remember that they have an enormous area to cover, and it's very inhospitable terrain out there." replied Mike.

Tony gasped, "Don't tell me how bad it is out there, I bloody live out there, the sods have got it cushy."

"At the moment we think that there are about thirty to forty terrs in the country, no one knows exactly, it's just a guess if you like." said Mike,

"Has no one ever asked the question, how many terrs are outside the county waiting to come in?" said Tony,

"The ones that are in the country we can deal with, just as soon as they make their presence known. It's the ones who are about to come into the country that should be of a worry to us all. I honestly think that the majority of the black population do not support any uprising," said Mike, "Yes they possibly would like more say in the running of the country, but they have seen what has happened to the other African countries that have been given independence."

"Then why don't the politicians, in all of the so-called do good countries, wake up to reality. Why does another country have to go down the same road to ruin." asked Tony.

Mike held up his hands, "I'm a police officer, I'm not in government, I just do as I'm told."

Tony shook his head, "Tell me this then, why don't we hit the terrorist camps across the border, why don't we just take them out."

"Bloody hell Tony." Mike said "Can you imagine the international uproar if we just went in and bombed the shit out of the enemy, it's an act of war, and at the moment we are not at war. It is a police matter."

"Who said bomb them," asked Tony, "Why don't we send in our special forces, the S.A.S. or the Selous Scouts, they are perfect for the job."

Mike smiled, "You're ahead of your time." he said,

"What do you mean, ahead of my time?"

"Let's just say that people much higher than you or I, are thinking along the same lines, and it is much more advanced than we would like to think." Mike looked at his watch and stood up, "Come on I will buy you some lunch, nothing flash mind, a sandwich and a pint."

Mike stood at the bar of the police club adequately named The Dungeon, and ordered two bottles of Lion Lager, and two cheese and pickle sandwiches.

"We will be sitting in the corner when they are ready." he said to the barman as he picked up the two ice cold bottles and the two glasses. Tony took a sip of the cold lager and gave a shiver. "That's bloody lovely." he said, "It tastes even better as it's free."

"And how are the family Tony?" Mike asked,

"Oh they are fine." said Tony, "In fact Joyce rang last night to see if things were any better. She wanted to know if it was all right for Benji and her to come back to the farm." Said Tony despondently. I know it must be difficult for them, but I feel it's too early for them to come back yet."

"And how did she take it?" asked Mike,

"Oh shit not well at all, she is moaning that when Mark and

Susie are out at work she is stuck in the house all day, and all that she can do is to walk around the houses, and now that's getting boring. So now she wants a car, but to be honest we just cannot afford one at the moment. No a car is definitely out of the question."

Mike downed his drink and stood up, "maybe I can help you" he said, "As you know my sister lives in Avondale, not far from Mabelreign, and I'm sure that she has, or had an old Ford Anglia in the garage. She has been talking for ages about getting rid of it, I will give her a ring when I get back to the office."

Chapter Nine

Tim Osby sat at his desk at Mount Darwin police station. He had been the member in charge for the last three years. Prior to this posting, he had been at Gatooma police station, after moving with his family from Sinoia. Since his most recent move, he had seen more of the African bush than ever before, his area was now right in the front line of the recent conflict, and this meant that he saw less of his wife and children. Tim's wife accepted her lot with quiet resignation. Having been married for a number of years she was well aware of how important Tim's job was, and how much it meant to him.

Tim flipped through the papers one by one, 'I've only been away for two days, and I come back to this mountain.' He muttered to himself. He put his cup down just as his phone rang, "Now Nigel and how the hell are you." he asked,

"I'm Ok," replied Nigel "but I have some news that I think you may be interested in. Early this morning one of my workers reported seeing four strangers on my land, not that it bothers me that much but he says they were armed. From his description it looks as if they were carrying AK47 assault rifles and an RPG rocket launcher. I have asked him over and over again, but he is sure that that is what they were carrying. Needless to say he kept out of sight, and as soon as it was safe, he came running to tell me."

"Stay where you are," said Tim, "and keep your man with you. I'll have someone with you as soon as possible, there are two sticks in your area at this moment. I'll contact them now. You don't have the exact location of the sighting do you?" asked Tim,

"I thought that you would ask for that, I have it right here." replied Nigel. Nigel and his family had been farming in the Mount Darwin area for the last eighteen years, he was a very quiet and private man, and even though he didn't often mix with the other farmers, he was still a very much respected member of the farming community.

Yankee Papa were the closest stick to the sighting area, and were instructed to head for that area as quickly as possible. The other stick Zulu Echo were heading in the other direction, following information given to them minutes earlier. They had been told of a sighting of two strangers both reported to be carrying what looked like weapons, and acting suspiciously. Lee was the stick leader of Yankee Papa, with him on patrol were brothers Howard and Norman. The two brothers worked on the family farm alongside their aging parents. Neither of the two sons had married, they had spent time in the Rhodesian Army, and now were part of the local P.A.T.U. stick. Mick was a farm manager but had been called up to do his stint in the bush, it was a break from the day to day work on the farm and he just hoped that this time he would see some action again. Tom was the youngest of them all, he had just qualified as a veterinary surgeon and was working as a government vet in the Mount Darwin area.

Lee looked at his map and checked the references that he had just been given, "That's Nigel's farm I'm sure of it." he said, "Check this out." he said to Howard,

"Sure is," Howard said, "the bastards are on the move, and this time it's on our land, and in daylight, it couldn't be better."

Lee briefed his men about the situation, "If we can get a live one that would be great." he said, "but let's have no heroics, if they want a fight then let's give them one. Then we take no prisoners; just kill every one that you get in your sights."

As the patrol moved on, Lee thought briefly about his wife back at their farm. They had moved down from Zambia three years ago to get away from the troubles there, and now it looked as if it was about to start all over again. 'Well this time I'm not moving for anyone,' thought Lee 'you can only be pushed so far.'

Tom was out at point, and as they approached the spot of the sighting, he concentrated on the ground before him. Soon he saw what he was looking for, broken blades of grass and slight indentations in the reddy brown earth; he indicated with his hands that he was on to something. Mick and Norman moved forward and took up positions alongside, but slightly to the rear of Tom. Tom's eyes were now concentrating on the ground before him, he knew that it was now that he would be most vulnerable to attack.

In formation they moved forward, Tom indicated that he was on tracks of four people, but he knew that they could possibly be the tracks of the local population, who were just going about their normal daily routine. It would be so easy to make a mistake. Tom took them deeper into the thick bush, the air was thick and humid, sweat ran down his face, it stung like hell when it ran into his eyes. The further they went, the harder it got. 'Bloody hell this is thick bush,' he thought to himself. After an hour at point, he could feel his concentration going, he signalled Norman to take over from him.

"I think that we are about an hour behind them." he whispered,

"OK. I'll go ahead for you." said Norman.

As Tom dropped back, he could feel the tension lift from him, slowly they made their way forward again. Norman soon realised that there were no sounds coming from the bush, sounds that you normally took for granted. He stopped and looked up, not a thing, not even a bird in flight. It was an eerie feeling, something had spooked them, he could feel the tension vibrating in the deep silence. As he moved forward it became obvious that whoever they were following were making no effort to conceal their tracks. This meant that they were either totally mad, very confident, or maybe, just maybe, he was following the wrong tracks.

It was now midday, and the sun was right overhead. They were now in a valley, and heading west. It was so humid, that everyone was now feeling the effect, "This has to be the most inhospitable place on earth." Howard said as he took over as lead scout, "There's bloody maggots hanging from the trees, the ground is soggy and stinks when you stand on it and disturb the surface. What a hell hole."

"Be careful." Norman said, "I think that we are closer than we think, I've just got this feeling, don't ask me why, I just think that something isn't right."

Howard took the lead, after a few minutes he stopped. "We are heading towards Umvukwes, and to get there we will have to cross the Ruya river", he turned to Lee, "they are heading towards the river,"

"Are you sure?" Lee asked,

"Yes I'm bloody sure, and the only place that they can be heading for is Umvukwes, and that is white farming land." Howard held up his hand, "Listen," he said, "Can you hear it,"

"Hear what?" asked Lee,

"Water." replied Howard, "Running water, we are almost at

the river."

Lee briefed his men, "Howard thinks that a contact is imminent, the tracks are leading down to the river, and he thinks that we are only minutes behind whoever we are following. OK let's get into extended line formation and move on to the river."

As the river came into view, the air was filled with the sound of gunfire, "Contact!" shouted Lee. As he ran forward, he saw Howard being flung backwards, as he landed on the ground, Lee could see the dark colour of blood pouring from his chest. "Contact! Contact!" he yelled into the radio, "This is Yankee Papa this is Yankee Papa, we have a man down, we have a casavac. I repeat, we have a man down, does anyone read me."

"This is ops, this is ops, we read you loud and clear, give us your loc."

Lee yelled his position into the handset.

"OK Yankee Papa we have three choppers airborne, keep your line open."

Lee clipped the handset to his webbing and ran towards Howard. He knelt down, totally oblivious of the enemy fire that was coming his way. He soon realised that he could do nothing for him, no one could survive the wounds that he had. There was nothing left of his chest at all, just a gaping hole. Lee knew that it was hopeless; it was just a matter of getting the body out of here and back to his family. 'Shit' he said to himself, 'Where's Norman?' He looked back to the position that he had last seen him, and there he was, laying down a steady rate of fire. As Lee looked in his direction, Norman looked straight at him and smiled, the smile drained from his face as he saw the body of his brother lying on the ground.

"No!" he shouted, "No don't let it be!"

In an instant he was up and running towards his brother, tears were pouring down his face as he saw the body, and realised that there was nothing that he could do.

The noise had now died down, gone were the deafening cracks of automatic fire and the heavy stench of cordite. Lee glanced around him and took account of all his men. Everyone seemed to be all right, Norman was still hugging the body of his brother when Lee patted him on the shoulder, "Come on mate, there is nothing that we can do now for Howard, but we can get after the bastards who did it."

Norman gently laid down the body, he wiped his eyes, "OK let's get the murdering bastards"." he replied in a choked voice.

Lee formed his men into an extended line, and indicated for them to move forward towards the river bank. As they moved forward they could see three men just getting out of the water on the far side of the river. They put down rapid fire and one man went down, the remaining two men quickly disappeared into the bush. Seeing that their enemy had made it to the other side of the river, Lee moved quickly down to the river bank. Again they came under fire, but from close quarters, it was very erratic shooting, and going wild. "I see him!" yelled Tom, "He is behind that old tree that has been uprooted and washed onto the river bank. "Grenade!" shouted Tom. Everyone hit the ground, the grenade curled in the air and landed about five feet from the target. Everyone waited for the crump as it exploded. Immediately they were up and running towards the contact area. The terr had been lucky, very lucky indeed, he was alive, but he would not be fighting again. His right foot was missing, and both his arms were torn to shreds. "Take his weapons, and leave him for the moment we have more important things to do." yelled Lee.

As Lee regrouped his men, he heard the welcome sound of the helicopters, as their rotors clattered through the air. His handset crackled as the lead pilot called him up "Yankee Papa this is Cyclone one, do you have me in your vision over."

"Yes Cyclone one, I have you, come straight as you are, but beware, we still have some hostiles in the area. We are OK on this side of the river, but they have crossed the river. The terrorists have been putting down some occasional fire, but at the moment it's all gone quiet, over."

The sound of cannon fire was fearsome as two of the choppers hovered high in the sky and gave cover as the first chopper swooped in low and deployed a stick of five men onto the river side next to Lee's stick. As soon as it lifted off the second chopper dropped a further five men onto the opposite bank, this was repeated by the third chopper. The first chopper then returned to pick up Howard, and the wounded terr. Lee and Tom lifted the body and gently placed it in the chopper, then they lifted the wounded terr and placed him alongside the body. "He won't survive the journey." said Tom, as he wiped the blood from his hands,

"Are you bothered?" replied Lee, "I'm bloody sure I'm not."

Norman stood looking at his dead brother; his eyes were full of sorrow, anger and unshed tears.

"In you get." Lee said to him, Norman turned quickly, "No chance," he replied, "I'm staying with the stick."

"Look mate I think it would be better if you went with your brother. There will be an awful lot to do, and I really think that your parents will need all the support that they can get at this moment in time. Now in you go."

Norman reluctantly jumped into the chopper and sat next to his brother's body. Slowly the pilot revved the engine and the chopper lifted it's cargo from the ground.

Lee shook hands with the stick leader who had just joined them, "So what's the news?" Lee asked,

"I was just about to ask you the same question."

"Well we were on tracks, and then we came under attack. We slotted one of them, but the rest of the group have crossed the river, they put down some fire but nothing that serious. As you know we lost one of our men in the initial fire fight, so now we will have to wait until the two sticks on the other side of the river have picked up tracks before we can do anything else. So, what's happening back in the civilised world?" Lee asked.

"Oh the shit's hit the fan big style, by the way, I'm Brian."

"Sorry mate I'm Lee."

"Yes there have been some significant things happening, three terrs killed, and one white farmer killed in the Karoi area. A farmers wife was shot at in the Sinoia area, she returned fire and the bastards ran off." said Brian.

"Well that's typical of them isn't it." said Lee.

"It proves one thing to me." said Brian, "There are more terrs in the country than we would like to think there are. I honestly think that the government have totally underestimated the situation."

"Well, whatever is happening on the political front, we certainly can't change things where we are at the moment." said Lee,

Brian nodded then looked at Lee and said, "I have been given orders to assist you and your men on this side of the river. As you're two men down, we are here to make up the numbers, so to speak."

"Well what can I say." said Lee, "Welcome aboard, bring your men over to the shade and I will introduce everyone, its best that everyone is on first name terms.

"OK," said Lee, "As we are waiting for things to happen on the other side of the river, and there is nothing that we can do until that news comes in, I suggest that everyone checks their kit, and get some food down their necks. 'Cos if the shit hits the fan, then heaven knows when the next meal will be."

Lee and Brian sat away from the men, and discussed the imminent battle plans. "As soon as we know in which direction the bastards are going, then we can get moving." said Lee,

"It's a waiting game, and there is nothing worse in a situation like this than just sitting doing nothing." said Brian. Just then the radio crackled into life, "Yankee Papa, Yankee Papa do you read me?" Lee grabbed the handset. "This is Yankee Papa over."

"This is Hotel Delta, confirm that you're with Zulu Echo."

"Affirmative." replied Lee, "We are waiting your orders, over."

"OK, terrs are now heading south, and keeping close to the river bank. I think that they intend crossing as soon as they feel safe to do so. They must know that we are on their tracks, and as far as we can determine there are four of them."

"Will you all make your way south of your position, keep as close as you can to the river bank without compromising your position. If they begin crossing then let us know immediately. We will keep you informed of any sightings that we have. If they try and cross the river, we don't want any of them escaping; wait until they are all in mid-stream. If they don't throw down their weapons, then tough, slot the bastards." "Good hunting Yankee Papa signing off" said Hotel Delta.

Lee led his men along the river bank in an extended line. Further in the bush were Brian and his stick. It was very slow going, trying to keep undercover and at the same time watching for any sign of movement on the far side of the river. After an hour, Lee called up Brian, "I think it would be better if we all moved further into the bush, you take your stick and move quickly ahead for about half a click, then take up a holding position and observe the river and the far bank. We will move slowly behind you, as at the moment we don't know where they are. They could be moving well ahead of us, and increasing the distance by the minute, or they could be directly opposite us on the far bank."

Brian's stick moved out, and started to make good progress as they pushed on at a very fast pace through the bush. Behind them were Lee and his stick slowly moving through the thick bush putting every ounce of concentration onto the far bank. Sometime later the crackle of Lee's radio broke the deep silence. Brian's strained voice echoed in Lee's ear. "We've got something I'm sure of it. Double up and join us as quick as you can" Brian whispered.

"What is it?" asked Lee,

"I think we have got a positive sighting on the far side of the river, twice we have seen a person or persons approaching the river bank, as if they are checking it out for a crossing. At the moment it's all gone quiet, no movement at all, but I'm certain that this is the point that they will try and make the crossing. It's ideal, it has the best cover on both sides of the river, the river at this point is fairly narrow. I've moved two of my men further along the river bank, just in case they decide to look for another crossing point, but I've just got this gut feeling that this is the point that they will use."

"OK" said Lee, "We are on our way." Lee and his stick moved at a quickened pace to meet up with Brian.

All eyes were on the far side of the river, everyone was waiting for the moment when the terrs would make their move. Lee's stick had now regrouped, and had their weapons trained onto the far bank,

"Wait until they are in the water." Lee said, "Once they are in mid-stream their movements will be very much more restricted, and hopefully they will surrender."

Everyone wanted to be in on the kill, but they also knew that a live terr would give them much more information than that of a dead one.

Slowly, out of the thick bush appeared a single figure, it was a male about thirty years of age. He was dressed in dirty blue jeans, a camouflage shirt and jacket, and was carrying an AK 47 assault rifle. Slowly he looked to his left and to his right before moving further out into the open. As he approached the water's edge he crouched down as if to make himself as small a target as possible. He beckoned with his hand to his hidden comrades in the bush, slowly two more appeared, again they were dressed in an array of military and civilian attire, one thing that they had in common, was that they were all armed. Directly in the line of fire were three terrs, one with an AK47and six magazines, one with a RPG rocket launcher and four rockets, the third was carrying a RPD machine gun. The three men stood together at the river edge as if they were discussing the best place to go fishing. One by one they entered the water, moving deeper, first up to their ankles, then up to their knees, then the water was past their waist level. When they were all mid-stream and Brian and Lee agreed that no one else was likely to join them, Lee put down the first warning shot. The three terrs froze, then started to return fire. It was obvious that they had no idea where the enemy was as they were all firing in different directions, the terr with the RPG fired his rocket down river and saw it explode into the water.

"OK" yelled Lee, "Let them have it." Almost immediately the river was like a boiling cauldron, slowly turning red, within minutes it was all over. The three bodies were floating down the river, all life had been extinguished in an awesome show of superior fire power.

Lee reached for his handset, "Hotel Delta, Hotel Delta, this is Yankee Papa, do you read me over."

"This is Hotel Delta, read you strength seven over."

"Job done." said Lee, "Three terrs down, we took them out in mid-stream. They are possibly still floating down river over."

"OK get your men back to the first drop off point. There are two choppers on their way in to lift you all out over." "Understood," replied Lee, "But what about the three floaters who is going to look for them and bring them out for identification?" "Don't worry about it, it's all in hand, just make your way to be air lifted out, over and out."

Chapter Ten

Tony sat on the veranda sipping a cold Lion Lager, 'Shit,' the place is bloody dead.' he said to himself. Cooking his own meals every night, no one to talk to when he came home. His mind went into the kitchen and to the pile of dirty pots and pans, dishes, cups and saucers that had been abandoned in the kitchen sink. He knew that he would have to make a planned attack or very soon he would have nothing to either cook in or eat out of.

The past three weeks had been intense for the farming community, all the work on the farms had been left to either the farm managers, the farmer's wives, or in Tony's case his boss boy Crispen. The call up of reservists had been increased due to the increased activity in the area. Out of the past twenty four days. They had only spent two days on his farm. He had been in the thick of it, at the so called sharp end, and he knew that the worst was yet to come. Last night he had phoned Joyce for the first time in three weeks, and she was not happy at all. She was worrying about his safety, she was missing him terribly, and Benji was playing up as kids do when dad is not around. She had no one to talk to during the day, as Mark and Susie were both out at work. Tony knew that he had to find some time to go and see his family or bring them back to the farm, and he knew that the second option was out of the question at the moment.

He put down the empty can of lager just as the phone rang, "Now Tony, and how are you?"

"I'm Ok Mike." he said, "What can I do for you?"

"Wrong mate it's what can I do for you," replied Mike.

Perplexed Tony asked Mike to explain.

"Elliot Dick, does that name ring a bell?" said Mike.

"Too bloody true it does," Tony said, "What have you got for me?" he asked,

"Slow down," said Mike, "There was a contact two days ago over in the Umvukwees area. We lost a man in the initial contact, a total of five terrs were taken out, three of them died in a river shoot out, and the two others were shot as they tried to make their way to the river. It was one of these two that had the name Elliot Dick, written in a notepad. It is such an unusual name, for an African, it has to be the same one that you were interested in, and it just has to be the same person that we had under surveillance in the Mazoe area. I think we could be onto something here, it's just too much of a coincidence."

Tony felt the hair on the back of his neck stand up, "What else do we have on him?" he asked,

"That's just it," replied Mike, "We have nothing else, all that we know is that someone else who is, or was a terrorist knew him, or at least had his name on him. He may be known to this person or it could just be a contact name, so it's back to square one again, but this time I'm going to have him brought in for questioning.

I have been in touch with the member in charge at Mazoe but at the moment he has no one that he can call on, everyone is out on ops, and I want to keep it low key. If I ask Crusader to go in and bring him in for us, we will never see him again.

"We will do it." said Tony, "When can we get cracking. I can have a stick ready to go within two hours, just give the OK."

Mike sighed, "Tony you and your men must be shattered, and you all need a good rest."

"Yes but this is what we have been waiting for." replied Tony, "Come on you have to give us the go ahead on this.".".

"OK it's a go, get your men at my office for a briefing, but I have got to clear this with my boss, so let's leave it until tomorrow. Be at my office at 1600 hrs, and be ready to move out as soon as dusk falls. said Mike.

"I've got one favour to ask," said Tony,

"OK what is it?" asked Mike,

"As soon as we bring him in, I want to spend a few days with Joyce and Benji." requested Tony.

"I've no problem with that, once he is in our custody, then off you go. Oh and I have got some news for you, do you remember that Ford Anglia that we talked about, you know the one that I said was just stuck in the garage at Avondale?" said Mike.

"Yes, I remember it, I mentioned it to Joyce but thought no more about it." said Tony,

"Well she has picked it up."

"You are joking." said Tony,

"I'm not," replied Mike, "Joyce picked it up two days ago; I got a phone call the day that she picked it up. She is over the moon with it, obviously she is going to keep it as a surprise, so when you see it act as if you didn't know OK."

Tony smiled and said, "My mouth will be sealed, see you tomorrow."

The following day two Land Rovers pulled up in front of Mike's office. Tony and Colin stepped out of the first vehicle and were closely followed by Buz, Alex, and Ken.

"Keep an eye on the kit Alex." said Tony as he led his men into Mike's office.

Mike smiled and put down his cup of coffee, "Grab yourselves a cup." he said, as he cleared his desk. As the men gathered around his desk he opened out a large roll of drawing paper. "I only got the green light an hour ago. It wasn't what I would call easy, as it is out of my area, but when you drop a few names, and remind people of a few favours that are owed, they saw it my way. Let's go through it once again, you will leave here as soon as the sun starts going down, it will take you about an hour to get to the drop-off point. From there you will go on foot through the bush to this point."

Mike indicated with his finger to the area circled on the map, "We have almost no intelligence as to the reception that you can expect if you are seen by the locals. We don't know if they are hostile towards us or friendly It may be that this chap Elliot Dick is the local hero, and the locals want to help him. On the other hand the locals could well be frightened of him and would be glad to see the back of him, so obviously use caution. We also don't know if he has any terrorist support at hand or if he is acting alone. One thing is now certain, he is involved in terrorism, he may not be active, but my guess is that he is either a safe house for the terrorists, or he is in control of handing out weapons and ammunition. Either way I want him brought in for questioning. If he makes a run for it, then slot him, I don't care what state he is in when you get him here as long as he is alive, any questions?"

"Just one thing," said Tony, "It's not a question, but this may take more than one night. He may not be there, we have had people watching this village before and they came up with nothing."

"Good point." said Mike, "All I can say is, stay as long as you can, but keep in touch, I really want this son of a bitch brought in for questioning. If you have no questions lads, I suggest that you go to the armoury and draw whatever you want to take with you, but please leave something on the shelves. I've got two more sticks going out tomorrow, good luck."

Tony walked into the armoury, and called out to the officer in charge, "Come on Vince, we have a war to fight, let's see what you have got for us."

Vince smiled as he came to the counter, "Now gentlemen and what do you want this time?" he asked,

"Five men, two hundred rounds each, three mills grenades each, five rifle grenades, five batteries for the radio, two pencil flares, and five canisters of flot. We will also need enough rations for lets say four days, and give us the decent stuff, the rat packs H and J are bloody foul, so don't even think about it," laughed Tony.

An hour later, Tony and his men were ready to move out, magazines loaded, all the rat packs had been ripped open, and anything that had to be cooked, warmed up, was binned. All the equipment was checked again,

"OK," said Tony, "Everyone ready?" he got the nod from everyone, "Let's just check the radio again, Colin, make a few calls, then shut it down and save the battery."

Soon the sky darkened as daylight started to fade. Tony looked at his watch again, 'I will give it another half an hour,' he said to himself. Then with a hard confident look at his team, Tony shouldered his equipment and said "Let's move out."

Chapter Eleven

Under the cover of darkness, two Land Rovers slipped out of Bindura Police Station. Tony sat in front with the driver, the remainder of the stick sat in the back, making themselves as comfortable as possible. The second Land Rover, that was travelling about thirty feet to the rear, was carrying an armed guard for the first Land Rover on its return journey.

Tony looked at his watch again, they had been travelling for forty minutes, anytime now and he would give the word to the driver to slow down, but not to stop. "Now," said Tony, "Slow down, we are getting out here."

As the vehicle slowed down Tony and his men leapt from the vehicle and quickly disappeared into the night.

The stick of five men lay low in the bush watching the tail lights of the two Land Rovers quickly fade into the darkness.

"OK Ken you take point, Alex your tail end Charlie." whispered Tony.

Tony placed his hand on Ken's shoulder and pointed into the night sky, "If you look carefully on to the sky line you can just make out a high tree line, well that is your marker, just head for that. As far as I know there should be no rivers to cross, if there are they should be insignificant, as there are none marked on the map. It's a full moon tonight, so use as much cover as you can...I know that speed is the essence, but the last thing we want is to be compromised, OK let's move out."

In the distance Tony could hear the two Land Rovers on their return to the relative safety of Bindura. Tony thought about them and the cold beers that they would soon be enjoying in the Dungeon, he licked his lips, 'press on,' he said to himself, 'press on.'

Tony and his men had now been in the bush for three hours, progress had been good, but hard going. Every tree and every bush seemed to move, and the longer you looked at it the more convinced you became. The moon was casting shadows that seemed to dance in front of them as if playing a game. "OK let's take a breather," said Tony quietly the welcome order was passed on, everyone quietly adjusted their webbing, took a sip from their water bottles and within a few minutes they were on their way again.

It was now Ten o'clock, quietly they skirted a small village that was in total darkness, only the dying embers from the fire gave away its existence. As they moved away into the bush a dog started to bark, "Shit," said Tony "This is all we need!"

Everyone froze, the dog barked again then silence. "OK let's move on" he whispered. Buz was now at point, and soon came upon a river, it was slow moving and about six foot wide, "I will cross it first." he said,

"Careful as you go." Tony said, "You don't know how deep it is."

"If it's not on the map then it can't be much of a river can it?" Buz replied. Within fifteen minutes everyone was on the opposite bank, and heading towards their objective.

Suddenly in front of them, silhouetted by the moonlight was the village, "OK," said Tony, "Let's skirt it and get to a good vantage point. If you look at the village, all the huts are together with the exception of one, and that is the hut we want to be near to." Tony led his stick into a good concealed spot that gave them a good view of the village, but most importantly, a very good view of the mud hut that they were confident Elliot Dick would be sleeping in. As dawn broke, the women went to work in the fields, leaving the children to play, and the men sitting in the shade playing dominos.

In the thick undergrowth the five men kept watch, watching every hut, counting every person who was in the village. How many dogs, that was their biggest enemy of all, the dogs were constantly looking for food, and the slightest smell would draw their attention. This meant that no one would risk opening a rat pack, even though they were all now feeling the pangs of hunger.

The midday sun beat down unmercifully, it's searching rays finding any exposed parts of the bodies, not concealed by the hastily erected camouflage. Everyone's throat was parched leaving all of them feeling like shit. The day dragged achingly on until finally the mud door slowly opened. Straining his eyes against the glare of the sun Tony watched as Elliott Dick emerged into the light.

Tony nudged Colin, "Bloody hell he's a big sod." Said Colin. Elliott raised his arms above his head and stretched. Slowly he looked round the village, his gaze flickering over the exact spot where Tony and his men were hidden. With an idle gesture he turned blew his nose onto the ground and went back into the hut.

"He's a fuckin' Albino," said Tony, "Elliot Dick is a bloody Albino," "Almost white skin, pale pinky eyes, and white tight curly hair."

"He must be at least six foot six." said Colin,

"That's why he didn't see us." said Tony, "Albino's have very poor eyesight; normally they are regarded as outcasts, by their own people. This guy must have some power over the locals, they either are afraid of him or they have great respect for him, No doubt about it though, he is our man."

Tony wiped his brow; sweat was running down his forehead into his eyes and dripping off the end of his nose and chin. 'Thank god he had gone back into the mud hut,' he said to himself, at least now he could move slightly and make himself more comfortable, all they had to do now was to maintain their cover and wait until darkness.

As night fell Tony and Buz slipped out from their concealed hiding place, and stealthily moved through the shadows towards Elliot's hut. The warm night air was accompanied by a slight breeze that was blowing away from the village. At this moment in time everything was going their way, hopefully any small sound that was made would be carried away from the village. The three remaining members of the stick were now totally silent as they watched Tony and Buz heading towards their objective, they knew that the slightest incident could compromise the whole mission.

Tony stood in front of the mud hut and indicated to Buz to force the door. With a strong thrust of his massive shoulder Buz flung the door wide open, immediately they both rushed into the small dark room, the beam of their torch quickly flashed across the room searching for Elliot before his eyes had time to focus. Almost immediately he was up and at them, his massive hands were tugging at Tony's webbing, the torch was knocked to the floor and cast hideous shadows along the walls. Tony brought his knee up as hard as he could into Elliot's groin, Elliot gasped for air as the pain surged through his body, at that moment Buz brought the stock of his FN rifle down hard on to the side of Elliot's head. Unconscious

Elliott slumped to the floor and lay motionless.

"OK, let's tie his hands and gag him before he comes round." rasped Buz. Within minutes they emerged into the warm night air again, Tony carried Buz's rifle as Buz lifted Elliot onto his shoulder and quickly stumbled for cover. Tony covered his movement until it was safe to follow; the snatch had taken four minutes, now it was time to get away from the village back through the bush and to the pre-arranged pick up point.

Elliot was now awake and struggling with his captors. He had to be dragged every inch of the way, blood was caked on his head and face, and he was cursing and making threats through the gag that was wrapped around his mouth. With Elliott's continuous efforts to escape, progress seemed to be excruciatingly slow.

Tony knew that speed was always the essence in a snatch; get in and out as fast as you possibly can, any delays only meant more chances of a compromise, a follow up by the enemy and a possible contact.

Dawn had broken as they approached the pick up point; everyone was tired, wet, and very hungry. Quickly Colin got on to the radio and called for transport to lift them at the pre-arranged point, within the hour they were back at Bindura Police station.

"With much back slapping and congratulatory banter, Mike praised Tony and his men. Elliott has been seen by the medic, and he is about to start his interrogation with Special Branch. Make no mistake he will talk, we are convinced that this one is a big fish."

Tony stood his men down and walked outside to his Land Rover, "A bloody good job Tony! I wish I'd been there with you." Said Mike enthusiastically. "Me too," replied Tony, "A couple of times I thought it was going to go pear shaped though. Anyway just to remind you, I will be away for a couple of days, if I don't spend some time with Joyce and Benji, life just won't be worth living. I'll call in to see you on my return from Salisbury."

"OK drive carefully and don't do any thing that I wouldn't do." said Mike with a smile.

Chapter Twelve

Hugh Russel was in his element at the thought of interrogating the prisoner. He didn't have much to go on, as very little was known about Elliot Dick no criminal record, not even a traffic violation. He finished his coffee, placed the mug onto his desktop, got up out of his chair and walked out of his office; it was time to meet Elliot Dick.

Since the start of the terrorist incursions Special Branch had been responsible for most of the interrogations of captured terrorists or their sympathisers. In Bindura they had their interrogation room at the main Police Station, they also had facilities at an old isolated farmhouse, this is where Elliot was being held.

Behind the Police Station near to the football pitch was a corrugated building called the Fort. It had a very high corrugated iron fence enclosing it; this was the headquarters of the intelligence branch of the Selous Scouts. Hand-picked men, some from the SAS, but all highly trained and motivated. They were a lethal unit of fighting men.

Hugh drove to the fort and picked up Henry, Warren Henry was a highly intelligent man who was considered one of the top experts in the interrogation of hardened terrorists. No matter how long it took or how hard they thought they were, they all cracked under Henry.

They drove in silence as Henry looked briefly at the limited amount of information that had been given to him. "Not much to go on." he said, "In fact there is sod all."

"Well we are certain that he is a main player." said Hugh, "His name has come up so many times from other terrorists, that everything seems to focus on him. I am sure that he holds the key to a lot more than we think."

"If he has any information, you can be sure of one thing , I will crack him." muttered Henry.

Inside the farmhouse it was bleak; all of the windows had been taken out and bricked up. A large wooden beam had been fitted into the walls across the room about a foot from the ceiling. The wooden door had been replaced with a heavy steel one with large heavy bolts on the outside. In the middle of the room was a solitary wooden chair, and a wooden table. Sitting in the chair was the now miserable Elliot Dick; his head was bandaged from the wound that he had received during his capture.

Henry walked into the room carrying a chair from the corridor, "Now Elliot what have you got to tell Me." he asked,

Elliot raised his head and slowly shook it from side to side, "My name is not Elliot." he said,

"I have done nothing wrong; you have got the wrong man. It's typical of you white colonial bastards; you just pick on anyone, don't you. I have nothing to say to you, nothing at all. I can promise you one thing," he said, spitting his words out, "You will all be very sorry, I can promise you that."

"Why what are you going to do?" asked Henry, "Call on your terrorist friends to come looking for us?"

"Terrorists what terrorists, what are you talking about? I don't know any terrorists?" shouted Elliot.

So you don't know any terrorists, what about Joshua, he knows you." queried Henry, "I think that you should start talking that's if you want to see tomorrow."

Elliot sat in silence, "I would advise you to cooperate my friend, it will be so much easier for you." said Henry.

"Go fuck yourself." spat Elliot, "You will get nothing out of me, I'm just a poor farmer." he said, as if he was having second thoughts.

"You're a bloody farmer!" shouted Henry, "You're the only farmer that I know, who doesn't have a bloody farm.

I want to know who you are, who you work for, who your friends are, where they live. I want to know who is supplying the terrorists with arms and ammunition. I want to know the names of all the terrorists who you know, I want to know where they are operating, how long they have been in the country, how many groups and how many men in each group. I also want to know what country they were trained in, and I want to know where they entered Rhodesia, and when, now start talking."

"Go fuck yourself." said Elliot, "You know nothing, but very soon you all will be wishing that you had never heard the name Rhodesia." Henry stood up and walked to the door, he nodded to

Hugh, "Let him stew for a while," He said. Think about it Elliot, we have all the time in the world. You will soon get sick of the discomfort, the lack of sleep, you will tell us what we want to know, believe me you will tell us." said a solemn Henry.

Tony explained to Crispen his boss boy that he would be away for a few days, and gave him instructions for the work that he wanted doing, "If you have any problems then don't hesitate to ring me on this number in Salisbury." he said.

Tony drove away from the farm wondering if he was doing the right thing. In the last month or so he had hardly spent any time at all on the farm, but believed that he could trust Crispen and had no doubts that the farm would be in good hands.

The journey to Mabelreign was uneventful; it had only been three months ago that two vehicles had been fired upon as they travelled on the same road. It was only a matter of time before the terrs got lucky and took someone out.

It was only as he drove onto the drive at Mabelreign that Tony realised that he could relax and start to unwind. His first thoughts at this time were of downing a cold lager. He got out of the Land Rover and walked over to the Ford Anglia that was now parked in front of him. 'Smart' he said to himself, he looked through the driver side window and gave the interior the once over, 'very tidy.' "Do you like it?" a voice called to him; he turned to see Joyce standing at the front door with a huge smile on her face. Tony grinned and walked towards her with his arms open wide, "How are you darling?" he asked,

"I feel much better now that you are here." she laughed happily.

"And yes I do like it" he replied in answer to her question. "It's a cracker; it's just what you need."

Joyce led him into the house, and closed the front door, "Come here." she said, "I just can't wait to get my hands on you." They stood kissing and holding each other, Tony's hands were all over her body, "Wait until tonight." she said "And we can do it properly," the desire clear in her eyes.

"Where's Benji?" Tony said, as he made for the fridge.

"He is in the garden." Joyce said, "Come on through."

Tony opened a can of lager and made his way into the back garden, "Bloody hell he has grown." he said, "Come here big boy, give your dad a big cuddle."

Benji ran over and flung his arms around Tony's neck, "Have you been a good boy for your Mam while you have been staying here?" Benji nodded and wriggled to be back down again, and ran off to play. "He certainly seems to have missed me." he said with a wry smile.

"So what's new?" asked Joyce, anxiously.

"Nothing other than what I told you the other night on the phone" said Tony, "The terrs are still active as ever, but we may have a breakthrough. We think that we may have captured one of the top men in the area. We will just have to wait and see, but it is too soon for you to start thinking about returning to the farm at the moment."

Tony sat in the garden as Joyce started to prepare the evening meal, "Mark and Sue will both be in soon." she shouted from the kitchen, "Why don't you get a quick shower, as I am sure that you and Mark will have plenty to talk about when he gets in. If you're going upstairs now, then take Benji with you would you, it's almost his bath time. If you could give him his bath, it will give me plenty of time to prepare the evening meal."

Tony was sitting in the garden with Benji on his knee when a deep welcoming voice called out, "How are you my mate." Tony turned and saw Mark walking through the patio doors towards him. "Now Mark." Tony said, as he stood up lifting Benji on to his left arm, they enthusiastically shook hands. "And how are you?"

"I'm Ok," replied Mark, "How are things at the sharp end?" Mark asked,

"Hairy, really hairy." replied Tony, "The situation is not getting any better at all. Obviously I haven't told Joyce everything about what is going on, it's no use having her worrying about things that she doesn't have to know about. But it's not good at all, the movement of terrs has increased, the sightings and the contacts are more of a daily occurrence. But the fight must go on, it is now imperative that we all stay strong and do not weaken our resolve. All they are is bloody thugs, they strike at night, or they hit isolated farms, or people out on the farm by themselves. Then they run off into the darkness. You know that I have said it many times before, we are too bloody soft with them, the politicians seem to be afraid of what the rest of the world will say if we hit back hard. Let's bomb the training camps, if the surrounding countries want to train and arm these bloody cowards, then they must be prepared to pay the price." said Tony bitterly.

"I'm surprised by what you have said." said Mark, "You know that on the radio or the television we don't hear any of this. We do hear about the odd sighting or the occasional contact, but we certainly are not getting the full picture. "It's obvious isn't It." said Tony, "If the government told the public everything then it could do two things. Firstly, it could panic the white population, and secondly it would give the terrs the information as to how they are doing. Remember this is a psychological war; it's a war of the hearts and minds, as well as a war of killing the enemy. It was suggested that there were only about twenty to thirty terrs in the country, I would think the figure is more likely to be nearer the hundred mark, if not more."

Tony sat in silence then said, "In the 1960's there were two parties formed, the Zimbabwean African Peoples Union, lead by Joshua Nkomo, known as Z.A.P.U. then came Z.A.N.U. the Zimbabwean African National Party, which was controlled by the Reverend Ndabaningi Sithole. At that time the white population was about two hundred thousand. In 1964 the two parties were outlawed as they constituted a threat to the stability of Rhodesia. The same year Britain gave independence to Northern Rhodesia, now known as Zambia, and to Malawi, with majority rule going to the black population. The Rhodesian government lead by Ian Douglas Smith could see what was going to happen to Southern Rhodesia, so in 1965 they declared U.D.I. By this time Z.A.P.U. and Z.A.N.U had gone into exile, and now this year the first incursions have started, you don't have to be a brain surgeon to work it out do you, it's so obvious who is behind the attacks.

Zambia and Mozambique are the two main players in the training of the terrorists. Mozambique have had the Cuban soldiers assisting and training the locals, and helping to fight the war against the Portuguese Government for years. Zambia is also assisting the terrorist movements, with training facilities and safe havens. Can you imagine this country if it were to be run by a black government, it would be chaos within a year, the whole structure would just collapse." said Tony despairingly.

Joyce and Susie came out into the garden, "Dinner will be ready in about five minutes." Susie said as she leant over and gave Tony a big kiss on the cheek, "Nice to see you again, Joyce has been missing you terribly. You should have seen the smile on her face when you said that you were coming to stay for a few days. It was such a relief for her to know that you were safe.

For the last three weeks Tony had survived on rat packs, and now he was sitting down to a slap-up dinner. He looked at the plate and thought 'I will never finish all of that, bloody hell I need a rope to climb it,' After struggling through the main course he knew that he was beaten, he couldn't face anymore food, no matter what it was, or how good it looked.

"What do you want for pudding?" asked Susie,

"You have got to be joking." said Tony, "I'm as full as a gun."

"Not even room for a brandy?" asked Mark with a grin.

"Well I may be able to squeeze a small one down." replied Tony. After his fourth brandy Tony said "I'm sorry but I just can't keep my eyes open, I've had very little sleep in the past two or three weeks, so if you will excuse me, I'm off to bed. The meal was great, the company even better," said Tony with a contented sigh as he slowly ambled his way to his room.

Tony undressed; he lay on the bed and waited for Joyce to come to bed. As tired as he was, he still had enough energy to make love to her, his body ached with desire.

Tony woke up to find the sun shining through the bedroom curtains. He reached out with his hand searching for Joyce, he turned over to find the place beside him empty, 'What time is it?' he asked himself, he raised his left arm and looked at his wristwatch. He could not believe the time, it was noon, he must have fallen asleep almost as soon as his head had touched the pillow, so much for his night of passion.

In the living room, Joyce was doing the housework and looking after Benji. She looked at the clock, and decided to give Tony a call to get up, "Tony it's noon are you going to get up today or not?" she shouted. Tony got out of bed and walked to the bathroom and washed his face, he quickly dressed and made his appearance. "Morning darling."

Joyce said, "Do you fancy a beer for your breakfast?"

"Don't mention drink to me." he said "I will never touch another drop of the stuff again,

"I don't know how many times I have heard you say that." Joyce said, "Come sit down and I will make you a cup of coffee, and some scrambled eggs on toast."

Joyce watched him eat his breakfast and drink his coffee, "How do you feel now?" she asked,

"Like a new man." Tony replied,

"That's good." said Joyce, "Benji is fast asleep, Mark and Susie won't be in until tea time, so what about the night of passion that you promised me yesterday?" Joyce reached out and took his hand, "Come on," she said tenderly, "Let's think of something other than killing and terrorists for a while."

Chapter Thirteen

Hanging from a wooden rafter, Elliot Dick was now completely naked, hands tied above his head. The rope was looped over the wooden beam and pulled tight. If he stretched hard enough his toes would just touch the floor. Lines of fear and fatigue etched his haggard face. "We know a lot more about you, than you could possibly think." said Henry, as he put his hand into his trouser pocket. Slowly he withdrew his hand and opened his IXL penknife in front of Elliot's staring eyes, "Hold his legs" he said to Hugh. Slowly he raised his hand and placed the blade onto Elliot's pectoral muscle. With a definite push, the tip of the knife entered through the taught skin just piercing the top layer of muscle. Elliot screamed with pain, his eyes rolled back into their sockets, as he saw the trickle of blood running from the wound. Henry moved the knife to the other side of his chest, "Do you have something to tell us?" he asked, again he pressed the blade into the skin on the now panting and heaving chest. Elliot opened his eyes, looked at Henry, and spat into his face. As Henry walked out of the room, he said to Hugh, "Blind fold him; I will be back in a few moments."

Elliot hung in silence, beads of sweat were now trickling all over his naked body, his laboured breathing echoed in the suffocating stillness. Henry walked into the room carrying a bucket of water, filled with ice cubes, "Are we going to talk, or do you want me to start all over again?" he asked, "I must say Elliot, I am getting a little impatient with your arrogance." Henry once again opened his penknife, he quietly placed the blade into the ice-cold water, then withdrew the knife and using the blunt side of the knife made a two inch scratch on Elliot's chest. Elliot arched his body in an attempt to evade the stinging pain. The ice-cold water that had started to run down his chest from the blade of the knife felt as if he was being cut again. The trickle of water felt just like the trickle of his blood. Again Henry placed the knife onto Elliot's chest, but this time he had moved lower down to his ribcage. Again Elliot's body moved away from the knife as soon as he felt the scratch and as he thought the oozing of blood down his chest "Are we going to talk?" Hugh asked, "Tell us what you know and all this will stop."

Elliot hung in silence, his chest rising as he gulped in lungfuls of air, "Talk to us," Hugh said, "Come on be sensible, just answer our questions and all this will stop. You will be able to have a shower, put on some clean cloths, have a hot meal, and have a good night's sleep."

Henry and Hugh looked at each other, and shook their heads, stubborn bastard they mouthed to each other. Henry moved quickly, he grabbed the knife out of the ice bucket and made two long quick scratches from Elliot's ribcage down to his groin. Elliot yelled with fright and the sudden pain, Henry grabbed Elliot's penis, and shouted to Hugh "Pass me the cutters; I'm pissed off with this bastard!"

Elliot screamed, "No! I will tell you everything, but don't cut me down there!"

"OK Elliot," said Henry, "Start talking, give me some names, or I promise you one thing, you will never be of use to a woman again."

Elliot could take no more; in his fear his bowels opened, the nauseating stench permeating to the rafters of the old farmhouse. "The only two people that I have seen are Joshua and Magumbo," He cried, "Joshua lost his men in a contact with security forces after hitting a white farmhouse at Shamva and Magumbo, and he also lost all his men in a contact at Mtoko. They came separately to see me for weapons, and for ammunition."

"And where are they now?" asked Hugh, who was now all ears. This was in his operational area, he was certain that the farm that had been hit was River Bend, where the Hastings had all been killed. 'You bastard,' he said to himself, 'I could kill you with my bare hands,' His fists were clenched and his knuckles were white, he was shaking with anger. "They left together, they said that they were going to team up, and hit back at the whites." "Hit back where?" asked Hugh,

"I don't know," replied Elliot, "They just said that they had a score to settle, one of their friends was killed when Joshua attacked a farm. I think I heard Joshua say it was called Camburo farm or something like that."

Henry and Hugh sat in silence; this had all come so quickly

that it had left them both wondering if Elliot was just stringing them along. Hugh shook his head, "No" he whispered to Henry "It all adds up, Camburo farm belongs to Tony Marshall, and he killed a terrorist on his farm recently, I'm telling you it all makes sense, he is cooperating I'm sure of it."

"OK Elliot, describe this Joshua to me."

"He is about six foot tall, slim build, he has a long thin scar on his right arm it runs from his elbow down to his wrist."

"Anything else?" asked Henry,

"No nothing else." answered Elliot, "But he does wear thin-rimmed glasses, I remember now he told me he cannot see any thing without them."

"And what about the other chap, the one called Magumbo, what does he look like?" asked Henry,

"He is a very powerfully built man." said Elliot, "I am sure he could kill a lion with his bare hands, everyone who meets this man Magumbo is afraid of him. He is very evil."

"And what does he look like?" asked Henry,

"Apart from being powerfully built, he is about five foot six, but very broad and strong. He is the man who cuts off people's lips and noses, and ears. He then makes the families cook and eat it. That is why everyone is so scared of him."

"He does what!" said Henry, "The man's an animal!"

Elliot shook his head and said, "He is a very evil man, he uses a rusty knife and a pair of pliers when he cuts off their lips, ears and noses. He enjoys every minute of it."

"What else can you tell me about this bloody animal?" cursed Henry,

"He was injured recently in a battle with your security forces somewhere in Mtoko, he lost the little finger on his right hand. You can see the bone sticking through the skin, he is in constant pain, and is very angry. He says he will kill every white person that he sees." babbled Elliot.

"So, you're the local Quartermaster." asked Hugh, "You're the man who supplies the terrorists with all their arms and ammunition. Who is your contact? How do you contact each other? Where do all the arms and ammunition come from?"

Elliot started to say something then stopped, "You know that we mean business, so stop pissing us about and give us all the answers, who is your contact?" asked Hugh, "And tell us, how were you recruited and by who, and when and where. Give us all the names of the terrorists who have been in contact with you."

Again silence. Hugh banged the table, "Now listen to me and listen good," "You either answer the questions and answer them now or I can promise you one thing for sure. I will personally take you outside and blow your fuckin' brains out do you understand me?" Elliot nodded, "OK let's start from the beginning."

Ten hours later Henry and Hugh had all the information that they needed, "OK," said Henry, "Take off his blindfold."

Hugh undid the blindfold and lifted it off Elliot's head. Elliot's eyes were all puffed up; slowly he opened them and tried to focus. "Give him a drink of water." said Henry, Elliot gulped down the water and started to cough it back up. He slowly looked around the room, first he stared at Henry and then he turned and stared at Hugh, he then moved his eyes to look at himself. As if not wanting to see the blood and the cuts. He closed his eyes again; he opened his eyes and looked shocked when he saw no blood or any cuts on his body except the first two, below them were only deep scratches where he thought he had been cut. "Bastards!" he yelled, "You will die for this; I can promise you that you will die a slow death for this!"

"I don't think so." replied Henry, "You are going to spend an awful long time in jail, you want to think yourself a very lucky man, very lucky indeed. You could hang for what you have done." As they walked towards the door Henry turned to Elliot and in a mocking voice said "Thank you for all the information, you have been most helpful."

As they walked down the corridor, Henry stopped at the last office he knocked on the door and walked in. "We are finished now, thanks for your help." he said to the officer sitting behind the desk, "He is all yours now, I would suggest that you throw away the key."

Mike Johnson sat at his desk and read the report. He had already spoken to both men concerning the interrogation, but had requested that all the details were put in writing. At least he now knew who was responsible for the murder at the Hastings Farm. And this animal Magumbo; so he was the person responsible for all of the mutilations, and for terrorising the local population. People who were completely innocent, but who Magumbo thought were possibly friendly towards the security forces. Mike then thought of Tony, so he was a target now, he had killed Ticky the night they were trying to lay a mine and to booby trap his farm gate. Mike made a note in his diary, Contact Tony Urgently.

As things were now hotting up in the area, Mike decided the best thing to do was to contact the Army and request their help to locate the arms cache, and then remove it, or blow it up, Knowing the Army as he did, Mike was certain that before moving it or blowing it up, an awful lot of souvenirs would be taken. Trophies of war as they were known.

Chapter Fourteen

Deep in the African bush, Magumbo sat silently scanning the surrounding countryside for any movement that would indicate that security forces were still looking for him. After collecting more ammunition from Elliot Dick, he once again met up with Joshua. They spent most of the night talking about recent events and of the losses that they had both had in recent contacts with the security forces. It was then that they both decided to join forces and together continue the war against the white farming community. The next day they started on their journey back to the Matepatepa Tribal Trust Lands.

Tembe Magumbo was nine years of age when his father was arrested for voicing his opinion against the white government that was ruling Rhodesia. His mother, who was not in very good health, continued to support the struggling family by taking on two jobs. She had three children to support, Tembe who was nine, and his two small sisters were aged three and five. His father had worked at the same factory since leaving school. During those years he had been a very reliable worker and had been promoted to boss boy As a result of his increasing militant activities his father was constantly being threatened with the sack. Eventually he was arrested by the police and was never seen again.

It was at this stage that Tembe also had to look for work. He could see that his mother's health was failing, and being the eldest of the children he decided that it was his responsibility to help in supporting the family.

When he was thirteen his mother died of TB, his whole world fell apart. On the small wage that he was earning there was no way that he could possibly support the family. It was then that the elders of the village said that they would look after his two sisters so that he could leave the village and find full time employment.

He said goodbye to his two sisters and with tears in his eyes he left the village and headed for Salisbury.

When he arrived in Salisbury he was in awe at the size of everything. He had never seen so many white people, so many motor cars, and the building and so many shops. If he had the money he could buy anything that he wanted. 'One day' he said to himself, 'one day I will be rich.'

For the first week he slept on the streets. Each day he knocked on every office door begging for work, but it was always the same reply, maybe tomorrow, come back in a few weeks time.

One evening as he sat outside a beer hall in an African township, begging for food, an old man took pity on him. He told the old man his sorry story, Tembe felt that he could trust this old frail man who stooped as he walked, supported by a branch of a tree that he used as a walking stick. The old man listened silently as Tembe's story filled his saddened heart. "Look my friend," the old man said, "I am a poor man but if you wish you are welcome to come back to my humble home, I can offer you warmth for the night and somewhere to rest your head."

Sitting at the table, Tembe listened to the old man's story. Two of his sons were in jail for distributing subversive literature, his third son was working away, but would be home in a few days' time. The old man said it maybe in Tembe's interest to meet his son; he may have something for him.

Tembe was eager to meet the old man's son. For the next few days he called at the old man's house hoping to meet him. On the third evening the old man told Tembe to come into the house and to close the door, sitting in the room was his son. "So you are Tembe." the young man said,

"Yes" replied Tembe, "But everyone calls me Magumbo."

"Come over here and sit down. My name is Tombei. My father has told me all about you and I am sure that I can help you."

As the evening past Tombei listened to Magumbo's story, "You have had a hard time young man," Tombei said, "and now you are looking for work. Well let me tell you something you will never be wealthy, you will always be poor. As long as we Africans are denied the right to govern ourselves we will never move on. What we must do is fight for what we are entitled to, and I can help you, believe me there are many people just like you who I have helped. "

"What do I have to do?" exclaimed Tembe enthusiastically "What kind of work is it?"

"Don't you worry about things like that." replied Tombei, "But first you must promise me one thing, you must swear that you will never tell anyone about our meeting. You must never mention my name, and you must forget about meeting my father and never ever return to this house."

"I will, I will, I swear to you I will." said Magumbo, "You have my word."

The following week, Magumbo, along with five other young men, followed Tombei through the bush and into Mozambique.

Magumbo knew that he was no longer in Rhodesia and guessed that he was now in Mozambique. The language that the local tribesmen spoke was totally different to his own.

After travelling through the bush for a further three days, Magumbo with growing awareness realised that instead of travelling at night, and constantly on the lookout for security forces, they were now travelling during daylight, and resting at night. Soon they saw troops who were friendly towards them, people who looked different, who spoke a different language. "They are here to help us in our struggle, they are Russians, they are also helping us." said Tombei.

Within weeks of his arrival, Magumbo had been indoctrinated by his new masters, and now believed that this was the answer to all of his problems. Overthrow the government, and everyone who helped to do it would be rewarded. A very good, and well paid job; a lovely big house to live in and wealth beyond his wildest dreams.

All of these promises encouraged Magumbo to train hard and to prove to everyone that he was the best recruit in the camp. As the days went by more recruits entered the camp and soon there were over two hundred fit young men who were eager to complete their training and return to their homeland to wage a war of terror on the white population.

It was now two years since Magumbo had started his training, he was now a strapping seventeen year old well-trained terrorist. He had proved to his communist masters that he was a proficient fighter with the determination and the will to return to his homeland and to lead his own unit of terrorists.

On his return to Rhodesia, Magumbo was accompanied by four other terrorists. For the first few days they travelled by night and rested by day. Magumbo thought that on his return to the tribal trust lands he would be treated as a hero, but at every village that they entered their presence was regarded with suspicion, and slight hostility. No food or shelter was ever offered, soon Magumbo came to the conclusion that they were definitely not welcome at all and that all of these villages must be supporters of the white government, and the security forces. It was at this point that Magumbo decided to take a much tougher approach, and soon he had all of the villages living in fear of his methods. Anyone that he thought was an informer, or a supporter of the government, was savagely beaten in front of the whole village.

In a short period of time he became the most feared and hated man in the whole area. The news of the beatings and of the mutilations spread to every village in the north east of the country. As darkness came, everyone locked themselves in their mud huts, all of the cooking fires were put out, there was no singing and dancing around the fires, just silence. Occasionally there was the sound of a dog barking in the distance, but even that sound brought fear, what was the dog barking at? Was someone coming to the village? Magumbo's answer to this was to burn the huts with the people still inside. Knowing that he had little support from the local tribesmen, who he thought would help and support him, Magumbo decided to continue with his plan and to hit the white farming community. Within weeks he had become the most hunted man in the north east of the country.

Mount Darwin was his first target, and then he moved west to Umvukwes, leaving a trail of attacked farmhouses or attacks on the farmers as they worked in the fields. Two white farmers were killed, and one injured.

Almost a year had passed; Magumbo knew that he was causing turmoil in the area. He sat thinking of his two sisters; they would be some size now he thought to himself. He missed them terribly but he knew that what he was doing, he was ultimately doing for them.

Staring up at the stars, he sat silently as he rubbed his injured right hand, he could feel the bone sticking through the skin. 'Bastards' he thought to himself, 'at least I'm alive,' not like his comrades who had all died at Mtoko.

Joshua sat in silence reflecting on the time he had spent back in his country, he remembered Ticky, Robert, and Isaac. The times that they had spent together planning their next attack, and the times when they had to run for their lives when things did not go exactly to plan. As he sat in silence looking at the stars, he could hear Magumbo muttering to himself, "Are you OK?" he asked,

"Yes I'm fine." replied Magumbo, "I'm just thinking. Thinking of what the future holds for us when all this is over, what will we be doing in a few years from now. Anyway." he said, as he stood up "It's time for us to be on our way, we have work to do at Matepatepa."

Chapter Fifteen

As a beam of sunlight filtered through the half open blinds, the smoke from the well-used pipe seemed to dance in time to the fan that moved slowly from left to right.

Mike Johnson waited patiently as Commissioner Adam Ross Stapleton flicked through the pages of the report. He tapped his chin with the stem of his pipe and nodded his head, "This is very interesting," he said, "It's an exciting development, do we have any thing else on this chap what's his name," he looked back at the file, "Elliot Dick, do we have anything else on him, not that it really matters now does it."

"Nothing." replied Mike, "Nothing at all, his name has come up within the last few days from other terrs that we have interrogated, and that is why we went after him. And since his interrogation, the information he has given us, is invaluable."

"Did he talk voluntarily, or did we have to persuade him to talk?" asked Adam,

"No, he spoke to us with no problem at all." said Mike with a smile, "No problem at all."

"Coffee?" asked the Commissioner

"I don't mind if I do." replied Mike, "Milk and one sugar please, do we have any news on the other area's?" asked Mike,

"Stick around." said the Commissioner "And you will get all the information first-hand. Alan Cross and Tim Osby will be here within the hour, you know them don't you, you met them at the last meeting."

"Yes I know them." replied Mike, "I went to school with Tim, and as for Alan, I've still got the stud marks from his rugby boots on my back, hell what a dirty player he was."

The Commissioner laughed, "I never knew that you or Alan played rugby."

"Hell, it's a great game, I used to love it, but due to injuries I had to hang up my boots years ago."

The Commissioner sat down and lit his pipe for the third time in an hour, "Look Mike stay for the meeting. If you don't want to travel back tonight why don't you book yourself into the same hotel as Tim and Alan, they won't be driving back until tomorrow, chill out, have a few beers together.

The reason for the meeting is to get the facts straight from the horses' mouth, if you know what I mean. I really want everyone to know that I am not just a name that sits behind a desk in an office in Salisbury. I do know exactly what you guys are going through out at the sharp end." A sharp knock interrupted the Commissioner.

"Come in." he called. The door opened and in walked Tim, followed by Alan. Both men smiled as they saw Mike sitting in the room, "And how are you?" said Mike as he stood up and offered his outstretched hand.

"We are well, and how are you doing?"

"Oh I am fine."

"Afternoon sir."

"Afternoon." replied the Commissioner, "Make yourselves comfortable, tea or coffee, serve yourselves, and lets get down to business."

The Commissioner sat and contemplated the three men facing him.

"Well gentlemen, I don't think that I need to tell you why you are here today. The situation is not getting much better as I'm sure you all know. Mike here has had a busy week or so to put it lightly, but if you will give us a report on what is going on in your area Tim, and when you're finished Alan can fill us in with all the details of events in his area."

Tim placed a closed file on the desk in front of him; he opened the file and pulled out four sheets of typed notes.

"Last Friday at 0200hrs, the Guilford's farm which lies twenty miles north east of Mount Darwin, sustained a rocket and small arms fire attack, this attack lasted almost an hour. The Guilford's, I don't know if any of you know them, well the family have been farming on the same farm for three generations. Old man Guilford and his wife returned fire from their bedroom while their son Andy who now runs the farm, took up a firing position from the veranda. I spoke to Andy the following day and he has identified four firing positions that were used by the terrs.

Andy is fine, but needless to say his parents are badly shaken, fortunately it was their dogs that warned them that something was up. At about 1.30am the dogs went berserk, looking back on it now, the dogs really saved their bacon, if it were not for the dogs then the terrs may have been able to get into the farmhouse. As it happens, as soon as Andy heard the dogs barking, he went out onto the veranda, he saw figures crossing the garden in front of the house, he immediately opened fire. It was then that his parents, who were woken up by the dogs barking and the sound of gunfire, also opened fire. Sporadic fire was returned. When Andy thought it was safe to do so he contacted Mount Darwin Police Station. At first light I deployed three P.A.T.U. sticks to the immediate area, tracks were found and follow up operations are still ongoing.

"That was the most recent event, two days earlier, Chemtoman farm was hit, well not exactly the farm. Peter Shaw, the farm manager was shot at while inspecting the crops, he says there were two terrs in the attack, as soon as he returned fire the terrs ran off. Now this is something new, this attack took place in broad daylight.

"And the latest report came in just as I was leaving my office to come to this meeting. Seemingly there have been four sightings of terrs in the Mount Darwin area; again I have deployed four more P.A.T.U sticks to the areas. I have asked for any updates to be forwarded to this office."

The Commissioner put down his pipe, "Anything else to report?" he asked,

"No," replied Tim, "That's it."

"Well nothing has come through to my office as yet." he said, as he once again started to light up his pipe, "Now Alan, and what have you got for us."

Alan sighed, "Not much different to Tim's," he replied, "Over the last two days, we have had four attacks. Two on white farm's, I'm pleased to say there were no casualties, but a new incident took place on the third attack. Instead of hitting the farmhouse, the terrs killed ten of the farmer's cattle. They were not killed for food as we first thought, as they were untouched, they were just left lying where they fell.

The next incident is really worrying, Jean and Fred Massey farm right out in the sticks, and I mean right out in the sticks, they must be in their late fifties, and have been on the same farm for the last twenty years. Jean was travelling by car as she has done for years, from Mount Darwin back to Centenary; it's all dirt roads where they live, no different from most of the farming community. As she was nearing her farm she saw three African males crouching down in the middle of the road. As she got nearer they stood up but made no move to get out of her way, Jean slowed down it was then that she saw that they were armed, with she believes were AK47 assault rifles. She had the presence of mind not to stop but hit the gas and drove straight for them. As she drove away from them they opened fire, I'm sorry to say that she was hit in the arm but carried on driving and made it back to the farm.

As soon as the report came in from her husband I deployed two P.A.T.U. sticks to the scene of the attack, a number of cartridge cases were found, but the most worrying thing is what was found next. A land mine had been planted in the road, had she been say half an hour later then I shudder to think what we may be talking about now.

"I don't have to say that everyone is most concerned about this recent development, and I'm not afraid to tell you that my arse was twitching as I drove here to day."

The Commissioner sat forward in his chair his head wreathed in pipe smoke.

"Well gentlemen, firstly let me say one thing to you all, I'm very proud to say the least, very proud indeed of the work that you and your men are doing. Don't think for one moment that it goes unnoticed, because it does not, I can assure you. Last night I was with the Prime Minister, and he asked me to say a very big thank you to everyone at the sharp end for the magnificent work that you are all doing. He knows that it is a very trying time at the moment, but things will get better, things are going on behind the scene that you don't know about, but I will come to that in a minute." said the Commissioner.

"In the Umvukwes area we have had some good results. In the Mangula area two terrs were shot dead, and one captured. Again in the Karoi area, a farmer was shot at in broad daylight, but when he returned fire the cowardly bastards ran off, no stomach for a fight. This is why we will win this war; they are cowards, nothing more and nothing less. Just bloody cowards, who strike at night, hit soft targets, women and now defenceless animals. We are fighting the scum of the earth, and they want to run the bloody country." The Commissioner shook his head in despair.

"In Marandellas two unconfirmed sightings, and right up on the Northern-most border at Mukumvura, two of our patrols came under fire from across the border. I will tell you more about that in a moment.

It is now accepted that there are more than just a handful of terrs in the country. It is my guess that there are at least eight groups of terrs operating in the North Eastern areas. How many in each group no one really knows, at the moment it's all guess work, but I would stick my neck out and say possibly three maybe five per group.

"Coming back to what I said before, what is being done about it, well I can tell you this. The Army is now fully committed. At first we all thought it was just one isolated incident. OK we got it wrong, we now know that it was the start of a much bigger offensive. The Army is deploying a lot more men throughout the country as the farming community as a whole are taking the initial brunt of it all. They are now finding it very difficult indeed to both work the land and to sleep and still be vigilant. So, we are going to deploy Police Reservists, two to each farm for a two week stint. After the two weeks are up they will be replaced with other volunteers.

Opening another file the Commissioner continued:

"As I mentioned earlier, two of our patrols came under fire in Mukumvura, the reason why we have men in that area is twofold. Firstly, we want to catch anyone trying to cross the border from Mozambique, secondly and most important the Government has decided to spend millions of dollars in erecting a high fence along our border with Mozambique. I know what you are going to say, what good will it do, all anyone has to do is just climb the fence. Well let me tell you something, let them climb the bloody fence, because there will be two fences, about thirty feet apart. In-between the two fences the Army Engineers are going to plant tens of thousands of anti-personnel mines. So let them climb the fence. Sensors will be fitted to our side of the fence and when they are triggered a signal will be sent out and a helicopter will be sent to

128

investigate.

"How long will the fence be?" asked Tim,

"As long as it needs to be is the answer." replied the Commissioner.

"Right down the whole length of the border if needs be."

"All reservists are to be called to a state of readiness. This includes Army, Air Force, and of course Police. The Rhodesian Light Infantry Support Unit, the Rhodesian African Rifles are now on full alert. A new unit The Grey Scouts, has been formed, they are a horse mounted unit. Needless to say the Rhodesian S.A.S. and the Selous Scouts are both playing a very important part in all of this, but their role must remain top secret, so please don't ask for anymore details."

The Commissioner sat and looked at his cold cup of coffee. He picked up his phone and asked his secretary to bring in the lunch that he had ordered, "Sandwiches are on their way."

"The sooner we get through the agenda the sooner we can call it a day."

"As I said earlier, I had a meeting with the Prime Minister, he was heading the meeting of the Joint Chiefs of Staff, a lot came out of that meeting I can tell you, a lot more than I expected. The green light has now officially been given to take off the gloves. If it means crossing the border in what we call hot pursuit, then we will do it. When our special forces identify the exact location of the terrorist training camps we will hit them hard either by sending in troops, or bombing them out of existence."

Tim gave a gentle cough, "Yes," asked the Commissioner "Is there something that you want to say?"

"Well I'm just a little bit concerned about the international outcry if we cross the border into either Zambia or Mozambique. Can you imagine the outcry if we bombed a neighbouring country, there would be hell to pay?" said Tim.

"Who cares." "It seems to me that the whole world is against us anyway, so what difference will it make. What are we supposed to do, just sit back and do nothing as these murderers kill innocent people. Stuff the rest of the world; it's time they woke up to what is going on in Africa." said the Commissioner angrily. "Don't misunderstand me." said Tim, "I agree with you completely; all I am thinking of is if the rest of the African countries join in against us."

"They won't," replied the Commissioner "They know which side their bread is buttered on, they will rattle their sabres as they have been doing for years. They don't have the backbone for a fight."

Mike looked up at the large clock that dominated the office wall, he looked at his own watch to check the time, it was three thirty, 'bloody hell,' he thought to himself time has flown. The Commissioner noticed the sudden lack of interest; he looked at the clock and was himself surprised at how the time had passed. "All right gentlemen, I think that we have covered a good bit of the agenda, let's have some lunch."

Chapter Sixteen

Tony kissed Benji and gave Joyce a long, lingering kiss before getting into his Land Rover and heading back to the farm. His thoughts were not on the road ahead but on the work that had to be done when he got back. It was now the time of year when the harvesting of the tobacco crops would begin in earnest. The leaves had to be cut at the right moment, taken into the drying sheds, and as this process was taking place the temperatures had to be monitored on a regular basis. It was a very busy time of the year. Once the drying process had finished, the leaves would be taken into the sorting sheds and sorted by hand. It was a long and very dusty job. When everything was sorted into piles it was then baled up and taken to the tobacco auctions. With all of this going through his mind, in no time at all he soon realised that he was approaching Bindura. As if by remote control he drove onto the tarmac parking place in front of the police station.

As Tony walked into the front office, he smiled at the African officer standing behind the desk, "Morning Chester." he called, "Morning Mr Tony." the officer replied,

"Is the boss in?" asked Tony,

"Mr Johnson is around the back of the station." replied Chester, as if to remind Tony that the name was Johnson and not boss, "He has just arrived, he has taken his Land Rover to the wash bay, if you want I will call him for you?" said Chester,

"No it's OK I will go myself." replied Tony, as he turned to leave the office. Just then, in walked Mike.

"Well, Tony, and how are you?" he asked, "I was just going to phone you in Mabelreign. I phoned you at the farm three times yesterday, but no answer. I was just about to drive out to see if you were all right when I remembered you had told me that you were going to spend some time with Joyce and Benji. Come on through, do you fancy a coffee? I'm going to have one." said Mike,

"OK" said Tony, "The usual one sugar and milk please."

Mike turned to Chester, "Do me a favour and bring us two cups of strong coffee please."

As Tony sat down, Mike closed the door. "Hell I'm so glad you popped in to see me before you drove on to your farm."

"Why? What has happened?" asked Tony,

"Nothing has happened." replied Mike, "At least not yet, we interrogated Elliot Dick the day you left to go and see your family. Well he was a bit of a tough cookie but we broke him in the end. He mentioned two names that will interest you, firstly Joshua."

"Yes," said Tony, punching the air "Tell me more."

"Well we now know that he was one of the terrs who attacked your farm, and the terr that you killed was called Ticky. Ticky was a good friend of this chap Joshua. Seemingly he has told Elliot Dick that he intends to go back and hit your farm again, but this time he intends to get his revenge good and proper. The other thing that now bothers me is, I have just come from a meeting with the Commissioner of Police in Salisbury. In the Centenary farming area, the terrs have started to use land mines. There is no doubt about it, they were seen planting one. The security forces found it and made it safe, it's of Russian origin, and this confirms our suspicions, we have been right all along, the commies are well involved, big style.

"So as you can imagine, this now puts things into a different perspective, everyone now has to be much more vigilant, not only do they have to be watching their backs, but now you will have to watch where you are driving.

"But now for some good news." said Mike, "How would you like to have company on your farm?"

"What," asked Tony, "Are you going to move in with me?"

"No you daft sod." replied Mike. "The government has finally realised that the farmers are in the front line. They also realise that it is anything but a perfect world for them at the moment, and as most of the attacks have been at night, it goes without saying that the farmers are on edge and will obviously not be getting a good nights sleep. This can only go on for so long, and someone is going to crack up under the strain, or make a terrible mistake. So they are offering the farmers the opportunity of having two guards on the farm twenty four hours a day. By day they can relax, sleep, or do whatever they want to do, but as soon as the evening comes then they will be on duty. It goes without saying, they will be armed, they have had basic training in the use of the FN rifle, they know what to do if they get a jam, they can strip their weapons down in the dark, so in the role that they are doing they should be OK. They will also be in radio contact with the nearest police station, but they will be under the command of the farmer at all times. What do you think?" asked Mike,

Tony smiled, "I'm all for it actually, yes I think it is a good idea, count me in."

"Well, you surprise me." said Mike, "I really thought that you would have said no chance as I know what a stubborn sod that you are. From now on if you hear the expression Bright Lights, then you will know what the conversation is about. If you're still interested, then you can pick up your two Bright Lights the day after tomorrow, they will be arriving here at about thirteen hundred hours. Mike relaxed back into his chair.

"Now that we have sorted that out, how were things at Mabelreighn? How is Joyce and the little fellow?" he asked.

"Oh they are fine; I certainly saw a big change in Benji. He is going to be a big lad when he gets older, but he is a little terror, there is no stopping him. And didn't Joyce do well, that Ford Anglia that you arranged for her it's a cracker. I can tell you one thing, she is over the moon with it.

"Joyce is starting to feel broody, she never stopped talking about having another child. Her excuse is that it would be good company for Benji, but I'm not too keen on the idea at the moment. I don't mind the practising, but I just don't think it is a good idea, not with the present situation anyway." said Tony frowning.

"So what is on the agenda now?" asked Mike,

"Well it's back to the farm, then to find out how things are doing. I'm sure everything will be alright, Crispen is a really good worker, he is so trustworthy and honest as the day is long. Then, I'm going to do some work on beefing up the Land Rover; I don't like the sound of these land mines.

"I suppose you will be having a day of rest?" said Tony with a smile,

"You must be joking." replied Mike, he pointed to a pile of paper work on his desk, "I have to go through all of that lot before I go home tonight."

"Late one tonight then." Tony said,

"Oh thank you for reminding me." said Mike, "I have got to phone just about everyone to invite them to a party this weekend. The Selous Scouts are here in Bindura, the Boss of the unit is throwing a party. It's an open house; it's really a moral booster, as at the moment. Everyone is on edge or just generally pissed off, so I think it's a way of getting everyone together, and for every one to let their hair down. He has invited just about everyone and his dog to the party. All the local community, the shop keepers, Trojan Nickel Mine, he has sent out invitations to them as well."

"I doubt if any of the farmers will be there." said Tony, "Can you imagine them wanting to travel back home at night? I certainly wouldn't be doing it, no bloody way it's far too dangerous. It's bad enough travelling during the daylight hours at the moment, never mind at night."

"You can always stop over at my place." said Mike, "It's up to you."

"Thanks for the offer." said Tony, "I will think about it and let you know, anyway I must be on my way, I will see you when I pick up my two so called Bright Lights."

As Tony left the tarmac road, the thick red dust swirled behind him. Normally he would be looking for any signs of movement on either side of the road, as well as watching the road ahead, but today his eyes were also looking for any signs of disturbance on the road surface. Anything that would indicate something had possibly been planted. News that the terr's were now using land mines was not encouraging at all, a land mine was the most indiscriminate of all weapons. It could lie undetected for any amount of time and the most innocent person could detonate it.

Tony knew the speed that he was driving went against all the advice he had ever been given, speed kills. If you are speeding and you hit a land mine the chances of surviving are greatly reduced, but he was so intent on getting off the dirt road that he thought it was a risk he had to take. In the distance he could see his farm, the closer he got to it the safer he felt. As he drove through the farm gates, Crispen, who had obviously heard him coming, came running out to meet him, "Morning Mr Tony." he said with a great big smile on his face, "Everything is fine. The tobacco has all been harvested and is now being hung up in the drying sheds."

Tony stepped out of the cab and stood next to him, he put his arm around his shoulder and said, "Crispen, I just don't know what I would do without you and the workers."

The next two hours were spent talking to his workforce, and checking that everything was just as Crispen had said it was. It was the first time that Crispen had been given so much responsibility, but Tony had to admit he had done an excellent job, "Are the workforce OK?" Tony asked,

"They are well." replied Crispen, "But they do have one problem."

"And what is that?" asked Tony,

"Well they have not been paid for three weeks, and they have had no rations for two weeks."

"Bloody hell" said Tony, "Look please tell them that I am terribly sorry, I am going into town the day after tomorrow, I will get their wages for them then. Come with me I will give them their rations now. Infact to make up for my mistake I will give them all double rations for this week."

"OK," Crispen smiled, "That will make them very happy sir."

As Crispen sorted out the rations, and gave it to the workforce, Tony drove his Land Rover into the workshop. First he jacked up the front of the vehicle, took off the front wheels. He hunted through tins and boxes, until he had about fifty or sixty nuts and bolts of various sizes. He then went out into the sorting sheds and looked amongst the old machinery. There, covered in canvas, he found what he was looking for. Two large rolls of old three-ply conveyor belting. He unrolled the belting onto the floor and then went back into the workshop and started to measure the undersides of the wheel arches, the underside of the cab, and the inside of the doors. Having cut all the belting to size he then started to drill holes into the bodywork of the vehicle. Bit by bit he bolted the conveyor belt to the vehicle. The floor was now covered on both the inside and the underside, the fire wall was covered, the insides of the doors were now finished and the wheel arches were done. Under the two front seats were two small storage areas. These he filled with Hessian bags filled with sand. Tony now put the front wheels back on, and took off the two back wheels. Again he repeated the work that he had done on the front of the vehicle to the back of the vehicle. Once the job was completed he stood back and looked at his work, it looked bloody awful with bolts sticking through the body work. It looked as if the vehicle had in fact been hit by a land mine, but Tony knew that at least he would be a lot safer now the work had been done, or at least he hoped so.

On his return to the farmhouse, Tony showered, shaved, and then opened a welcome can of cold lager. As he sat on the veranda he thought about the work to be done over the next few days, and the increasing threat of terrorist activity in the area. He was suddenly startled by the phone ringing Tony placed the can of lager on the veranda floor and went inside to answer it. "Now Mike," he said, "Hell your working late, true to your word."

"Too true I am." Mike replied, "An hour ago I was told that the Bright Lights will definitely be arriving the day after tomorrow, so I am now frantically phoning all of the farmers in the area to see who wants them,

"The best way of getting in touch with them is obviously when they get in from work. As you welcomed the idea, you are one of the first on my list."

"As I said, I'm all for it, what time did you say they would be arriving?" asked Tony,

"About 13-00 hrs." said Mike,

"OK, I'll be at your office in good time, how many are coming through?" asked Tony,

"Well I have been given a number of twenty, so that means that I can cover almost all of my area, but it all depends on who wants them and who doesn't. As you know there are some stubborn sods out there. Anyway I must get on, so I will see you at the pick up."

"OK Mike," said Tony, "See you soon."

Tony went to the fridge and helped himself to another lager; he was looking forward to the company. At least he would have someone to talk to on the long evenings. Television was rubbish, the programmes were poor, and the reception was even worse. The news bulletins only gave half the story, he knew this first hand, as things had happened in which he had been involved in, and the story on the television bore no resemblance to it at all. So all in all, he was looking forward to the company.

The following day Tony jotted down some figures, 'I will give them to the accountant tomorrow while I'm in Bindura,' he said to himself. He then went out to the curing sheds to check the temperatures. This was the part of the farming year that no farmer relished. It was not just a case of putting the tobacco into the sheds and forgetting about it. The temperatures had to be checked at regular intervals, day and night, and that meant losing out on some sleep. Now that the terrs were more active, it could be quite hairy at times, walking from the warmth of the farmhouse, out into the chill of the night air. Crossing the dark, unlit ground where every footstep exploded into your ears, the door of the curing sheds creaked as it opened, warning anyone that you were coming in. Even to the most hardened person it was not a pleasant duty.

Once he was satisfied that everything was alright, he went to see his workforce who were having their first break. "Morning everyone." he said as he walked towards them, "Thank you for all of your hard work while I have been away, and I'm sure that Crispen has told you all that you will all get paid tomorrow. Did you all get your double rations for this week?" he asked. They all smiled and clapped their hands, "Thank you Mr Tony, thank you!" they all called to him.

The following day Tony rose early and made himself a good breakfast, he looked around the room and wished that Joyce and his son Benji were back with him. It was no life he thought to himself as he quickly washed the dishes. At noon he drove his modified Land Rover out of the workshop and stood looking at it in the daylight. 'This will be the topic of conversation when I arrive in Bindura,' he thought to himself. He filled it up with diesel, checked the oil, and the tyre pressures, then drove around to the farmhouse. He quickly went inside, picked up his shotgun, and checked that it was loaded, slipped a full magazine into his FN rifle and cocked it. Satisfied that every thing was in order he went outside and fired up the engine.

The journey to Bindura was uneventful; in no time at all he was parked in front of the bank. He withdrew enough money to pay his workforce and left the bank, he then made the short walk to his accountant's office. The main road was fairly busy for the time of the day, he nodded to the various people that he knew, but made no attempt to stop and make conversation with anyone. He knew that once the conversation started the topic would soon be about the present situation, and he felt that the least said about it the better. Ten minutes later he was sitting with a cup of coffee in his hand talking to Mike, "These men who are coming, you know, the ones that you call the Bright Lights. You say that they have had some kind of training but have they ever been in the bush before?" he asked,

"All I have been told is that twenty of them have volunteered to do their bit to help out. Give them a chance." said Mike, "Even if it is their first time in the bush, they are eager to do their bit, you can't knock them for that now can you."

"No, not at all." replied Tony, "I'm just curious that's all." Mike looked at his watch, "They will be here any minute now." he said, "Or at least they should be."

No sooner had he spoke than he heard a truck pull up outside, "This must be them." he said as he got up from his desk, "Come on Tony let's go out and meet them."

Outside sitting in a large Scania truck, were twenty men of all different ages, some looked as if they were well past the retirement age, and some looked as if they needed their parents with them.

"Right." shouted Mike, "Let's get you lot off the truck, and bring all of your gear with you. If you can sort of stand in either a line or at least one group, then I will try and allocate you to a farm. If any of you wish to pair off with someone that you know, and would prefer to do your tour of duty with that person then please feel free to come and see me before I start, OK?"

Within minutes everyone had been allocated to a farm, and the farmers went over and introduced himself to his guests.

Tony shook hands with the two young men who had been allocated to him, "I'm Tony, and it's about a half hours drive to my farm, so I think it would be a good idea if we had a quick beer. It will also give you a chance to meet some of the other farmers." he said. The two young reservists followed him into the bar, the atmosphere was alive, and everyone was talking at the same time, and shouting their orders across the bar. "I think we may have to wait a while before we get served." said Tony, "Anyway what're your names?" he asked,

"I'm Kevin." one said, "And this is Martin." Again they shook hands, "Are you from Salisbury?" asked Tony.

Both men answered at the same time and then started to laugh, "Yes we are." said Martin, "We have known each other for about a year now, we both joined the Police Reserve at the same time, did our training together, and decided that we wanted to do a bit more to help out. When we heard that they were looking for volunteers to do a two week stint, we both jumped at the chance, and here we are, ready to do our bit."

"Have you done much training with your FN?" asked Tony,

"Too true we have." said Kevin, "We have done our initial training, and then we asked for further training, and for the last three weekends we have been doing instant action training. We are also in the rifle club, which means that we keep our rifles at home. We think this gives us an advantage, as we know that it's in perfect condition at all times, and it' s zeroed in, exactly as we want it."

"I'm impressed." said Tony, "You both seem to be serious about what you are doing, and it certainly puts my mind at rest. I honestly thought that I was going to get a couple of guys who were out for a bit of a laugh, well I can tell you it won't be a laugh." Tony raised his hand to attract the barman's attention, "Three lagers." he said, "And make it snappy, a man could die of thirst in this place."

Within half an hour the bar started to empty, everyone said goodbye to each other, Tony looked at his watch, "OK let's go." he said, "Where's your gear? Let's get it on to the Land Rover, and then we can get moving."

The journey took just over half an hour, even though Tony felt a lot safer since he had worked on the vehicle, he was in no rush to put it to the test. As he passed each farm, he gave a running commentary on who lived there, and how long they had been farming in the area. "If you look straight ahead you can see my farm, we will be there in about ten minutes." he said.

After showing Kevin and Martin their living quarters, Tony took them on a tour of the farm buildings, "Wherever you go on the farm always take your rifle and your ammo. You will never see me without mine." said Tony, "If we take a hit and you don't have your weapon you are stuffed believe me, when you're in the bush you must regard your weapon as your third arm.

"I doubt very much if you will ever have to leave the confines of the farm, but if you do have to, then it's more than likely that I will be with you. At the bottom of the garden is a large swimming pool, if you feel like a dip then by all means use it. Just past the pool area you will find a tennis court, anyone for tennis?" Tony asked with a smile, "You know I built that for my wife, she went on and on for one, and guess what, she has never used it. Waste of time and money." Tony looked up at the sky and then at his watch, "Right, I think it's time for a bite of lunch and a cold beer."

Over lunch he told them how long he and his family had been farming, and how his grandparents had bought the land and built this very farmhouse with their bare hands, "How long have you been in Rhodesia?" he asked Martin,

"Three years." said Martin, "My parents were farming in Kenya, up in the white high lands, but as you know things got so bad that eventually they sold up and went back to the England. There was no way that I was going back with them, the weather is terrible, and to be honest I could never work behind a desk. No, an office job would drive me crazy so I immigrated to this country and I love it."

"So what are you doing at the moment?" asked Tony, Kevin.

"I'm a rep for a printing company in Salisbury, that's where I met Kevin, he works as a printer."

"Yes," said Kevin, "If you want anything printing, then I'm your man."

"And how long have you been in the country?" Tony asked,

"Well my parents lived in Zambia, my father worked on a copper mine. They had been in Zambia for about twenty-six years, but when he reached his retirement age he decided that it was for the best to return to England as things were happening in Zambia that he was not happy about. Law and order was out of control, and with the conflict in this country, the locals, well their attitudes were changing towards the white population, so my parents decided to leave. I must say they were not too happy when I said that I was going to move to Rhodesia. They said it was like jumping out of the frying pan and into the fire, but I'm here and I have no regrets at all."

"Well I must say that you two have cheered me up no end." said Tony, "Let me fill you in on the situation as it is at the moment. Due to the terrorist activity at the moment in this area, the farmers are just not switching off; they can't get a good night's sleep as most of the attacks come at night. Even though at the moment some attacks have been during daylight hours, the purpose of your presence on the farms are to rest up during the daytime and to be on guard at night, dusk till dawn. I would suggest that you use the veranda. If you sit inside you won't see or hear any thing until it's too late. In your sleeping quarters there is a radio, you will be expected to radio in to a sitrep when you are on duty every hour, on the hour. Your call sign is the name of this farm, should the shit hit the fan, believe me I will be out of bed and out here with you. One of the first things that you must do is to get to the radio, don't piss about with small talk, just give it straight. For example, 'This is Camburo farm, we are under attack, I repeat this is Camburo farm we are under attack, over,' then wait for a response. If for any reason you get no reply, then ditch it, get back outside and put down some fire. If for any reason you are suspicious, either, you think you have seen something, or maybe you have heard something then wake me up, and I mean, wake me up. Drag me out of bed if you have to, it's better to be safe than sorry. Remember, that when you first come out into the night from a lit room it may take your eyes awhile to focus properly again. Make sure that when you move outside of the farmhouse, before you open the outside door, you must switch off the room light. If you don't, then you are making yourself a perfect target, you are a dark target surrounded by light. Also remember, at night, shadows can play tricks on you. You will be certain that a bush has just moved closer to you, you may even think to yourself, that tree wasn't there last night, believe me it does happen."

Tony left the two men to make themselves at home, and he went out to speak to Crispen, "As you will have noticed" he said, "I have a couple of people staying on the farm. They will be here for a short while, but will be out of sight most of the time, if you see them then just ignore them, unless they speak to you." Crispen

141

nodded but looked puzzled, "Don't worry." said Tony, "They are not here to spy on anyone; they are only here to do a very important job." Crispen didn't look too happy, "What is the problem?" Tony asked,

"Nothing." said Crispen, "It has nothing to do with the two men who are staying at the farm, it is something that I heard this morning."

"And what is it that's worrying you?" asked Tony,

"Well there is talk of two strangers in the area, no one knows them, but they are asking lots of questions."

"What sort of questions?" asked Tony,

"Oh, how many workers are on your farm? Do you have a house servant? How big is the house inside? Where are the bedrooms? Do you have dogs? All questions like that."

"Who are these two men?" asked Tony,

"Does anyone know them or has anyone ever seen them before?"

"No" replied Crispen, "No one knows them, they are not from this area."

"OK." said Tony "Don't let it worry you, but if you hear anything else then please let me know straight away."

Tony was now in a dilemma, he had a good idea who the two men were, should he contact Mike and tell him the news? If troops were deployed into the area then the two men would just go to ground, and then wait until the area was safe for them to come out of hiding again. He decided not to make the phone call. Now, the other thing that bothered him was should he tell the two farm guards. They were undoubtedly nervous as it was, and to tell them the latest news would possibly spook them totally. But if they were not warned and something did happen then it could end up in disaster. Tony decided that it was for the best that he should tell them and tell them soon.

The first week passed without incident, and soon the second week was almost over. The two men seemed to have taken everything in their stride, and all the nervous signs disappeared. They now showed more confidence in everything that they were now doing. During the day after they had slept they were now spending more time in the swimming pool and relaxing. Tony noticed that the tennis court still had not been used, 'what a bloody waste of money that had been,' he muttered to himself, 'nobody wants to use it.'

It was the last night of their stint on the farm and Tony thought it would be a good idea to finish it of with a barbeque. When he came in from work, he started to prepare the meat, and soon the smell of burning wood filled the air. It was now seven o'clock and the meat was cooked. He brought out three cold beers, and they got stuck into the food. The conversation was rugby, then more rugby, then jokes. As the night drew on Tony could not remember the last time that he had laughed so much, he looked at his watch and said "Look guys it's time that I hit the sack, let's put out the flames, we don't want to give any one a target, the less light the better."

After making sure that all of the embers were well and truly out Tony left the two men on the veranda and went to bed.

At nine o'clock Kevin made the first sitrep of the night, he returned to the veranda and sat down in the shadows. Both men were ready for home, but had enjoyed the experience enormously. They were whispering to each other as if they were hiding from someone, but they both knew that in the night air your voice could carry for along way. Martin had just returned from making a sitrep, and was sitting on the veranda when Kevin said to him, "I'm sure I saw movement out there."

"Where?" asked Mike,

"Just to the right of the pool." Kevin replied. Martin now concentrated his eyes on the area to the right of the pool, "I can't see anything." he said,

"I'm telling you I'm sure that I saw something." said Kevin, "Someone, or something, is out there."

"OK" said Martin, "Let's just stay silent, and wait a few minutes."

Both men sat in total silence hardly wanting to breathe. "There said Kevin "I'm sure I heard a voice." B

Both men were now looking and listening, "There" said Kevin, "No doubt about it, there is something out there."

Suddenly two figures moved in the shadows, "OK" said Martin "I'll go and wake Tony."

Slowly and quietly, Martin left the veranda and went inside the farmhouse. Both men knew the layout of the inside of the house, so

143

Martin knew exactly where to find Tony. Softly calling his name first, then gently giving Tony a shake, he woke him. "It looks as if we have company."

"Who? Where?" asked Tony,

"Out on the front garden, near to the swimming pool, we have heard voices and just now we are sure that we saw two figures."

'Two figures' thought Tony, his mind was now in attack mode, he jumped out of bed and slipped on a pair of shorts, a pair of trainers, a dark shirt, and then grabbed his webbing with six FN magazines. He picked up his rifle and slipped off the safety catch, and led the way out onto the veranda. "Anything else?" he said quietly to Kevin,

"No, nothing at all, but there's no doubt in my mind there is someone in the garden, and I'm sure I saw two figures."

The words were hardly out of Kevin's' mouth when the farmhouse was raked with automatic fire. "Get down!" shouted Tony, with his experience of recent contacts, Tony immediately pinpointed the firing position, and returned fire.

"Give me covering fire." he shouted to both men, "I'm going to get to the radio." Tony leapt to his feet, ran across the veranda, jumped over the two foot wall and into the sleeping quarters and made for the radio set. With the handset in his hand he stood facing the door with his rifle ready to blast anyone who entered.

"This is Camburo farm, I repeat this is Camburo farm, we are under attack, and does anyone read me over."

"I read you Camburo this is Bindura, do you have any casualties over?"

"No, we have no casualties, but we are presently under attack by numbers unknown."

"OK Camburo help is on its way over."

Tony dropped the handset and ran outside and back towards the veranda. As he was about to jump the wall he called out "It's me don't shoot."

"OK!" they shouted to him, "Shit they are determined bastards aren't they, it looks like two firing positions." said Kevin, "And they are certainly pouring the lead our way."

"How's your ammo." shouted Tony,

"We are OK." replied Martin, "We are only on single shots, let them waste theirs, they have been firing on automatic since the attack began."

Suddenly the firing stopped, the silence was deafening. "Keep down." said Tony, "They're still out there, let's just wait for a few minutes."

The next two minutes seemed like an hour, Tony put down some probing shots hoping that it would draw their fire, but nothing happened. Suddenly they heard a great whoosh and a roar, "Get down!" shouted Tony, "It's a fuckin' rocket."

He saw the tell tale sign as the black powder filled the night sky; suddenly it exploded, destroying the outbuilding.

"What did it hit?" asked Martin,

"The bloody outhouse." said Tony, "The washing machine, the freezer, and a fridge with all of my beer in it, the bastards." he said. "Well there isn't that much that we can do about it at the moment." Tony turned to Kevin and said, "Can you go into the house and watch the back through the kitchen window, just in case they decide to attack us from the rear. If you see anything just open fire and I will come straight to you."

Tony could see the outhouse burning, but there was nothing that he could do about it. He knew that everything in the building would have been destroyed by the initial blast. As it was quite a distance from the farmhouse, he felt confident that the fire would not spread to it. For the next hour they silently waited for a further attack. As the night drew on, it became more certain that whoever had attacked the farm was now long gone. Tony was not going to take any chances by leaving the veranda and walking out into the garden while it was still dark.

Kevin soon appeared from the back of the farmhouse, "Nothing to report." he said, "It looks as if who ever hit us has done a runner." Martin who was still lying on the veranda floor, with his rifle pointing in the direction of the swimming pool said, "I'm not really bothered where they are, I am not moving from this spot until daylight."

"OK" said Tony, "No one is hurt, the outhouse and its contents can be replaced. So apart from the initial shock of the attack, everything else is fine. Martin, do me a favour,"

"It depends what you want me to do." replied Martin, "If you want me to go and take a look to see if they have gone or not, then you have got no chance."

Tony could not stop his laughter, "I'm not asking you to do anything like that." he said, "Just go and make three cups of strong coffee, I think we all need one don't you."

The three men were now sitting on the veranda. As daylight started to chase away the darkness of the night, they all felt a lot more confident. Tony knew that the help that he had been promised would not start out until daylight broke, to travel at night would have been madness, the terrorists would just love it.

He went inside and made some more coffee and some toast. As he looked out of the window, he could see Kevin and Martin walking around the perimeter of the garden, and searching the position from where the attack had come from. He shook his head, the two of them had shown incredible bravery, this was the first time that either of them had been in the bush, and they had been in a contact situation. 'Well done' he said to himself, before they could do more damage to the possible foot prints that the attackers had left, he went outside and called them back to the veranda for a quick breakfast.

As they finished the toast and coffee, they heard the sound of incoming helicopters. They stood up and looked into the direction of the clatter of the rotors, there in the distance were four helicopters thundering towards the farm. Within seconds they were hovering in the air as the first one deployed its men. As soon as they were on the ground it soared into the sky to give cover as the next one off-loaded its men. When all the troops were on the ground the helicopters disappeared as quickly as they had appeared. Tony walked over to meet the troops, "Morning" he said, "It's nice to see you."

"I'm Captain Tim Salmon." a voice said.

Tony shook his hand and pointed to the terrorists firing position. Tim immediately called one of his officers over and pointed to the position that Tony had just indicated to him, "Get the trackers on to it straight away." he said, "How many do you think there were in the group?" he asked,

"Hard to say." replied Tony, "Two, possibly three I would say no more than three though. All we saw were shadows at first, or at least that's what the two Bright Lights saw When they were sure there was someone out there, they woke me, it was then that all hell broke loose." said Tony,

"And what time did it kick off?" asked Tim,

Tony rubbed his chin, "It must have been about three o'clock." he said, "If you check with Bindura police station, they will have a record of the time that I radioed in."

"It's OK" said Tim, "I'm just trying to get a picture in my mind of exactly what happened, and the time will help the trackers.

"What I want you to do now is to stay put. I want to do a complete three sixty of the farm building just in case they have left a surprise behind for you. I am well aware of your last incident and the booby trap that they were preparing for you. So just sit tight and I will let you know when it's OK to move about." Tim started to walk away then he turned on his heels and said, "Don't worry about your workforce trampling over everything; they won't be coming to work today. We will want to talk to each and every one of them."

Tony was now getting impatient, he had last spoken to Tim three hours ago and since then no one had been to see him. As he put down his fifth cup of coffee he heard a vehicle approaching the farm, he stood up and walked into his garden to see if he could see who it was. All he could make out was a Land Rover that had been stopped at the front gate and was surrounded by the Army. As they waved the Land Rover past, and into the farm forecourt, Tony could make out the face of Mike, "Over here!" he shouted to him, Mike waved to him and made his way to the veranda.

"Well someone doesn't like you." he said,

"I'll give you two guesses as to who it was." said Tony, "It's too much of a coincidence isn't it, you told me that those two shits Magumbo and Joshua are out for revenge, and then this happens. There is no doubt in my mind at all, mind you I must say one thing, it could have been totally different if it were not for the two young lads that you sent me two weeks ago. I shudder to think what would have happened if it had not been for them. The bastards were on the front garden. If I had been on the farm on my own, they would have been up to the window of my bedroom. I honestly cannot praise the two of them enough. When the shit hit the fan they did not flinch, they gave back as good as they got."

"So what have the Army found?" asked Tony,

"Seemingly not a lot." replied Mike, "It looks as if you were right, there are two sets of footprints leading to the garden. Then they crossed over behind the swimming pool, and took up a firing position at the point that you showed Tim. From there it looks as if they made their way over to the east side of the garden, possibly when they came under fire from the farm. The tracks lead down to the river but they did not cross it Instead they made their way to the village, then they drove the cattle out of the stockade to cover their tracks. At the moment the trackers are looking in ever increasing circles to see if they can pick up fresh tracks, but quite honestly I don't have much hope. Whoever hit your farm, seems to know what they are doing, they certainly are not raw recruits."

Mike turned and looked in the direction of his demolished outhouse. "I hope you know a good builder." he said with a smile.

Chapter Seventeen

Magumbo and Joshua had been moving slowly north for the last five days. They now had the target in sight, but it was now time to wait and plan their attack. All the details were in place to hit the farm when they saw the Land Rover return to the farm, but rather than just the farmer getting out of the vehicle they saw three people. One was the farmer, but the other two were in combat uniforms and were carrying rifles. "This changes things." said Joshua, "Who the hell are the other two?" he asked,

"How should I know." replied Magumbo irritably, "You said that you knew the farm."

"I do." replied Joshua, "The last time I watched this farm there were three people but it was the farmer, his wife and a child."

"Maybe the wife and child are inside." Magumbo said, "We have come this far to hit the place I don't feel that we should just abandon it just because two more people have turned up."

"I'm not saying that we should change our plans." replied Joshua, "All that I am saying is that I don't know who they are, let's just sit tight and see what they are on the farm for, and what they are doing."

As the days and nights passed, the plans remained the same; they were intent on attacking the farm. First they were going to hit the farmhouse at night, then they decided to hit the farmer as he was working in the fields. But despite their plans they could not agree on when to make the attack. It was decided to hit the farm at night. What they could not decide was where the two newly arrived men were staying on the farm. During the first week they never saw them during the daytime, then on the second week they appeared to be spending more time in the garden area, and using the swimming pool, or just lying in the sun. "What were they doing on the farm?" asked Joshua, "Surely if they were just friends of the farmer they would be dressed in civilian clothes and not combat gear."

As they could not agree on their presence or purpose on the farm they decided to go ahead and hit the farm at night in two days time.

It was late on Friday night when they made their move towards the farm. Keeping in the shadows, and moving very quietly and slowly, they made their way onto the farm premises. In the light of the moon they could now make out the swimming pool that the two men had been using. Closer to the farmhouse was a dip in the ground, lying in the dip they could now see the farmhouse silhouetted in the moon light. Nothing moved, just the slight sound of the night breeze as it whispered through the branches of the trees.

Joshua lay next to Magumbo, they were breathing as quietly as they could. Joshua raised his AK47 assault rifle, and took aim; Magumbo moved into a more comfortable position and also took up a firing position. "OK" said Joshua, both men opened fire at the building. The noise was deafening, the smell of cordite filled their lungs. At first nothing happened, then they ducked as return fire came back at them from the veranda. The bullets whistled over their heads, and then the bullets were thumping into the ground in front of them and at the sides of them. Magumbo dropped his assault rifle and quickly picked up his RPG rocket launcher, taking aim, he held his breath, but instead of squeezing the trigger he tugged on it. The rocket veered off to the left and exploded in a sheet of flame demolishing a small building at the side of the main building. The return fire was now getting more intense, and a lot more accurate. "Come on let's get out of here." he said to Joshua, he dropped his rocket launcher; picked up his assault rifle fired off a few shots and they both made a hasty retreat.

Once they were out of the garden they started to run, leaving the farm which was now silhouetted by both the moon, and the fire that was blazing in what was once a small outhouse. They ran down to the river and made their way along its bank. As they ran into the bush, they could make out a small village in the distance. As they got nearer, the moonlight cast shadows on the mud huts. At the far side of the village, they saw a stockade where the villagers had herded the cattle for the night. Skirting the village, Magumbo and Joshua listened for any sign of life, only the occasional chicken caught their attention as it hunted for its next scrap of food. In the distance the bark of a dog, or a jackal, broke the still silence of the night air. A muffled cry of an infant came from a mud hut. Slowly they made their way towards the stockade. As they approached, the cattle suddenly moved away from the fence. Joshua whispered to the cattle, slowly making his way closer to the gate, taking great care not to startle them. He lifted the heavy wooden tree trunk that was used to jam the gate shut and opened it. As he entered the stockade, the cattle moved quickly passed him and into the open bush. Moving away from the village, both men knowing that they were safe as the cattle would cover any tracks that they would leave behind.

As the sun started to rise in the early morning sky, they abandoned the cattle, and made their way into the thicker bush. In the distance they could now hear the sounds of low flying aircraft. Looking into the sky they could see helicopters flying towards Camburo farm. Magumbo smiled at Joshua, "They will be chasing their tails long after we have left the area." he said.

Within minutes of the helicopters passing they then saw them flying in ever increasing circles in a definite searching pattern. For the next three hours both men knew that it would be madness to move from their position. They also realised that ground troops would very soon be swarming over the area.

As the evening came, the sound of the searching aircraft receded, both men knew that it was time to move. Crawling out of the thick undergrowth they stretched their arms and legs, picked up their weapons and slowly moved away from the area and headed east.

For the next two days, both men continued to move away from the area, travelling at night and resting during the daylight hours. Water was no problem, as the bush had a plentiful supply of rivers and watering holes, but food was now in short supply. They had seen a fair amount of wild game but knew that it would be a big mistake to shoot any for food. The sound of gunfire would bring any troops who may be in the area racing to the scene.

In the distance they could see a small village. They decided to rest up during the day, but at the same time they would observe the locals and check to see if it looked safe enough to approach. As the dawn broke the first signs of life were the dogs and then the children, followed by the women who prepared breakfast before going into the fields to work the land. Much later in the morning the men appeared, and as custom dictated, they all sat in the shade, and started what would be hours of conversation.

After a further two hours of waiting and watching, Magumbo and Joshua decided to venture into the village. After hiding their weapons they slowly walked up to the group of men who were sitting in the shade. At first everyone just looked at the two strangers, and said nothing. Obviously very suspicious, they listened as Joshua told them that he and his cousin were on their way to Nyamapanda where their family lived. Their father had died and they were trying to get there for the funeral. After many questions Magumbo and Joshua were made welcome. They were given food and water and offered shelter for the night. That evening they sat with the rest of the villagers and again shared a welcome meal. The conversation had no main topic and went from the weather to tales of the old days and the hunting trips that they used to go on. As the night drew on the effect of the home-made beer loosened their tongues. Normally politics was not something that you spoke about to strangers, but as the conversation got under way it became clear to Magumbo that the village was split. Some were in favour of the freedom fighters, and some just wanted to be left alone. Magumbo sat in silence, willing them to change the subject. He was taking note of who was saying what, when he noticed a young man sitting at the back. The young man took no part in the conversation, but every time Magumbo made eye contact with him he looked hastily away. Magumbo also found it curious that the young man was dressed in much better clothes than the rest of the people in the village.

Late that night Joshua and Magumbo were given a place to sleep. The next morning as they prepared to leave, they thanked the elders of the village for their hospitality. As they looked around the group of people who had come to say goodbye, Magumbo asked one of the elders, "Who was the young man that sat behind you last night?"

The old man frowned, then smiled, "Oh you mean Crispen, he is my grandson. He left very early this morning to get back to the farm where he works. He only gets home to see us now and again, he has a very responsible job you know, he is a boss boy at Camburo farm."

As the two men left the village behind them, Magumbo could not stop thinking of the young man, "That's the farm that we have just hit." he said to Joshua,

"I know it is." he replied, "It's the same farm that Ticky was killed on, I know the farm now as if it was my own, and one day it will be."

The following day, they decided it was now safe enough to keep on travelling. For the next three hours they made their way through the bush. Soon they could hear the sound of a vehicle in the distance; it seemed to be coming their way. As the vehicle came into view it slowed down and stopped. Both men crouched down and waited. From their concealed vantage point, they slowly crept forward. About fifty yards in front of them they could see an army truck, covered in camouflage paint and netting. Standing next to the vehicle were four heavily-armed soldiers adjusting their webbing. They then disappeared into the bush. No sooner had they entered the bush, when the vehicle roared into life and continued on it's way along the narrow dirt road, sitting in the back of the truck were eight more heavily-armed men.

Joshua and Magumbo stayed hidden in the undergrowth as the vehicle continued on its way. The last of the eight men were dropped off at two intervals, the final four about one hundred yards from the last drop off point. Again the vehicle didn't stop, it just slowed right down as it had for the last four men. As they jumped off the back and ran into the bush, the vehicle then continued on its way back to base camp. Alpha Bravo pushed deep into the thick bush. The three sticks were now about one hundred yards apart from each other, but moving in the same direction. Tango X-ray was slightly behind Alpha Bravo, with Hotel Zulu up front. It was more of an exercise than an operational assault on the area. No sightings had been reported, but the Officer in Charge had a gut feeling that if he was a terr, that would be the area that he would head for. Anyone who was being chased just had to take the shortest route that would eventually come to the Mozambique border and safety. The objective of the exercise was to either flush out anyone in the area, or to make them head away from the border areas, and into the waiting stop lines that had been put in place.

Magumbo watched the men disappear into the bush; the truck slowly moved along the dirt road was soon out of sight. The decision now was, should they go back the way that they had just come, or did they carry on regardless? Both men sat and waited. After an hour they decided it was now safe to continue on their journey. They made their way through the bush keeping parallel to the road, moving well away from the position where they had seen the four soldiers enter the thick bush.

Magumbo and Joshua now had to cross the road; slowly they made their way to the roadside. Crawling on his stomach, using as much cover as he could, Joshua inched his way to the edge of the dirt road. It was impossible to see the road in both directions without breaking cover. Hardly bearing to breathe, Joshua peered along the road; slowly he crawled back into the bush. "It's clear." he said. Both men moved closer to the roadside, staring into the bush on the far side of the road, Magumbo waited before he made his move. Once he had decided that it was all clear, he quickly ran to the other side of the road. He crouched down in the bush and waited for any sound or movement that would indicate danger. When he was satisfied it was safe he beckoned to Joshua. Magumbo broke a long branch off a tree; he reached out onto the road and swept away any signs of foot prints that they had left.

The sun was now directly overhead; it was noon, time to rest, both men now burrowed into the undergrowth. In the distance they could hear the sounds of fixed-wing aircraft, and the occasional helicopter as the rotors clattered through the still air.

In the distance they could see the hills that were beckoning to them, but they knew that it would take at least three days at the pace that they were going to get anywhere near them.

As the sun started to drop towards the horizon both men moved out of their makeshift camp. After walking for about an hour they decided that it was too dangerous to continue as they had no idea where the four soldiers maybe so they decided to find a spot for the night and rest up. Hopefully by morning the soldiers would be well out of the way. In the distance about three hundred yards away, they could see a small hill with a rocky outcrop halfway up the side, "Ideal." said Joshua, plenty of cover for the night, and a good vantage point to see any movement that may be coming their way.

At first light, Magumbo and Joshua were woken by the sound of movement at the foot of the hill. Joshua carefully looked over the top of the large boulder that he had slept next to, what he saw made his heart pound; four heavily-armed men were making their way up the hill directly towards their position. It was the four men that they had seen yesterday, they must have back-tracked, or dropped behind. "Shit" he said to Magumbo "They are onto us."

Magumbo jumped to his feet and grabbed his assault rifle, "How many?" he asked,

"Four," replied Joshua, "And coming straight for us, no more than twenty yards away."

"OK let's get out here."

Both men moved as quickly and as quietly as they could, moving from boulder to boulder, keeping out of sight as best they could. Every few minutes they stopped to listen, not daring to take a look. Eventually they skirted the hill and decided to make a run for it. Just as they broke cover they heard a voice shout, "Up there, just to the right of the rocks." the sound of automatic fire filled the air, both men dashed back to the safety of the large boulders. Suddenly their place of safety became a place of terrifying torment. As the bullets hit the boulders that were protecting them, slivers of stone were sent flying through the air, slicing through their skin. Both men ducked down, Magumbo held his assault rifle over his head, pointed it in the direction where the firing was coming from and opened fire, emptying the magazine. Quickly he clicked a full magazine back into his rifle, just as he was about to open fire again, there was a sudden burst of fire coming his way. Once again there was a shower of razor-like splinters of rock flying everywhere, both men ducked down and covered their heads with their hands.

"We have got to get out of here." said Joshua, "Or we will be cut to ribbons." As quickly as it had started, the firing suddenly stopped. In the distance they could hear someone shouting into a radio, "This is Tango X-ray, this is Tango X-ray, do you read me over." Magumbo nodded to Joshua, "OK let's go, I'll give you covering fire, when you get clear, cover me and I will join you."

Magumbo jumped up and raked the area with automatic fire; Joshua ran as fast as he possibly could, waiting for the moment when he would feel the pain of a bullet as it hit him in the back. As soon as he made it to the rocks, he turned and opened fire, spraying the area with his assault rifle. As Magumbo ran towards him, a rifle grenade exploded in the rocks where they had been hiding. Now with Magumbo at his side, they both loosened off another magazine each then ran as fast as they could into the safety of the thick dense bush.

Alpha Bravo stopped as they heard the firing; it was coming from the rear of their position and to the east. Then they heard Tango X-ray giving its call sign on the radio, they had made contact with the enemy. Immediately Alpha Bravo started to move towards Tango X-ray's position. In the thick bush, visibility at its best was no more than twenty yards, and in some places it was as little as four or five feet. It was madness to go crashing through the bush, all the enemy had to do if they heard you, was to just lie in wait, and when you came into view, spring the ambush. Every soldier knew that a proper and well prepared ambush would have a one hundred percent kill rate. Magumbo and Joshua ran on regardless, all they wanted to do was to get a good distance from the soldiers who would now be hot on their heels.

As they crashed their way through the bush, in headlong flight the lead scout of Alpha Bravo raised his right hand, indicating to his stick to stop. In the distance he thought he could hear the sound of someone, or something. He cocked his head to one side, and listened, yes, something was out there. He lifted his right hand with his fist clenched, indicating enemy, then signalled to his men take cover. Now to even the trained eye, the bush now looked as safe as it had ever been no one in sight, nothing moving, but every weapon now ready to open fire. Suddenly in the distance he saw two African males carrying weapons, and running like the wind through the bush. He leapt to his feet and opened fire, "At twelve o'clock!" he shouted. Everyone was now concentrating on the target area, the sound of five weapons, as they opened fire was deafening.

Magumbo was the first to return fire, instantly Joshua joined him. They both put down a hail of deadly fire. Not sure of the exact position of the enemy, both men sprayed the area until their magazines were empty. Quickly they reloaded and keeping as low as they possibly could, they moved into thicker bush, every few yards they stopped and fired a few rounds towards the enemy position.

Both men, now sweating profusely, and gasping for breath, ran blindly through the bush, the danger that they were now in was brought home to them very quickly. They knew that there were at least four Army sticks in the immediate area, but now they could hear the unmistakable clatter of helicopter rotors as they flew directly overhead. Looking up to the treetops Joshua could see the under belly of the helicopter as it hovered above them. The down draught from the rotors was blowing the branches in a mad frenzy, leaves were flying in thickening swirls, dust from the ground was being sucked up into the air. Both men were sure that they had now been spotted, there was no escape. They knew that the ground troops would soon be upon them, Joshua raised his assault rifle and fired a full magazine into the belly of the helicopter and then at the rotors. The whine of the engine changed note, and it started to cough and splutter. Black smoke started to bellow from the engine compartment, the air was now full of smoke and the smell of engine fuel. Suddenly the rotors started to disintegrate. The helicopter started to vibrate violently, it hung in the air, as if resting on the tree tops, and then it began its rapid decent to earth. Both men ran for their lives as it crashed through the tree tops, and hit the ground. The roar was deafening as everything exploded. A great big orange ball of flame sucked the air out of the trees. One minute everything was being sucked towards the flames, and then there was another massive explosion the force sending both men flying through the air. Dazed, and with their backs stinging from the burning embers that had landed on them, they crawled away from the scene. When they got to their feet and ran blindly into the safety of the thick bush.

In the distance they could hear the voices shouting orders, and more explosions as the ammunition on the helicopter exploded. Overhead they could hear more helicopters, but now they were high in the sky and taking no chances.

Both men were now two hours away from the scene. Totally exhausted they found their escape route cut off by a fast flowing river. Both men ran along the banks of the river looking for a place to cross. They ran for fifty yards one way, and more than a hundred yards in the other direction. Joshua slowly shook his head, he looked at Magumbo, "There is no chance of us crossing that with out a boat." he said. Both men stood ankle-deep in the water so as to leave no tracks, "Come on," said Joshua "Let's go back downstream." Tired as they were, both men splashed through the water, knowing that at any moment they could be spotted either by air, or by the troops who would now be hot on their trail and eager to spill their blood.

"There." pointed Magumbo,

"Where." asked Joshua,

"Over there just at the waters edge."

Joshua looked at the point where Magumbo was pointing, right at the rivers edge was a very large tree, its roots exposed by years of water erosion. The tree was now lying at an almost impossible angle. With its massive gnarled roots protruding out of the ground, it looked like a massive sea creature beckoning its prey with its outstretched tentacles. Running towards the tree they could now see insidea large dark cavern that now offered them safety. Stepping out of the water, and careful not to leave any footprints or any telltale signs that may give away their hiding place, both men crawled over the roots that were the thickness of a man's waist. Once inside they moved slowly to the back of the cavern, the smell of rotting vegetation filled their nostrils; this was a perfect hiding place. It was pitch black, very uninviting, and at the very back there was a large mound of earth that had been washed up by the flooded river, crawling over the mound of earth both men closed their eyes and rested.

Joshua woke with a start, voices, he nudged Magumbo. "Someone is out there." he whispered. Both men laid their assault rifles on the mound of earth, and took aim directly on the entrance. In the daylight they could see pairs of legs near to the river bank, and voices. "They must have crossed the river" someone said,

"Impossible it's flowing too fast, they would be washed away."

"Do you know how powerful that water is, without a boat, no one would be able to cross it believe me."

"Then they must have either gone upstream, or downstream."

Joshua nudged Magumbo, a pair of legs was moving towards their hiding place, both men ducked down. "Shit they are on to us." Joshua whispered.

Slowly a figure approached the cavern, bending down, he started to enter the darkness, his rifle was pointing straight at the two men as they lay hidden, moving his eyes from side to side the soldier moved slowly forward. Joshua took up the first pressure on the trigger, as the cavern got smaller; the soldier got down on his knees and started to make his way forward. Joshua was just about to open fire when a voice shouted, "Come on Robin, we are moving out, they must have backtracked and gone back into the bush."

As the soldier backed out of the cavern both Magumbo and Joshua let out a huge sigh of relief.

Chapter Eighteen

Kandeya is a sprawling Tribal Trust Land. It lies to the north east of the country, covers about three thousand to four thousand square kilometres, and is home to approximately seventy thousand Africans who live in scattered kraals. It is also a hot bed for terrorist recruitment.

In the late 1930's the Rhodesian Government appointed a new chief for the Kandeya Tribal Trust Land. The appointment was not the choice of the people. When the Rhodesian African Nationalism was born, the head of one of the families that had been overlooked as the candidate for the position of chief, became the Nationalist leader. The people of Kandeya soon realised that they could now hit back at the government by supporting the terrorists who now used their land to recruit the young men and to launch their attacks on the surrounding white farmers.

Pandama farm was very close to the Kandeya Tribal Trust Land. Bob Prosser had been farming in the area for the past thirty-five years. When he first saw the farm, it was just virgin land, one thousand six hundred acres of nothing. As far as his eyes could see, it was bush, rocks, and then more bush. It took him all of six months to build a farmhouse that he could call home. Once that was finished he plucked up the courage to ask Janet's father for her hand in marriage. As the two families had known each other for many years, and Bob and Janet had been childhood sweethearts, Bob was sure that the answer would be yes.

Over the years, Bob and Janet worked hard to make the farm a success. They now had two sons Glen and Harvey. Both the boys had shown a great willingness to work on the farm, but Bob had told them in no uncertain terms, get a good education first, regardless of the cost, then, and only then, can you take over the farm.

With the boys at university, the farm was dead. No laughter, no brotherly rivalry, but on the other hand there was no mess, for once the farmhouse was tidy.

Janet was the backbone of the business; she did all the bookkeeping, and ordered all the stock. She paid all the wages to the work force, made sure they had their rations on time, and looked after them when they were ill. She was even there when the women gave birth, the workers loved her.

Bob sat on the veranda with a glass of KWV brandy in his hand. He was looking at the sunset, the sky was a burning orange, he could make out faces in the clouds, and he could see the shapes of the last few birds as the raced home to their nests. "Yes it's a beautiful country." he murmured, "Penny for your thoughts." he said to Janet,

"Oh I'm just thinking about the future." she replied, "You know, what will we be doing this time next year, what is going to happen to the country. With all this trouble I often think about the boys, and what the future has in store for them."

"I often wonder myself." Bob replied, "But you know there isn't a lot that we can do about it now is there. I know that Kenya and Zambia have now got themselves self rule, but no one put up a fight did they, it was just handed to them on a plate. They are kicking up in South West Africa, and in Mozambique. How much more do they bloody well want, all of Africa. They won't be satisfied until they have the lot, I can tell you. At least we and the Portuguese in Mozambique are putting up a fight, and as for the problem in South West Africa, well the South Africans, they will never hand it over."

Janet put down her knitting, "How would you feel if there ever was a black government in Rhodesia?" she asked,

"It will never happen." Bob replied, "They are just not ready for it yet. You just have to look at any country that has been given independence; it has turned into total chaos. If and when they are ready, then I will be the first to say yes let's give it a try, but to share the running of the country, not just to hand it over to them on a bloody plate. You know, I was talking to our workforce the other day, and you know what, they don't want a black government. They would like more say in the running of the country, but they have seen what has happened in other countries in Africa. Once they have been given independence, they know that in no time at all, everyone would be starving, killing each other, or dying of disease."

Bob poured himself another brandy, dropped a handful of ice cubes into the glass, and sat back down, "You know what the biggest threat to the black population in Africa is, themselves. The different tribal factions hate one another, they could never agree on anything. If they could just stop their squabbling, and unite, then they could drive the white man out of Africa within months, but their hatred is too deeply engrained for them to change. That is why once they get independence, the so called President will declare it a one party state, and brutally crush any opposition."

As Bob topped up his glass again with another large brandy, he switched on the radio just in time to hear the news.

'It was announced today that the Prime Minister spent most of yesterday in talks with the Reverend Abel Muserawa. Although the talks were polite and friendly, no common ground could be found, but it was agreed to continue with the talks later next week.

'The security forces regret to announce the death of Captain Alan Maynard who was killed in follow-up operations in the north east of the country. Captain Maynard leaves a wife and two young children. Five terrorists were also killed in the operation. In the Madziwa Tribal Trust Land, follow up operations continue after a helicopter was brought down by enemy fire. We will bring you more details as and when we get them and that is the end of the news bulletin.'

Bob downed the brandy in one gulp, he went over to the radio and switched it off, and poured yet another brandy. "It's all bad news." he grumbled as he sat down.

Janet looked at his glass, and said, "Go easy on the brandy; with the trouble that is going on all around us, you will be no good to anyone if we get attacked."

"Don't be daft." he replied, "Why should they hit us, we have a very good relationship with our workforce."

"Don't kid yourself." Joyce replied, "We are white, and that is enough for those murdering thugs." Just as Janet put down her knitting, the telephone rang, "That will be the boys." she said, as she got up to answer it. Bob looked at his watch, it was nine thirty, a quick word with his two sons, and then he would have to do his rounds of the curing sheds, before turning in for the night.

Bob sat on the edge of the bed; the early morning light was just starting to peep through the bedroom curtains. He looked at the bedside clock, it was four thirty. 'God' he said to himself, 'you stink of brandy.' His head was fuzzy and his mouth tasted like the bottom of a parrot's cage. He wandered into the bathroom, cleaned his teeth, and splashed cold water onto his face, but still he felt like shit, 'early night tonight,' he said to himself. He made himself a cup of strong coffee, he took one sip, and decided that he just couldn't face it and poured it down the sink. He made a cup of tea, and took it through to Joyce, "Here you are love." he said, careful not to breathe on her, if she smelt his breath he knew that he would get hell for the next few days. Bob pulled on a pair of shorts, and a thin short-sleeved shirt. He reached for his shoulder holster and slipped it on, picked up his pistol from the bedside table and slipped it into the holster. As he walked to the bedroom door, he leant over and kissed Janet on the top of her head, "Your tea is there." he said. Next to the door he picked up his shotgun and walked to the front door. Shoving his feet into his muddy boots, he unlocked the door, walked outside, locked the door again and looked up at the morning sky.

As he walked around to the back of the farm buildings, Bob was thinking about the things that he had to do that day. Firstly he needed to check the tobacco curing sheds again. Then dip the storage tanks. Fuel oil was essential to the running of the farm. Normally it was delivered on a two or three week rota, but the order had to be placed well in advance, at least a week. 'Everything was fine,' he said to himself as he closed the shed door. Bob's next job was to service his Land Rover, not only did it need a good service, but he knew that he could no longer leave the exhaust pipe. If it was not replaced today it would most likely just drop off.

As Bob walked towards the garage, he looked around the farm buildings; he could see Janet through the kitchen window, probably starting her housework. Bob shook his head, 'she never stops' he thought to himself. He gave her a wave before disappearing through the large garage doors. He opened the doors as wide as they would go to let more light in. Walking past the tractor, he placed his shotgun on the work bench, and lifted the bonnet of the Land Rover. Bob looked down at the engine, 'I bloody well hate this job,' he said to himself; the job itself was of second nature to him now, as he had done it for years. It was just too expensive to take it to a garage. Not only did they charge the earth, but they took too bloody long to do it. Bob stood back and wiped his hands, he looked at his watch, 'not bad going.' he said to himself, 'now just the exhaust pipe to sort out.'

Bob crawled under the vehicle and soon saw the problem; the silencer was holed just where the pipe came out of the box. Within minutes he had the silencer on the work bench, and was now busy cutting a piece of tin that he could use as a patch. Satisfied that it was strong enough, he welded the patch over the holed silencer. Happy with his handy work he left it on the work bench to cool down. 'Breakfast,' he said to himself, 'then I'll finish it off, and get on with the rest of the days work.'

"You must have a very good nose," Janet said, "I was just about to give you a shout, go on wash your hands and sit yourself down."

Bob always said, breakfast is the most important meal of the day, no matter how late you are, never leave the house without it.

"So what's on the agenda today?" Janet asked,

"Well I have serviced the Land Rover, I've nearly fixed the exhaust pipe, at least I hope I have. Once I have finished that then I have some work to do in the fields, but I will be home as usual in time for lunch." Bob pushed the empty plate away, "That was lovely, I must say I was ready it."

"I'm surprised that you could face it, after the amount of brandy that you put away last night. Don't try and tell me that you don't have a sore head; you can't fool me you know we have been married to long. I can read you like a book." laughed Janet. She picked up the breakfast plates, "Go on, get back to work, before you fall asleep again, and don't bother trying to give me one of your forgive me kisses, you stink of drink. Go on get out." she said with a smile.

Bob lay on his back and wriggled his way under the Land Rover and started to bolt the exhaust pipe back into place. He was so engrossed in his work that he didn't hear the footsteps as two figures entered the garage. It was only when he reached out to pick up a spanner to tighten the exhaust pipe in place that he saw two pairs of feet standing at the side of the vehicle. A sudden rush of fear swept through him, it was the shock of not hearing anything, and then to see two people standing so close that made him jump. His first thought was his shotgun; it was out of reach, lying on the work bench. Slowly he moved on his back to the side of the vehicle, he could now see the two figures were armed, both with assault rifles. Bob's mind was racing, who were they, he was trapped; he was like a rat in a barrel. He reached for the pistol in his shoulder holster, but he couldn't get his hand to it, he was in too much of a cramped position. He tried to lie on his side, so that he could have a better access to his weapon, but still he couldn't get at it. Bob's heart seemed to stop as he saw a face looking at him, beckoning to him to come out from under the vehicle. The face had an obscene smile as if it was taunting him, Bob quickly shuffled his way to the other side of the vehicle, only to see the barrel of an assault rifle pointing at him, and behind the rifle another sinister face. Bob now knew that he had to either come out, or be dragged out, either way he was at their mercy. As he slowly emerged into the open, he was slammed against the side of the land rover. His pistol was taken from him, and the beating started. First he was kicked in the groin, and in the stomach and when he tried to curl up into a ball to protect himself, his face and head became the target. The beating continued, he was now gasping for breath, the pain was incredible, he could taste the blood as it ran into his mouth. The sound of his teeth breaking made him want to vomit. Trying desperately to fend of the blows, he struggled to see through blood filled eyes the identities of his attackers.. Who was the man with the missing finger? And who was the other one, with the scar that ran down his forearm. As the beating continued, the pain eased as Bob slid into unconsciousness.

Sitting in the living room, Janet looked again at the clock; it was now well past the time Bob usually came in for his lunch. 'I'll give it another half an hour,' she said to herself, 'then I will go out and ask the workers if they know where he is.' As she looked at the clock for the tenth time in the same amount of minutes, Joyce with a deep sense of foreboding decided to go out and ask the workforce if they knew where Bob was. No one in the sheds had seen him; in fact no one had seen him since early that morning. She asked two of the workers to accompany her to the garage, as she could remember Bob saying that he was going to do some work on the Land Rover.

As she approached the garage she could see his tool box open beside the workbench. "Your lunch is ready" she said in a relieved voice as she walked into the garage. "You must be starving." Janet stopped; her hands went up to her face. Agonised screams tore from her body. Again and again, she screamed, her mind unable to take in the horror of what lay before her.. Lying on the dusty floor was the body of her husband. His face was a mask of blood, both of his eyes were missing, and he had been repeatedly stabbed in the neck, chest and stomach. As a final insult he had been stripped naked and spread-eagled on the floor.

Chapter Nineteen

Tuesday brought high temperatures, and high humidity. In Salisbury the streets were quiet, and only those who had to be out moved quickly from one building to the other, not even a bird could be seen in the sky.

General Willis had called a meeting of Joint Operational Command [J.O.C.] Every senior member of the Police, Army, Air Force, Special Forces, and two Government Ministers were present.

"Well gentlemen," said General Willis quietly "I have called this meeting so that I can brief you all on the present situation as it is at the moment. Not only in the North East of the country, but throughout the country as a whole.

I know that we all keep in touch via the telephone etc., but I do believe that it is very important for us all to have these meetings so that we can share relevant information." Everyone nodded in approval.

"At present there are an awful lot of rumours flying around, and an awful lot of speculation, so today I also intend also to deal with that.

I'm sure you will want to know what the progress is concerning the operation to erect two parallel fences down our border with Mozambique. Well I am able to tell you that it is going very well indeed, and I am even more pleased to say that at the moment we are well ahead of our planned completion date.

"It has been decided to plant anti-personnel mines within the confines of the two fences, starting from Mukamvura down to Nyamapanda. I must say a big thank you indeed to the Police Commissioner for his involvement in the operation; the work could not have been carried out so quickly, and so safely, without the support of the Police Reserve, thank you Adam.

"Next is the erection of security fencing in the white farming areas. As you may remember from our last meeting, it was suggested that if the farmhouses and the outhouses were fenced off, it would give the farmers better protection especially at night. This idea was put forward, and I can confirm that once again, good progress is being made. As you can imagine all of this work is costing the government a small fortune, but they think that it is a small price to pay for the security it will give. The farmers in the sharp end at this moment in time need all the help that they can get.

"The response that we have had from the farmers is very positive indeed, and I know that with the Police Reserve, now known as the Bright Lights, they feel much safer when they are on duty guarding the farms at night.

"Now I want to draw your attention to the rumours and to the speculation that is going around. Yes, the Prime Minister has been having talks with various African Political Parties, including the Reverend Abel Muzarewa. Don't believe all that you hear about the talks, I can assure you that despite all their differences in opinions, they are still talking. The Prime Minister was quoted yesterday as saying that he thought the Reverend was a man that he could do business with, but in my opinion don't hold your breath.

"I can now confirm to you that Special Forces have identified two large terrorist training camps inside Mozambique. One is in the Tete district known as Chifumbo, and the other one, which is a worry to us, is called Mazangesi. This is giving cause for concern as it is right on our border. In fact too close for comfort. We have asked the Portuguese Army in Mozambique to help us, but they have their hands full with their war with Frelimo. Obviously the two terrorist camps feel safe because of this.

"The first camp Chifumbo is reported to have about three hundred terrs in various states of readiness. At the other camp, Mazangesi the number of terrs is reported to be in excess of seven hundred. I can tell you that these two camps will cease to exist within twenty-four hours. I will now hand you over to Air vice Marshal Raymond Vesting." concluded General Willis.

"General Willis has painted the picture for you. Let me if I may finish it off, without glossing over anything said the Air Vice Marshall. We have now received the exact positions of the two camps, and as I speak to you the operation is well under way to take both camps out. Last night I gave the order along with General Willis, to make heavy bombardment at first light this morning. Four Hunter bombers will lead the attack; this will be followed up by helicopter gunships and K cars. The Rhodesian Light Infantry, [Fire Force] will then be dropped in to do the mopping up and to collect any documents that may be of interest to our intelligence department. Prisoners, well," he paused with a smile, "I doubt if Fire Force will find any do you? he asked with grim humour. The main object of the exercise is to destroy the threat that exists on our doorstep, and to send a very clear message to the terrorists. That they have no safe havens; regardless where they are, we will hunt them down and destroy them."

General Willis stood up, "Thank you Ray. I can also inform you that a unit of the Selous Scouts have also identified two other large camps but of a different kind. The two camps are arms dumps, and even though they are a fair size they are not very heavily guarded. Needless to say as the two other camps are taken out, these two arms dumps will also cease to exist. I proposed to send in more troops to assist the Selous Scouts, but my offer was declined. They said, and I quote, 'No help needed, only about twenty terrs to deal with' unquote.

General Willis dropped the sheet of paper that he had just read from onto the desk, and smiled "Need I say more."

"I think that you would like to say a few words," said the General as he nodded to Vincent Morley the Minister of Internal Affairs.

"Yes" replied the Minister as he rose from his chair, "Over the last forty-eight hours we have been getting reports from the locals in the Melsetter area and also in the Chipinga area. These are possible sightings of what has been described as armed gangs. As I speak we have security forces in those area's but as yet they have found nothing to confirm the so-called sightings.

South East of the country in the Chimanimani National Park, which is over looked by the Chimanimani Mountains, once again sightings have been reported. This time two of large groups of armed men. I don't know if you are familiar with this area, but I can tell you that you could hide a small armoured division in it. So I feel that it may take some time before we get a breakthrough in that area. Needless to say as soon as information comes in it will be passed on to you all, thank you gentlemen." said the Minister.

"Thank you Vince. Well that is the picture as it is today." said General Willis, "Tomorrow it could be totally different, it's just a case of finding them. Once we do find them then as you know they are no match for our troops. No matter how many of them there are they are just bloody cowards, but still very dangerous, and they obviously cannot be underestimated.

"At the moment the north east of the country, which has now become known as the sharp end, is taking the brunt of the war, but make no mistake we will win the war. You will remember (Operation Nickel, and Operation Cauldron,) in both cases the terrorists failed miserably. Operation Hurricane will be the same, they will fail again, and the life expectancy of a terr that comes into Rhodesia and starts to take us on is only two weeks. Obviously there is the odd one who is a bit more switched on. He moves around a bit more and this makes it harder for us to pin him down. They all make the same mistake. They get too clever and start to think that they are invincible; they underestimate the fighting spirit of out troops. Gentlemen they will never win this war, never in a thousand years."

The room fell silent as General Willis started to gather up his notes and put them into his briefcase. The silence was broken by the sound of a telephone ringing in the corner of the room. Everyone turned as the young secretary walked to the phone and picked it up, "Yes" she said, "That is correct, I certainly will, one moment please."

The young lady placed the phone onto the table, "Commissioner," she said, "It's a call for you, it sounds rather urgent."

The Commissioner rose quickly from his chair and picked up the phone, "Stapleton here, don't worry about that." he said. His face changed from a half smile to a look of horror, "When did this happen, and at what time, they what!" he ground through gritted teeth, "Give me the farmers name again."

Quickly he indicated to the secretary to hand him a pen and something to write on, "Yes I have got it." he said, "Do you have the name of the farm, OK I am at a meeting with the J.O.C. so leave everything with me. Thank you for the call."

Adam placed the phone back into its cradle and stood looking out of the window; slowly he turned and looked around the room.

"Gentlemen" he said, "The nightmare continues. That was the Member in Charge at Fort Victoria, early this morning a farm on the Sabi River was hit. It's situated between the Odsi River and the Sabi River near to Cashel just north of Melsetter; the whole family have been wiped out. I don't know if anyone knows the Allsteads. No one said anything; I met Alister about a year ago, what a nice guy. He bought the farm Kymbani about nine years ago after emigrating from Scotland. He lived on the farm with his wife and two teenage daughters, no known next of kin I'm afraid, but under the circumstances, it's probably for the best."

The room remained silent as the Commissioner returned to his chair and sat down.

"Well what can I say," said General Willis, "It now looks as if we have a second front to contend with." He looked at the Commissioner "What action is being taken at Cashel?"

The Commissioner looked up and replied, "Follow up operations are in hand as I speak, there are five P.A.T.U. sticks in the area, and Crusader have deployed Support Unit to the area.

Once again the silence was broken by a knock on the door, as it opened a woman in uniform walked into the room and handed an A4 Manila buff envelope to the Air vice Marshal. Ray took the envelope, he said thank you as he opened the envelope. Every eye in the room was on him as he read the contents of the letter, when he finished he handed it to General Willis. After reading the letter, he took off his glasses, and looked around the table. "Well gentlemen, the two terrorist camps that we spoke about earlier today, I can now confirm that at 0400 hrs this morning the first camp Chifumbo was taken out. Two air strikes hit the camp, followed by an assault using helicopter gunships and Fire Force. There were no survivors, at the time of this report it was estimated that the body count was in excess of two hundred and eighty. There were also large amounts of weapons found at the camp, these have now been destroyed, and documents have been found and are being examined by Special Branch.

"At exactly the same time the other camp Mazangesi was attacked. Once again it was totally destroyed, but only two hundred and ten bodies have so far been accounted for. The figure of about seven hundred terrorists have been confirmed by documents found at the camp, so we have somewhere in the region of five hundred terrs running loose. Not good news I'm afraid." He put down the letter and looked around the room, "Well as you can see it was a great success, but the big question is where are the rest of the bloody terrs. Did they go back into Mozambique just before the attack, or did they cross into Rhodesia prior to the attack? Follow up operations are under way, and more troops are being moved to the area to be used as stop lines.

"Well gentlemen, I think that brings the meeting to a close, thank you all for taking the time to be here. I know how busy everyone is at the moment, I will keep you all informed as to the results of the follow up operations, and any news that may be of importance." concluded the General.

Chapter Twenty

On the eleventh of July at two thirty in the morning, four Hunter bombers stood on the runway. The crew were having their last briefing. Squadron Leader Dave Cockle sat taking notes as to the exact map references. Everything had been planned to the last detail, but for the last time he went through it again with his men. "OK," he said, "The weather is good, visibility is perfect, it just couldn't be better than it is tonight. You all know what is expected of you, you have all done it before, so as soon as they have finished loading we will be on our way. Get the job done and back here for breakfast."

Nearer to the Mozambique border, eight helicopter gunships were preparing for lift-off once the Hunters had passed over. Meanwhile in Salisbury four Dakota transport planes were taking off, their cargo, young members of the elite Rhodesian Light Infantry who would be dropped in by parachute, once the initial air assault had began.

At both the terrorist training camps, everyone was sound asleep, even the guards had dosed off. The general feeling in the camp was that no one would dare to attack such a large unit of men.

At exactly 0400am the camp was woken by the sound of aircraft screaming out of the sky towards the camp, then the ground shook violently as the bombs exploded. First the living and the sleeping quarters were hit, then the armoury took a direct hit. As the Hunters started on their return journey back to base, the helicopter gunships started to descend upon the burning camps, one by one they dropped into the camps and raked the burning buildings with 7.62 machine-gun fire and 20mm cannon. As they lifted into the air to give covering fire the Dakota's roared overhead. In the early morning sky parachutes opened delivering their cargo of death. The young men hit the ground at the run, shooting from the hip; they ran straight into each and every burning building. No fear, no pain, the adrenalin pumping, screaming as they ran, the enemy had no chance at all. Every vehicle was now on fire, small explosions rocked the air, and the smell in the camps was of burning flesh and cordite. Black smoke filled the air as the swirling ash and the glowing pieces of smouldering grass flew everywhere.

As the heavy plume of acrid smoke hung over both camps, the body counts started. Every weapon that was found had its serial number taken, then it was destroyed. The helicopter gunships were still hovering in the air to give cover in case of a counter attack. One by one the helicopters quickly refuelled and then they were back up into the air.

It was now 0525am and the job was done. The body count at Chifumbo was two hundred and eighty dead, no prisoners. The body count at Mazangesi was two hundred and ten, no prisoners. As reports had said the number of terrs was about seven hundred, the troops pushed on into the bush to look for any fresh tracks that would indicate that the terrs had infact run back into the bush and were now deep inside Mozambique. The only tracks that were by any means fresh, and they were about twelve hours old, all led to the Rhodesian border. It now looked as if the main group of terrs had in fact left the camp just prior to the attack..

Chapter Twenty-One

It was eight thirty in the morning and Mike Johnson was sitting at his desk reading the report of the J.O.C. meeting. He picked up his second cup of coffee and took a mouthful. The progress of the two fences that were being erected along the North Eastern border was very good news indeed, and the decision to plant anti-personnel mines within the confines of the fences was a great bonus. Harder for the terrs to get into the country and even more difficult for them to get out, especially when you have someone chasing you. Mike nodded to himself as he read on about the security fences that were being built on every farm in the North East of the country, again he said to himself, 'about time.'

The report gave a very brief report on the two terrorist camps just over the border in Mozambique. 'Shit' he thought, 'that's a bit too close for comfort.' As he read on he was alarmed to find that possibly he had about five hundred terrs heading into his area. He turned the page and started to read the rest of the report, amongst the bodies of those killed at both camps were ten Eastern Block Communist Instructors. Now this was bad news, all of our suspicions have now been confirmed, he thought to himself.

When Mike had finished reading the report, he dropped it onto his desk and let out a sigh, "The bastards are everywhere." he said out loud.

He turned to look at the map on the wall behind him. Standing up he took some marking pins and placed them in the positions of the camps that had just been taken out. He then drew a line from the nearest pin to Bindura, about ninety miles he thought to himself. If they break up into small groups then the farmers who live close to the border could be in for a real hard time. If they stick in one group, then the farmers have no chance at all, but it would give the security forces a much better chance of spotting them and then just bomb them. But deep inside, he knew that there was no chance of them staying in such a large group. 'Groups of say five men, bloody hell' he thought, 'one hundred groups, has any one thought of the implications of this.'

Mike's thoughts were interrupted as the telephone rang, he

picked up the phone but his mind was still in turmoil with the thoughts of the problems that lay ahead.

"Morning, Mike Johnson here." he said, "And how are you, I haven't spoken to you, or seen you for ages. How is life treating you then?" suddenly his face changed, he put one hand onto the desk to steady himself, then he sat down.

"When did this happen?" he asked, "I just can't believe it, where did it happen, in his bloody garage? You can't be serious, who found him? Oh no not his wife, how is she? Yes I'm sure she is, don't they have two sons? Yes I thought they did, and they are both at University. Have they been informed? OK leave it with me I will get things rolling at this end."

Mike put down the phone and immediately picked it back up again, quickly he dialled a number, "Morning sir," he said, "I've just had a phone call from one of the farmers at the sharp end and Pandama farm just been hit. Yes sir, Bob and Janet Prosser. No sir just Bob, seemingly he was in his garage working when he was attacked, his wife found him. No sir she is not there now, one of the farmers' wives has taken her to their farm. They are now trying to contact her two sons Glen and Harvey, they are both at University. No seemingly Bob is a real mess; he must have suffered terribly before he died. Yes they mutilated his body, it looks as if he was savagely beaten before they stabbed him, his eyes are missing. I can imagine the state of his wife Janet when she found him."

"OK Mike, I'll get on to Crusader straight away, you get things moving at your end, I want a good result on this one and I want it fast." The Commissioner put down the phone, Mike felt terribly alone.

Tony walked out of the front door; 'if that was lunch' he said to himself 'then roll on dinner.' He had just closed the front door when the phone rang, he stopped in his tracks. 'Oh sod it' he said to himself as he turned and walked away from the house. 'It can't be important someone ringing at this time of the day.' As he walked away he could still hear the phone ringing, feeling guilty he ran back and into the living room. 'Maybe it's Joyce,' he said to himself as he picked up the phone, "Hello Tony here." he said, "Oh shit it's you Mike, I was just on my way out, what can I do for you?" he asked.

"I need your help, and I need it urgently. Its bad news Tony, Bob Prosser has just been murdered on his farm, can you get your stick together as quickly as possible?"

"Leave it with me." said Tony,

"Great," replied Mike, "Believe me Tony it's a bad one, if you can ring me as soon as you and your stick are ready, then I will get a helicopter out to your farm to pick you all up.

"I 'm trying to contact as many of the farmers in the area as I can, and for them to organise their sticks, and to get them out there as quickly as possible. Crusader have been informed, and I would expect they will be on the spot within the next hour, I would imagine they will be out there in force."

"What's the name of Bob's farm again?" asked Tony,

"Pandama farm." replied Mike,

"It's right on the edge of Kandeya T.T.L, isn't it?" asked Tony,

"It is." replied Mike, "Why do you ask?"

"I know that area very well." said Tony, "The population there are very hostile to the Government, and they won't help the security forces at all."

"How come you know it so well?" asked Mike,

"Oh years ago when I was a teenager, my father used to take me hunting and camping there. I'm sure it will have changed a bit over the years, but it can't have changed all that much. I'll give you good odds on that the terrs are heading into Kandeya." said Tony, "In fact I will guarantee it."

"All I can say to you Tony is that you pass all this information to whoever is in charge when you get to Pandama farm."

As the helicopter rotors thrashed the air, Tony and his stick ran over to board it. High in the air they raced towards the farm. The noise onboard was deafening, everyone was shouting to make themselves heard. Below them the ground flashed past, and the occasional wild animal dashed for cover. Within minutes they could see other helicopters converging on the farm, they could also see a large number of troop carriers weaving their way along the dirt roads, clouds of red dust billowing into the air as they raced towards Pandama farm.

As the helicopter landed, Tony was first out and quickly made his way towards the solitary Land Rover that stood in the middle of the front garden. As he approached the huddle of men who were standing around the vehicle, he picked out Hugh Russell.

"Bloody hell you got here quick didn't you." he said,

Hugh turned to Tony and with a curt nod, "We were in the area on another case when the call came through." he said.

"Tony have you met Captain Vince Hall?" he said,

"Yes we have met before." said Tony as he held out his hand. "How are you Vince." he said,

"I'm fine how is life treating you?" Vince replied,

"Shit at the moment." replied Tony, "But life goes on."

"Well I want the whole work force taking in for questioning." said Hugh, "I don't care how long they have been at the farm, I want the lot to be taken in for interrogation, I just do not accept the fact that no one knows anything at all."

"So what exactly happened?" asked Tony,

"Well all we have to go on at the moment is that when Bob didn't come in for lunch, his wife went to look for him. She remembered him saying that he was going to do some work in the garage, and that is where she found him."

"I didn't know Bob that well." said Tony, "But one thing I did know about him and it's that he was ultra safety-conscious. He never left anything to chance, and now for him to go like this, well it's terrible."

"OK then," said Vince, "If we look at the map you can see that this is where we are at the moment. I have got men out at this point, and this point." He pointed at the map with a pencil, "All in all there are six sticks out there, Support Unit are moving into position to act as a stop line, and they should be in about this position as I speak." again he tapped the map, "The latest reports that are coming in are that trackers have found tracks, and it looks as if there are two sets of tracks. So it could be that they have split up, this could very well be to try and confuse us. The two sets of tacks that have been found indicate that there are only two persons, almost certainly male, and I would imagine that they will still be armed, and very dangerous." He turned to Tony, "I got a call from Mike Johnson,"

Tony nodded, "And what has he been saying?" he asked,

"Well firstly he mentioned that you and your stick were on your way but he also said that you know the area fairly well."

"Yes that is correct." replied Tony, "It was a long time ago, but I do know the Kandeya T.T.L. and I can tell you this it is a very hostile part of the country. The locals have very little time for anyone connected with the government."

"Well if we look once again at the map," said Vince, "You can see how close we are to the border with Kandeya, as the crow flies I would say no more than fifteen miles."

"The Crusader trackers are having difficulty at the moment following the tracks, as whoever it is that they are following are back tracking, obviously trying to make it as difficult as they possibly can. What I want you and your stick to do, is to go it alone, try and think like a terr. Would you head for the Mozambique border?"

"No chance." replied Tony, "They must know that there are troops and plenty of them all working on the two fences all along the border. It would be madness to try and make their escape there. No I think that they will head deep into the bush, and try and lose themselves amongst the locals. Once they do that then it will be almost impossible to catch them, but I doubt that they will just walk into the first kraal that they come to. They will first of all get well away from here, and then I think that they will lie low for a few days and watch the area to see where we send our troops. Even though the locals in the area are very much against us, we do have a small number of informers who put money before loyalty. I am certain that the terrs will be aware of this. I feel that for the next few days they will be very reluctant to show their faces and they will lie low. If we move in now, we may just beat them at their own game." Tony looked at the map, "I would like to go in from here in a straight line. Could you keep the air clear of all aircraft, let them think that everyone is concentrating in the other areas. You asked me to think like a terr, well if I was a terr then that is exactly what I would do and that is the direction that I would go in."

Vince gave Tony a strange look, "You're up to something." he said,

"What do you mean?" asked Tony,

"It's that look on your face." replied Vince,

"I'm just eager to get out there and get it sorted." said Tony. "Recently my Boss boy went to visit his family, and while he was there, two strangers came to the village and spent the day and the night there. During the evening the conversation turned to politics as most conversations do. Things were said by the two strangers that made Crispen suspicious; as soon as he returned to the farm he mentioned it to me. Now maybe I am just paranoid, but, and I say but, could these two strangers be the ones that hit my farm? When the farm was first hit, I shot and killed one of the gang, and I know that from information given by a prisoner, that the rest of the gang have every intention of getting revenge. Believe me I hope that these two are the ones. Yes I'm eager, too bloody true I am, the description that I got from both Crispen and a prisoner are exactly the same. I have a mental picture of them and I know I will recognise them when I see them."

Tony pulled his men to one side and briefed them on the situation and his plans, "OK" he said "Is everyone happy with what I think we should do. If anyone has any other idea's then let's have them." as no one spoke, other than to agree, he nodded, "OK let's move out, Colin you take point."

As they moved away from the farm, Tony knew that really he had nothing to go on except his instinct, but as no other information was forthcoming at the present time, he had a good feeling that he was going in the right direction. For the next two hours they moved through the bush in single file, stopping just twice for a sip of water and to check their directions.

Moving through the thick bush was a very slow process. You either push on regardless with no regard to the noise that you are making and have a very good chance of walking into an ambush, or you take your time, keeping the noise down to a minimum, and observe everything that is not exactly as nature made it or intended it to be. Animals leave totally different tracks to humans. Tony knew that the latter was the only way forward.

Ken was now at point, fifty yards to either side of him he could see open ground, but it was too exposed. Once again they stopped as they came to a river. Lowering himself down to the ground he signalled to the rest of the stick to slowly come forward. Everyone was now looking at the far river bank, from left to right they scanned the view in front of them, everyone knew that this was a very dangerous move to make, as once they were mid stream then they were at the mercy of the enemy. After deciding that it looked safe to make a move, one by one they crossed the river. As soon as the first man was across, he gave cover as the next man made his way across. As the last man came out of the water they moved into the bush and took a short rest.

Tony looked at his watch and decided it was best to look for a place to make camp for the night. As he led his men further into the bush he was mentally taking notes of places that they could return to for the night. He knew that it was the most dangerous thing to do, pick your spot and then just relax. As he moved through the bush he chose what he considered a good defensible position to initially make camp.

"OK let's do a three-sixty, and get some food down our necks."

".Tony knew from experience that the enemy could be watching their every move, and if they stayed in one place then during the night they could well be attacked. By moving to a different position under the cover of darkness, they had a much better chance of survival.

At first light Ken took point and the stick moved out again. During the night Tony had been thinking about the route that they were taking. Thinking back to his teenage years when he had gone hunting with his father in the Kandeya T.T.L. Tony knew that for the first ten or fifteen miles there were no villages, just thick bush, and very rocky land. This was the reason why no one lived in the area, it was just too hard to farm there. If his calculations were correct then tomorrow he would expect to see some signs of life, the odd small village, and possibly signs of someone trying to grow crops.

He also knew that the two terrs that he was hoping to make contact with would get all the help that they needed once they had made contact with their political supporters. He also knew that there would be no shortage of them as it was a hostile part of the country.

It was now nine o'clock in the morning, and the stick had been on the move since first light. Buz was now at point with the rest of the stick following him in single file. The sweat was running into his eyes, making them sting. Tiny mapani flies were all over his body searching for any form of liquid, everytime he brushed the sweat from his brow they got into his eyes. He turned to look back at the rest of the stick and saw that they were having the same problem; they were all covered in the tiny insects. They didn't bite, but you could feel them on your skin, moving in the sweat. The constant movement of the hands as everyone tried to chase them away soon became known as the mapani salute. Eventually everyone just gave up, and accepted the fact that they just could not beat the tiny insects. The constant waving of their hands was considered to be a real give away to anyone who may be watching.

As the stick stopped for a quick rest, Tony looked at his map; he knew that he had his work cut out this time. The direction that he was heading was north north east, he drew an imaginary line from his present position. If he followed this line then he knew that about sixty miles away he would come to the Zambezi River as it flowed towards the mighty Cabora Basa Dam. Tony studied the map, would the terrs cross into Zambia? 'no' he said to himself, Malawi? Again he said no, it's too far away. The terrs have come to Rhodesia to terrorise not to run away, but then it is me thinking like a terrorist, and I'm not the one being chased. 'No' he said to himself, 'I would take my chances in Kandeya.'

For the next three hours they moved through the thick bush. The midday sun was drawing every ounce of strength out of the men. In the distance they could now see smoke as it rose into the sky, as they got nearer to the source of the smoke they could see that it came from a village. Thirty mud huts could be counted, and at the edge of the village they could see two large huts probably used for storing grain. For the next two hours, each man took it in turn to watch the village through the binoculars. Nothing seemed suspicious, but then what were they looking for? If two men appeared carrying assault rifles then things would be different, but everyone seemed to be just going about their everyday chores. Children playing, dogs looking for that scrap of food, and the chickens pecking at anything that remotely looked like food.

"I think we are wasting our time here." said Tony, "Everything looks normal, let's move on."

As the sun started its slow descent towards the horizon, the torment of the flies started to subside. Even though the sweat was no longer running down their backs, their uniforms were soaked, and were now starting to chafe their skin. Their webbing felt like sandpaper through their shirts, making it even more painful.

"Right." said Tony, "Let's stop and have a brew."

One man quickly made the tea, while two kept guard. The remaining two men took off their webbing and made themselves a bit more comfortable.

Buz was lying under the shade of a bush looking out of the camp, his rifle was pointing out like a third eye. Moving his eyes from left to right then back again, he scanned the area in front of him, he then raised his eyes and looked further into the distance, again moving his eyes from left to right and back again. As he started to move his eyes to the right something caught his attention. His heart was pounding as he searched for it again. 'Bloody hell' he said to himself, 'what was it, and where is it?' Quickly he strained his eyes, searching for something that had caught his eye. 'There it is' he said to himself, a slight smile came to his face. Just visible through the thick bush he could make out the slightest flicker of a flame, and the slightest whisper of a spiral of smoke as it rose into the sky. 'Possibly nothing,' he thought to himself, 'maybe someone out hunting,' but it was enough for him to want to take a closer look. Slowly he moved backwards into the camp and gestured to Tony.

Both men now lay on the ground, Buz pointed to Tony, "If you look straight ahead about fifty yards away."

"Nothing." said Tony, "I can't see a thing."

"OK can you see that Acacia tree, standing on its own."

"Yes I can see it." replied Tony,

"Right now look to your left, slowly about four feet from the base of the tree, look past the tree and into the bush."

"Yes I've got it." said Tony, "I can see the flames, but there's no one there."

"Here, take the binoculars." said Buz, "Have a closer look."

Tony took the glasses and held them up to his eyes, "Just flames" he whispered, "Just flames." he was about to hand back the glasses to Buz when he saw movement, "Got something." he said, "Someone is there."

Tony focussed the glasses as a figure came into view and stood next to the fire. He could now see the figure clearly and by his gestures he was obviously talking to someone who was at the moment out of view. By the aggressive movements of his hands and his head it looked as if they were having an argument. Tony searched the area to try and identify who the other person was. Suddenly the second person appeared, but Tony could only make out the back of him as he stood pulling up his pants and doing up the zip. Tony was more than intrigued by what was going on. The second figure started to point towards the ground, and started gesticulating at someone else. It was at that moment that a young African girl stood up clutching a bundle of her clothes to her chest in an attempt to hide her naked body. She was crying and looked terrified. Suddenly she was struck across the face and fell to the ground, it was at this moment that the first man walked over and looked down at the girl. He started to laugh as he undid his pants, then he disappeared behind the bush where the young girl had just fallen.

"The bastard." said Tony, "He's raping the young girl."

"He's what?!" asked Buz,

"The son of a bitch is raping the young girl, and there's nothing that we can do about it." said Tony, "If I had the slightest inclination that these two were the terr's that we are looking for, then we would go in like a shot. Come on." whispered Tony, "Come on, just give me an excuse."

At that moment the figure who was standing watching, turned around and looked in Tony's direction. Tony froze, he knew that he could not be seen as he was well hidden in the thick bush; it was what he saw that made his heart pound. Standing now clearly visible, Tony saw not only the tall thin figure but the thin-rimmed glasses, and the protruding front teeth. He slowly moved the binoculars down to the man's arms, he was looking for the long scar that he had been told about, but he had his arms crossed in front of his body. 'Move your arms,' Tony said to himself. Suddenly the other man came into view, pulling his pants up and laughing as he spoke. His friend who thought the whole thing was something to laugh about as well slapped him on the back as if to say well done. He then bent down and when he came into view again he was holding an assault rifle in his hand. As he did so Tony saw the long scar that ran down his arm, "Got ya," said Tony, "OK Buz get the men ready we are going in."

Once Tony had briefed his men, he told Buz to take point.

Moving out in formation they slowly headed for the target area; keeping low they made their way closer and closer to the spot where they had last seen the two terrs. Tony knew it was risky, as he had only seen two terrs, could there have been more? He wouldn't know until they made contact with them. Putting it out of his mind; he now concentrated on getting the job done as quickly as possible.

Buz held up his hand, and signalled everyone to close in on him. Crouching beside him, no more than ten yards away the clearing was now in view. The young girl was frantically trying her best to get dressed as quickly as possible in fear of the ordeal being repeated Once she was dressed she waited until the two men were looking the other way, then she fled into the bush. The two terrs were now standing in full view, each had an assault rifle and across their chests they had bandoliers of ammunition and pouches all full of magazines. Joshua also had an RPG Rocket Launcher, and tucked into a shoulder bag were three RPG 7 rockets. On his other shoulder he was now carrying another bag which looked fairly heavy. Just as they were about to leave the clearing Tony gave the order to attack. Noise was now of no concern as the five men raced through the bush. Before the two terrs knew what was happening, Buz was in the camp. He gave the first figure he saw a double tap in the chest and down it went. Raking now the area with a burst of automatic fire, he ran through the clearing quickly changing magazines. He saw the figure of the terr that he had just shot, he was lying on his back, blood was pouring from the two holes in his chest. As he looked at the figure he could see the colour of the shirt changing from green to a dark red, already the flies were starting on their free meal. Buz quickly kicked the body, no sound or movement, just to be certain he put another double tap into the body and ran on. In front him he could now hear the sound of return fire. As he moved further into the thick bush, someone shouted, "He went to your left Buz!"

Tony had seen the first terr go down, and then he had seen the second terr. Joshua was running like the wind as he fled into the bush. "OK" Tony shouted, "Spread out."

At that moment a burst of automatic fire made everyone duck for cover. "Over there!" a voice shouted, "He is over in that direction!" Within seconds the stick were moving forward in buddy-buddy formation. Still the occasional shot came their way, but now it seemed to be getting further and further away. "This is a switched on terr," said Tony, "He could be drawing us into an ambush, so be bloody careful. I don't want to lose this bastard."

For the next hour the stick slowly eased their way through the thick bush, looking for any tell-tale signs, a broken twig, a bent blade of grass, an over-turned stone. Anything that would give them that all important lead. Before initiating the contact, Tony had sent out a sitrep and his position. He was now waiting for the distinctive clatter of the helicopters that would have been airborne as soon as the news broke.

It soon became obvious to Tony that Joshua had once again given him the slip. Reluctantly he pulled his men back. Once back at the contact site they cleared a site large enough for a helicopter to land and lift the dead body to be taken away for identification.

As dusk was starting to set, the helicopter lifted out of the clearing. Slung below it was a net carrying the body of the dead terr. Tony looked up as it banked steeply and started its journey. Tony watched as the black shape of the helicopter was silhouetted against the burning orange of the setting sun, "There should have been two of the bastards in that net." he said quietly to himself.

Chapter Twenty-Two

Tony looked at his watch, it was eleven o'clock. He had spent the last three days catching up on the paperwork that he had neglected due to the time he had spent in the bush over the last few months. He knew that he would have to spend a lot more time on the farm and not just take advantage of his hard-working and totally reliable Boss Boy.

Joyce had been on the phone and was now bending his ear to return to the farm. As much as he wanted them back home, he was just a little bit unhappy with the situation at the moment.

He was making himself a cup of coffee when the phone rang, "Now then Mike," he said, "What can I do for you, and before you ask I just don't have the time to go out on patrol at the moment. I've got so much to do on the farm that I just don't know where to start first."

"Relax Tony," Mike said, "It's not a call out, all I want to ask is, can you possibly be at my office tomorrow about ten o'clock? The reason I am asking you, is that I have asked all the stick leaders in the area to come in and have a chat. I want to make sure that everyone in the area knows exactly what is going on, in each others area's, and in the area in general. I also want to brief everyone on the minutes of the recent J.O.C. meeting. It should only take about two hours at the most, and I really think it will be worthwhile. Can I take your silence as a yes then?" asked Mike,

"Shit you're a hard task master." said Tony, "Do you realise how much work I've got to do on this bloody farm? Yes I'll be there, ten o'clock you said."

"Yes thanks Tony, see you tomorrow at ten then."

Tony picked up his cup of coffee and sat down at his desk, 'I bloody well hate paperwork.' he muttered to himself, 'the sooner things quieten down the better. Hell Joyce used to have it done in no time at all, and now look at all of this mess.' he said as he shuffled the paper into a large pile. 'Stuff it' he muttered 'it will have to wait.'

The following morning Tony left the farm and made his way to

Bindura. It was less than an hour's drive but it was almost all on dirt roads, so not only were you looking for the possibility of an ambush, but it was now very likely that a land mine could take you out. Tony smiled, at least he would see how good his armoured Land Rover was, his smile faded as he thought, 'well maybe not.'

Mike welcomed everyone to the meeting, "There's fresh coffee in the corner, and would you believe it biscuits, chocolate ones at that."

"Bloody hell Mike," said Tony, "Who is paying for all of this?"

"Nothing is too good for you lot." Mike replied,

"Now I know you are after something." said Tony, everyone laughed, the atmosphere was soon very relaxed as the meeting got under way.

"As you will all be very much aware of, over the last month or so we have had an increased activity in terrorist operations. Tony has just returned with his stick from a rather nasty incident near to the Kandeya T.T.L. The white farmer in this incident was mutilated, and I'm sure died a terribly slow and painful death. Follow up operations resulted in one terr dead, but one got away. "Needless to say he will return to fight another day. This escape is by no means a reflection on Tony and his stick, who did an excellent job."

Mike turned to Hugh Russell, "You all know Hugh, and so I will let him give you some more information."

Hugh stood up, "Right let me give you the details as I have them at this moment. There is no doubt at all that the terr who was killed by Tony's stick was involved in the killing near to Kandeya. The dead terr has been identified as Magumbo, this has been a very good result indeed Tony, and I would like to thank you and your stick for this success. Magumbo has not only been a thorn in our side for some time, but he has been terrorising the local population. Hugh picked up a handful of photos and handed them around the table. "This is the animal who was responsible for cutting off the lips, ears, and noses, of anyone who he thought were possibly a supporter of the government. Once he had cut off the various parts of the body he would then make the family cook it and then eat it. He did all of this with a rusty knife and a pair of pliers, and believe it or not, he still had them on him when he was killed, one very evil bastard. The local population throughout the North East will be greatly relieved once the news gets out. In the Madziwa area, he even forced women and children into a mud hut, secured the door, and then set fire to the hut. No wonder everyone was terrified of him.

"The identification of Magumbo was made easier for us, as during a contact in the Mtoko area, he lost his little finger, and all that he had left was a bit of bone sticking out."

He turned once again to Tony and smiled, "Again the thanks go to you and your stick Tony, as it was the same contact that you and your stick were involved in. Other information from the ballistics of his assault rifle shows that he was also present in the attack on your farm recently Tony. It is now almost certain that his accomplice is the same person who attacked your farm when the terr called Ticky was killed. He has now been identified as Joshua. The identification details of this one is as follows, tall and very thin, rimmed glasses, protruding front teeth, and a long scar running down his right arm from his elbow to his wrist."

"That's him" said Tony, "I would know him anywhere, he was the one that got away in our recent contact, no doubt about it."

"Well that is all the news that I have at the moment." said Hugh, "The moment that I get any further details I will pass them on to Mike, thank you." Hugh sat down and put all of his documents back into his folder.

Mike stood again.

"As I am sure you all know, we have had two very good operational success results inside Mozambique. But the bad news is that it looks as if about five hundred terr's are unaccounted for. Everything points to the fact that they may have slipped across our borders, and could become active at any time. All I can say to you all is be extra vigilant, I don't want to sound like an alarmist but we must be prepared for the worst.

"Reports are coming in all the time from the local population of possible sightings, some have proved to be nothing at all, but as you can imagine we cannot afford to ignore these reports. It's very easy for people to ask what are we doing, but over the last two weeks we have had twenty-three reports. Eighteen were a total waste of time. I'm not stupid, these reports could be given to us to draw us away from the areas where the terrs are, it is a very fine balancing act, believe me.

"There are things going on in all of your areas that I am sure not all of you know about. Can I ask each of you to give us a brief account of what is going on in your area."

Bob Shepard raised his hand, "Yes Bob." said Mike,

"Well over the last few days we have had a bit of a rough time. In the Umvukwes area, two farms have been hit, one white farmer wounded. I'm pleased to say it was not a serious wound, but he was still attacked. Follow up operations resulted in the death of two terr's and the capture of one terr. It is very obvious to us all that there is an awful lot of intimidation going on out there. I think the locals want to talk to us, but are too frightened, they just don't know who they can trust."

"I can identify with that." said Peter Stoppard, "As you all know the area that I farm in has been very quiet. In fact everyone thought that the war was just going to pass us by. Then this week the Amanda's and the Concession areas got some real stick. Four farms hit in one night, and that was with the Bright Lights on the farm, the poor sods they must have crapped themselves. Follow up operations were set up immediately, but they led to nothing. Whoever was responsible for the attacks just seemed to vanish into thin air."

Mike looked across the room, "How is your area?" he asked Ray Cooper, "I know that you have been out and about."

"Yes" replied Ray, "The Raffingora farming area has been very quiet for awhile. All we have been doing is recce patrols it was really, just to let the locals see that we were in the area. We were moving north towards Sipolilo, when we came under fire. It was totally out of the blue, it wasn't as if we were on tracks, or on a follow up or anything, it was totally unexpected. The contact lasted about fifteen minutes, but when they heard the choppers, the terr's thought better of it and ran. Really it ended up like shooting rats in a barrel; they just didn't have a chance. But would they give up and surrender, would they hell, at the end it was five dead terr's, two adults and three young teenagers. Shame about the teenagers, but if they are old enough to fire a weapon then they must accept the inevitable, and they did."

Mike looked around the room, no one seemed to have anything else to say, everyone had heard of the recent contacts that Tony and his stick had been involved in, and Tony had no intention of going through it all again.

"There is one thing that is bothering me." said Tony, "We seem to be letting them bring the war to us, why don't we take the war to them. If we continue fighting the war the way that we are doing at the present then it will last until our grandchildren take over the fighting from us. Why don't we just go in and take out the top brass, no one can tell me that we don't know where they have their headquarters. We know who they are; we must know where they stay during the day and at night. Well let's just go across the bloody borders and take the bastards out once and for all, and please don't say it will cause outrage through out the world, the whole world is against us as it is anyway, so stuff them, let's just get it done."

"Bloody hell Tony," said Mike, "We can't just go over the border and bomb the shit out of the enemy.

"We have just done it in Mozambique." replied Tony, "What's the difference?"

"When we hit Mozambique it was a different thing completely, for one thing the government in Mozambique are fighting a war just as we are. The government in Mozambique are Portuguese, not African." replied Mike, "And the other thing is we were hitting legitimate targets, two terrorist training camps. The targets that you are talking about are in civilian areas."

"So what is the problem with that." asked Tony, "When did I ever mention bombing the targets? Why don't we use our special forces to do the job."

Mike looked around the room and saw that everyone seemed to agree with what Tony had just said, "Don't look so surprised." said Tony, "Nothing could be easier, they could either be dropped in at night, or go across Lake Kariba by boat. They could even cross at the Chirundu crossing. Once the target area has been positively identified, it would be a simple matter of hitting the target and then getting choppers in quickly and lifting out our men. I'm pointing my finger at Zambia, because everyone knows that the terrorist leaders are living there. It's a safe haven for them, and I think it's about time we made it an unsafe haven, what do you say."

"I know where you're coming from and honestly I do agree with what you say, but you know that decisions like that are made well above my head." said Mike.

"Fair comment." said Tony, "But can you promise us this then, will you mention it to the Commissioner the next time you talk to him?"

" I will mention it to him at our next meeting, but I honestly cannot promise you anything. Right," said Mike, as he moved some papers into a neat pile, "Can we now move on to the next thing that I would like to discuss with you."

Chapter Twenty-Three

Since his last stint in the bush, Tony had spent almost every minute of the last two weeks working on the farm. On his return in the evenings, he would first phone Joyce, then Benji would want to say something to him, eventually Joyce would take the phone again. Normally she would ask about coming back to the farm, but this time she sounded more determined than she had ever done before, "I feel as if I am in the way." she said, "You know what I mean. How would we feel if we had two people staying indefinitely with us. You know how disruptive Benji can be; it's not fair on them. I feel that it is for the best that I come back to the farm as soon as possible."

"I can see your point." said Tony, "But I think it would be wiser, that you both stay where you are for a little while longer."

"I don't think that you are being fair to either me or to your son, and certainly not to Mark and Sue." hissed Joyce angrily.

"OK leave it with me for a few more days, and if things are still calm in the area then I will come through and bring you both back, how does that sound?" said Tony trying desperately to mollify Joyce.

"No going back on your word." said Joyce,

"No going back." said Tony "I promise you."

Tony put down the phone and shook his head. She just can't see that what I am doing is in their best interest. Deep down he wanted them back on the farm so that they could be a family again, but he knew that Joshua had certainly escaped the latest contact and that Camburo farm was one, if not his main target.

Tony showered, cooked a meal and shouted to his current Bright Lights, "Dinner's ready come and get it!" As they sat around the dinner table the conversation was mainly about farming and the situation in the area.

"Is this your first stint in the bush?" Tony asked. Both men started to answer at the same time; they looked at each other and started to laugh.

"It's my first time, in fact it's my first time away from a town or city, but Adrian here is almost an old timer at it."

"You must be joking." said Adrian, "I've only done three stints, and this one is my fourth. "You must love it" said Tony with a smile, I wouldn't say that I love it but I certainly want to do my bit. The first time I was called up I was excited, really looking forward to it, but when we got to the farm and night came, then it was a different story. But after it was all over I must say I enjoyed it. said Adrian seriously.

"The second time I was called up, well I knew what to expect, I was much more at ease and more confident. Both times there were no incidents, and yes it was interesting. The last stint that I did was at Shamva, Richard and Wendy, I can't remember their surname." he said,

"You must be joking." said Tony, "Richard and Wendy are very good friends of ours, we have known them for years, what a small world."

"It's bloody hairy on that farm." Adrian said, "The trees in the garden come almost up to the farmhouse, the slightest breeze and the leaves start rustling, it's spooky."

"You know something," said Tony, "The last time that we were at their farm, it was for Sunday lunch, and I suggested then to Richard to get those trees cut down. Believe me I know how you must have felt; it certainly wouldn't have filled you with confidence. Anyone could get almost right up to the farm without being seen."

Tony pushed his dinner plate away from him, "Well I can tell you all of the trees that were anywhere near this farmhouse have been removed. Right around the farmhouse you have a clear line of fire, no one can creep up on us, I can promise you that. At least not if everyone is on their guard. You may remember the outhouse that I showed you when you both arrived at the farm? Well that was taken out by terr's when they hit the farm recently. If it's any consolation to you, they were aiming at the veranda at the time. The firing position that they used has been flattened, so now they have no cover except for the large rock to the left of the swimming pool. If they decide to hit the farm again then I hope that they use it for cover."

Both men looked at each other, "You hope they use it as cover." Adrian said, "What the hell for?" Tony smiled, "It's booby trapped, I've planted explosives around the base of the rock, and it's wired back to the house.

"I've installed three magnesium flares to the outside of the farmhouse, so should we take a hit then at least we can light up the night sky."

Both men looked at Tony with some trepidation.

"What's wrong?" Tony asked,

"What's wrong." they said, "No one told us that the farm had been hit recently."

"So what." asked Tony, "The chances of it happening again are very slim indeed." he lied. Tony decided that it was a good time to change the subject as they were about to go on guard in a hour. 'One thing is for sure.' he thought to himself, 'they will be wide awake tonight.' Tony cleared away the dinner plates and placed them into the sink and turned the tap on. When he had finished the washing-up he went out onto the veranda and sat down.

"When it gets dark out here it really gets dark." a voice said,

"It sure does." replied Tony, "Just sit back and relax. All you have to do is to stay quiet, stay still, and listen. There isn't much that you can see at night so it's pointless straining your eyes for nothing. If you do, all that will happen is that they will start playing tricks on you and you will probably start shooting at shadows." Tony stood up and looked up at the stars, "I've got some work to catch up on then I'm off to bed, see you both in the morning."

As dawn broke Tony stood at the bedroom window and watched the two men as they did a sweep of the front garden. He smiled to himself; they were doing everything that he had told them to do. 'Leave the veranda before it became light, if there was anyone watching the farm don't let them have any idea where you spend the night, but be on your guard. Don't think for one moment that daylight brings safety.' As the two men returned to the veranda, they could smell coffee and toast, "Morning." they said, "Morning to you." replied Tony, "Quiet night?" he asked,

"Very quiet." replied one of the men, "But it was bloody cold out there."

"Believe me." said Tony, "It can get very cold especially if you're just sitting, and not moving around. You will have to wrap up with something warm tonight. While I am on the subject of tonight, you will be on your own. I will be staying in Bindura but I should be back early, but don't wait up for me. I will leave a couple of phone numbers just in case you need to contact me."

"Party time?" one of the men asked,

"Well sort of." replied Tony, "A few weeks ago I was invited to a braai by the Member in Charge of the Selous Scouts, and his parties are famous for going on until the night. More booze than you could shake a stick at. I doubt if I will be in a fit state to drive home, and even if I was it would not be the wisest thing to do at this moment in time."

Chapter Twenty-Four

Tony stood at the bar with a can of Lion Lager in his hand, he felt a tap on his shoulder. "Now then Mike." he said, "I was starting to wonder where you were, free drink and no sign of Mike. Something must be wrong."

"I want you to meet someone." Mike said, "Infact it's someone who wants to meet you. Tony this is Chief Superintendent Mac McGovern of the Selous Scouts."

Tony held out his hand, "Pleased to meet you Sir."

"Call me Mac, everyone else does, I've heard an awful lot about you." said Mac. He placed his hand on Mike's shoulder, "But it was all good reports, I can assure you. You farm up at the sharp end don't you?"

"I do." said Tony, "And believe me at the moment it is bloody sharp."

"Your farm, is it called Camburo?" Mac asked,

Tony looked stunned "It is, how do you know that?"

"As I said I have heard a lot about you and your stick. I want to shake your hand again and say thank you to you, and to everyone who is in your stick for the magnificent work that you are all doing. You know something, and I'm not speaking out of turn, but without the farmers who are taking the brunt of all this, we would have no chance at all of winning this war. Look Tony I must go as I've got a meeting with my men before they go out tonight, but I will catch you later, it's been a pleasure meeting you."

"Nice guy." said Tony,

"One of the best." replied Mike, "He is in charge of the Intelligence Unit of the Selous Scouts, and believe me they are switched on guys."

"So how does he know so much about me?" Tony asked,

Mike smiled, "It's his job to know everything about everyone, and believe me that was one of the greatest compliments you are ever likely to get from anyone." Tony nodded to the barman, "Two cans," he said, Tony took the two cans of cold lager, pulled the ringpull on one of them and handed it to Mike, "Here get this down your neck, what time do they start the braai he asked, I'm starving."

"So what's new at the farm?" Mike asked,

"Nothing much has changed since I last spoke to you." said Tony, "The Bright Lights have made a great difference, at least I am getting a good night's sleep now knowing that someone is watching out for me at night. Mind you I must say that the two guys I have got at the moment, even though they are very willing, they have very little knowledge or experience of the bush. I just hope that they have a quiet night tonight, I can just imagine them shooting at every shadow."

"Don't worry they will be OK." said Mike, he nodded to the barman, "Same again, it looks like headaches in the morning, that's for sure." he said with a grin.

As the evening drew on, Tony found himself relaxing and enjoying the company that he found himself in. Everyone was laughing and thoroughly enjoying themselves. No one would think that the country was at war, and that they were almost on the front line. No one seemed to have a care in the world. Tony nodded to himself and smiled, 'you're a shrewd man Mac' he thought to himself, this was his way of getting the community to let off some steam, to relieve the tension.

The following morning Tony woke up with a blinding headache. As he raised his head off the pillow he could hear someone moving about in the next room, startled, he jumped out of bed. It was only then that he realised that he was not on his farm but at Mike's house. 'Shit' he muttered to himself as he held his head in his hands. Slowly he stood up, pulled on a pair of shorts and went into the living room.

"Morning and how are you feeling?" Tony looked across the room and saw Mike about to start preparing breakfast. "How do you want your eggs?" he asked "Nice and runny to go with your stringy bacon."

"Sod off." Tony said as he dashed to the bathroom. Mike brought his breakfast into the dining room and noticed that Tony who had returned from the bathroom was now sitting on the veranda with his eyes shut. Mike was about to go through and join him, but at the last minute thought better of it. After finishing his breakfast he sat down, looked at the state that Tony was in and said, "Would you like some black coffee and something for your headache?"

Tony grunted, "How often does he throw parties like that." he asked,

"Oh not all that often but when he does everyone goes mad Believe me Tony you won't be the only one nursing a sore head.

"I've never seen so much booze in all my life."

"Yeah" replied Mike, "And I think you tried to drink it all yourself. You obviously don't remember much about the night do you? But no harm was done everyone enjoyed themselves. So what is planned for today?" Mike asked,

"Well first of all I'm going to have that strong cup of coffee, then a shower, and hopefully if I feel up to it go back to the farm.

"Last night when I was at the bar, enjoying myself, I just couldn't help thinking, Joyce would have loved it, she would have been in her element."

"Well there is nothing stopping you from bringing her back to the farm now, you have the farm guards, and I think deep down you would much prefer it if they were with you."

Tony looked up and nodded, "I'm right aren't I?" said Mike,

"Yes I will ring her tonight."

"Ring her now if you want to. There is no time like the present you know, and as you are aware as from next week the contractors will be starting on the erection of the security fences on your farm."

"I'll wait until the fence work is all done then I will bring them back to the farm." said Tony.

Chapter Twenty-Five

The following week the contractors arrived and immediately the work started. There was a limit to how much fencing could be used on each farm, so Tony took it to it's utmost limit. He wanted the fence as far away from the buildings as possible, that would give him added security and it wouldn't make the place look as if it was a prison. Within three days the posts were all up and concreted in place. The main gate was large enough to get heavy farm vehicles in and out. The side gate would be alarmed, and could be both opened and closed from inside the farmhouse, Tony looked over the plans that he had agreed to and nodded in approval, yes he was happy with what was being built. Now he would be more than happy to bring Joyce and Benji home.

Joyce just couldn't believe it when Tony phoned to give her the good news, "So when can we come back?" she asked,

"The work will be finished in about eight days time," said Tony, "And as soon as it is all done then I will come through and collect you both, so don't start packing just yet, be patient."

"Mark wants a word with you." said Joyce,

"How's things Tony?"

"I'm fine." Tony replied, "Things are moving at this end and I was just saying to Joyce that very soon now and they will both be returning to the farm."

"That's great news." said Mark, "I thought she was getting some good news by the look on her face."

"All I can say Mark is a very big thank you to both you and to Sue for all that you have done for us."

"Don't you mention it." said Mark "Both you and Joyce would have done the same for us."

"Well as you will possibly know we now have two guards on the farm, and we have the added security of the fencing. I really don't think that there is much more that can be done to make it any safer."

Mark handed the phone back to Joyce, "So when are you coming to get us?" she asked,

"As soon as the fence is finished." replied Tony,

"I can't wait." she said, "At last we will be together again."

"Just calm down." said Tony, "I can't give you an exact date yet but it will be soon, give Benji a big hug for me, and I will speak to you later."

Tony put the phone down and shook his head 'I should never have phoned her' he said to himself, 'she will be on the phone every minute of the day now.'

During the next few days Tony spent most of his time overseeing the completion of the security fence. It was not that he didn't trust the workers to do a good job. He just wanted to identify any weak points that he could improve on. After all, the fence was there to protect him not the contractors. On the last day he was asked to give the fence a final inspection and to sign an acceptance form. "I'm more than happy with the work." he said, "So where are you going next?" he asked the foreman,

"Back to the depot and load up for the next farm. We have four more to do then hopefully that will be our lot."

Tony smiled, "What's wrong? Don't you like the open air?" he asked,

"I love the open air." the foreman replied, "But we don't like being shot at, that happened twice at the last farm. You farmers must be a special breed to live out here, I wouldn't sleep at night."

"We don't." said Tony, "Well I lie, we do sleep but with one eye open."

Chapter Twenty-Six

Mark and Sue came home to find Joyce packing all of her clothes. Little Benji was trying his best to drag his suitcase across the floor towards the front door. "Moving out." said Mark,

"No" replied Joyce "I'm just getting things ready for when Tony arrives,

"It won't be for days yet." said Sue, "Come on and sit down, when it's time I will give you a hand, come on let's have a cup of tea."

Joyce sighed "Make mine a strong one then, with plenty of sugar." Joyce took a sip of her tea and placed the cup on the table, "Please don't think that I am being ungrateful, but I miss Tony so much and when he said it was all right for us to return home, well I just can't wait. I was going to drive to the farm to surprise him."

"You must be bloody mad." said Mark, "Have you any idea how dangerous the roads are up there at the moment. Tony would go berserk if he found out what you intended to do as a surprise for him."

Joyce picked up her cup of tea "But I'm only going home, I live out there, all the other farmers' wives drive on the dirt roads."

"That may be so, but what about Benji? Do you really want to risk his life never mind your own, just wait until Tony comes to collect you. Come on let's get your suitcases back upstairs and get the dinner on."

The following day Joyce fed Benji, washed the breakfast dishes, tidied up the house and once again started to pack everything into the suitcases. She waited until Benji was having his afternoon sleep, then packed everything into the car. She placed Benji on the backseat. Quickly she locked the front door, put the keys through the letterbox, got into her car and reversed off the drive.

Joyce drove past the Feathers Pub, then turned right passing Bon Marche supermarket. She glanced at her watch it was half past two, she put her foot down and was soon through Avondale and heading into the country.

Tony, who was totally unaware that Joyce had left Mabelreign to return to the farm, was on his way back to the farmhouse. As he drove through the main gates he could see the two Bright Lights playing football on the front lawn. As soon as they heard the Land Rover engine they walked briskly over to the parked up vehicle. "Anyone for a bite of lunch?" Tony asked,

"Too true." one of them said,

"It will only be sandwiches" said Tony as he wiped the sweat from his brow, "Just give me a couple of minutes and it will be ready. While you two are sitting waiting why don't one of you open some cans of beer, there are plenty in the fridge. Tomorrow I will be away for most of the day as I am going to pick up the family and bring them back to the farm. In fact I must give Joyce a ring right now and let her know that I will be coming." Tony walked into the living room and picked up the phone, a few minutes later he returned to the veranda and sat down, "No answer" he said, "Either they have gone for a walk or they are both sound asleep, I'll try again later. Anyway who is for another beer?"

It was later than usual when Tony returned to the farm that evening, "Bloody hell," he said, "Nothing but problems today."

"There has been a phone call for you, about an hour ago someone called Mark, he said he would ring you later." said Adrian.

Tony frowned, "I'll give him a ring." he said,

"Now then Mark and how the hell are you?" Tony's face changed as the blood drained from it, "And what time was this?" he asked,

"I'm not really sure." Mark replied, "When we got home we found the house all locked up and a letter saying that she had decided to drive to the farm and to surprise you."

Tony looked at his watch, "Hell man it's almost seven o'clock, look I will have to go, I will give you a ring as soon as I know anything."

Tony put down the phone and immediately picked it up again and dialled Mike's number, he looked at his watch again and shook his head, 'he won't be at the office at this time of the evening,' he muttered to himself, "Hi Mike," he said, anxiously.

"You just caught me," Mike said "I was just leaving."

"Joyce has left Mabelreign, and is driving to the farm."

"Who with?" asked Mike,

"She is on her own," replied Tony, "but she certainly would

not drive at night, and there is no sign of her, to say that I am worried is to put it mildly."

"Hold on now." said Mike "No news is good news."

"It's Ok you saying that." said Tony "But where are they?"

"Right," said Mike "I will contact Salisbury and get someone to drive out to Mazoe, someone from here will drive to Mazoe, that will cover the main road. I will get a party together and drive from the police station up towards your farm. You drive towards Bindura and we will meet halfway, and don't worry I'm sure every thing will be OK."

As the night sky closed in, Joyce switched on the head lights. She had pulled off the road when she saw the engine was overheating, she lifted the bonnet and was met with a face full of steam. She sat for an hour realising that there was nothing that she could do until the water temperature dropped. When at last she removed the radiator cap she saw that there was no sign of water. She looked up and down the road but could see no traffic. She looked into the bush on either side of the road, no sign of life at all. For the next two hours she waited in the car hoping that someone would drive past. As she was about to give up hope of any help she saw two African figures walking along the road towards her. As they approached the car she indicated to the radiator, "I need water." she said, "Manzi, water, I need water." Both men just looked at her and shook their heads and wandered off into the bush. Daylight had long gone, Joyce sat in the car cuddling Benji, she could feel the cold night air and knew that it was going to be a long night. Startled by a knock on the driver's window, Joyce looked out and saw the two African men who she had spoken to a few hours ago. One of them held up two plastic bottles, she opened the driver's door and got out of the car, the eldest of the two men indicated to her by pointing to the car engine, "Manzi" he said with a smile,

"Oh thank you." replied Joyce, she quickly lifted the bonnet and poured the water into the radiator, when the radiator was full she replaced the cap, closed the bonnet, and handed the two bottles back to the two men. "Thank you very much." she said, "I'm ever so grateful for your help."

The two men just stood looking. Joyce went into the car, opened her handbag and handed them a ten dollar note. The two men, now smiling, clapped their hands, turned and walked away into the night. Not realising the danger she had possibly been in Joyce started the car and headed for Bindura. As she drove past the Coach House Inn on her right she could see people sitting in the bar, and in the dining room. Ahead she saw the sign saying Welcome to Bindura, she turned left at the sign and drove past the Police Station. She gave a brief look at the Dungeon Bar and saw that it was full of eager drinkers, some still in uniform and others in civilian clothes. On her left she could see Lincoln Road, with people relaxing on their patio's and veranda's. "Not long now," she said to Benji, "Not long now and you will see your Daddy, won't he be surprised." As the lights of Bindura faded behind her, she had now left the tar road and was now driving on a dirt road. She could remember Tony telling her of the dangers from landmines. Unconsciously her hands tightened on the steering wheel. Either side of the road the trees seemed to beckon her on as they swayed in the evening breeze. With her headlights on full beam she now started to feel uneasy as shadows seemed to dance in front of the car. She had never liked driving at night at the best of times, and asked herself why she hadn't left earlier in the day. She quickly glanced over her shoulder and saw that Benji was fast asleep on the back seat, 'not long now' she said to herself. Suddenly she saw a pothole in the road and swerved to miss it. 'Slow down,' she said, 'slow down.' Before she had a chance to reduce her speed she had to swerve to avoid another pothole but this time she overcorrected the steering, and instinctively hit the foot brake. She immediately lost control and the car skidded on the dirt road. All she could see was trees and grass as she ploughed into the bush. It was the cool night air and the smell of petrol that brought her to her senses, then she heard Benji crying. She quickly turned to look at the backseat and saw that he was now upside down on the floor. Joyce quickly got out and lifted Benji out of the car. As the car had spun off the road Joyce had no idea in which direction she had been heading. All around her everything was now pitch black, the rustling of the leaves on the trees, and the movement of the long grass made her skin crawl. She opened the boot and pulled out two blankets, she wrapped one around herself and the other one she wrapped around her little boy. The smell of petrol was very strong and she decided to get well away from the car, she couldn't even see the road as it was so dark. She hugged

Benji close and moved a few paces away from the car, when she turned around again she couldn't even see the car. 'Which way do I go?' she asked herself, 'Oh please, someone come and help us.' Joyce stood looking into the darkness. Benji, who had cried himself to sleep, was now becoming too heavy to carry. Joyce made the decision to find some kind of shelter where they could get out of the cold night's breeze, hoping that in the morning someone would find them.

Tony picked up his shotgun and shoulder holster, checked that he had plenty of ammunition and that both his weapons were loaded, left the farmhouse and got into his Land Rover. He had thought about calling his stick out but he just couldn't wait. With the farm disappearing behind him, Tony drove towards Bindura, he was looking straight ahead and also to the sides of the road. 'Where the hell is she?' he kept asking himself, 'what on earth made her do something as stupid as this.' After a few miles he stopped his vehicle and killed the engine. He sat for a few minutes then got out of the cab and stood in the middle of the road. Slowly he moved his head from left to right, straining his eyes as he searched the night sky. 'Nothing' he said to himself, he moved his head to one side and listened for the slightest sound of maybe an approaching vehicle, again nothing. He was now starting to fear the worst, every possible scenario passed through his head. He got back into the Land Rover, started the engine and started to chase his headlights along the dirt road. Tony glanced at his watch, it was now eight fifteen. 'Come on!' he shouted, 'Come on Joyce where are you!' He really didn't expect a reply, and he didn't get one. He continued to drive towards Bindura as he approached the next bend in the road something caught his eye way out in front of him. It looked like a white sheet spread out on the grass. His heart was pounding as he drove up to it. Suddenly his mouth went dry, there it was, Joyce's Ford Anglia, nose down in a ditch. Tony slammed on his brakes and pointed his Land Rover in the direction of the car. He left his headlights on and jumped out of the vehicle. With his shotgun in his hand he approached the car, the driver's door was open but the car was empty. Tony looked at the backseat, again nothing. He looked around the outside of the car at least there were no bullet holes, 'thank god for that,' he said to himself, 'no signs of damage other than a crumpled wing, and broken headlight.'

"Joyce!" he shouted, "Where are you, are you both OK?" The deafening silence pressed down on him almost like a physical weight. Tony waited for a few more minutes the got back into his Land Rover and slowly drove along the road. In the distance he could see lights coming towards him, he stopped the engine and waited. As the headlights got closer he flashed his lights. When the vehicles stopped in front of him he got out and walked over to them, "Are they all right?" the driver asked.

"No idea." replied Tony, "It's definitely her car, but no sign of her or the little fella. Can someone please contact Mike for me. I believe he is heading towards Mazoe, let him know that I have found her car but that they are still missing."

Everyone had a good look at the crumpled car, "One thing is for sure they can't be very far away." Tony nodded in agreement, "I've just spoken to Mike, said the other driver. He is heading back, and said he will be as quick as he can."

"OK" said Tony "Let's spread out, has everyone got a torch? OK then half of you take that side of the road and the other half take this side with me." Tony shone his torch on the dirt road and moved it from side to side,

"Here I've got something!" a voice shouted, "It looks like a set of footprints heading into the bush, and by the size of them I would say that they are a woman's and she is wearing shoes. It must be Joyce's."

Tony quickly went over and looked at the prints, "Yes" he said "There are more over there, everyone over here!" he shouted, "Get into an extended line and let's move slowly into the blackness, bloody dangerous this." he said to the man next to him, "We are sitting ducks if anyone wanted to take us out,."

"Cheers mate, you fill me with confidence." the man replied. Tony shone his torch into the thick bush, nothing. Slowly they moved forward going deeper and deeper into the bush. As they shone their torches they could see dozens of pairs of eyes of small wild animals staring at them as they were caught in the light. As they moved forward someone shouted, "Over here I think I have found something." Tony's heart was pounding as he ran over to where the man was pointing his torch into the thick bush. There next to a small tree were two figures huddled together in blankets, their hands were held up in front of them to shield the light from their eyes. "Is that you Joyce?" Tony shouted, "Tony!" came the reply. He ran over and knelt down beside Joyce and his son Benji. He grabbed hold of them both and hugged them, "Are you both alright?" he asked,

"We are fine." she said through the sobs, "Oh Tony I'm so glad to see you, I'm sorry I know that I should have waited for you to come and get us but all I wanted to do was to surprise you." she said,

"It's all right now you're both safe, and as for surprising me, well I think you did a very good job of that." Tony stood up and lifted Benji into his arms, "OK lads, thanks a million for all of your help, I'm going to get the family back to the farm. Could you do me one more favour please, let Mike know that everything is OK, and that I will ring him later."

Once they were back into the safety of the farm, Tony made some tea as Joyce put Benji to bed. "Whatever made you do such a stupid thing like that?" asked Tony struggling to keep his temper. Joyce knew that she had made a massive mistake and just shrugged her shoulders, "I just couldn't wait to see you again, and I felt that I was cramping Mark and Sue's style. It was all right for the first few weeks, but you know what a mess Benji can make and their house is like a show home. There is nothing out of place it's always so immaculate."

Tony could see that she was really sorry for what she had done, "OK" he said "Let's just drop the subject, you're both safe and well and that is the main thing. After a good night's sleep you will be fine." After Joyce went to bed, he first phoned Mark to give him the good news, checked on Benji, then went out onto the veranda and sat down with the two Bright Lights for a chat. "How do you lads feel now that the fence is up?" he asked,

"Much better." they replied, "It may sound daft but it certainly gives you a feeling of security knowing that if anyone wants to get to the farm then they have to first of all get either over or through the fence." Tony nodded in approval, "Just don't get too complacent." he said, "They can still give you a good revving from the far side of the fence. Just remember one thing and that is we have to be lucky all the time, they just have to be lucky once. If they find a chink in your armour then they will use it."

The following morning Tony was up early and ready to start work. As he passed Benji's bedroom he peeped in to see if he was OK. Tony smiled at him as he sat up and held out his arms to be lifted up. "Now then big fella," he said, "And how are you this morning, come on we will make your mammy a cup of tea."

"I'm up." said a voice behind him "But you can still make me a cup of tea though."

"Did you have a good night's sleep?" he asked,

"Not bad." she replied, "So what is there to do today?"

"Nothing." said Tony "You just relax, I will be back about lunchtime." he kissed her on the cheek, handed Benji to her and went out closing the door behind him.

The following two weeks were uneventful, Joyce caught up on all the outstanding paperwork. Benji acted as if nothing had ever happened, and Tony felt much better. At least he was getting well-fed now, and no housework to do. The workforce seemed more relaxed now that Joyce was back on the farm. Everyone was smiling and the singing started again, but by the end of the third week he noticed that when the workers finished work the singing stopped. The week before he had stood on the veranda with Joyce and listened as they all sang and danced around the open fires in their villages. The following day as Tony said goodbye to the workers he called Crispen over, "Is everything all right?" he asked,

Crispen looked slightly worried. "

"I think that there is something worrying you all, if there is then you must tell me so that I can sort it out for you." said Tony.

"The women are concerned." Crispen said,

"What are they worried about?" Tony asked, "Don't they have enough food? if not then tell me."

"No, food is not the problem." he replied, "The women are worried because they have seen a man watching them when they go down to the river to get water, and it is not the first time that this man has been seen. But when the men go down to see if they can find him he has gone."

"What does he look like?" asked Tony,

"They say he looks very dirty, as though he hasn't been washed for a long time and that he is very thin."

"Don't worry about it." said Tony "I'll go down to the river tomorrow and see if I can find him."

After dinner Tony sat outside, it was not long before the two Bright Lights came out to join him. "Well how's things?" Tony said, "Are you feeling fit and ready for another night on duty?"

"I don't know about fit." one of them said, "I had a terrible sleep. It was so hot, I spent most of the time tossing and turning and eventually I just sat and read a book. So I just hope we will have a very quiet night."

"I was talking to Crispen late this afternoon, and seemingly there is a stranger on my land and it's unsettling the workforce. So if you see anything at all let me know straight away. I know that it is difficult for you to spot a strange face as you don't know all of my workers, but if you see anything that looks suspicious then give me a shout, or send one of the workers for me." said Tony.

"Five days to go and we may be going to get some action after all." one of the men said,

"Don't count on it." Tony replied, "It is possibly nothing more that an innocent Bantu just travelling through the area, but we just cannot be too complacent."

For the next two days Tony stayed very close to the farmhouse. He knew that Joyce was well aware of the situation but he wanted to give her as much time as she needed to settle back in to the usual routine of things again. He only moved away from the farmhouse when the two Bright Lights were up and moving around in full view of anyone who may be watching the farm. On the third day Tony decided to go down to the river where the stranger had been seen and to have a good look around. "I'll be away for about an hour." he told Joyce, "If you want anything just ask our two guests." he said with a smile. Tony walked over to his Land Rover and as he passed the two men he said "I will be away for about an hour, I'm going to have a look around the river and see if I can see anything of this stranger. Do me a favour stay around the farmhouse just in case Joyce needs anything. I'll see you in a while." Tony parked up the Land Rover and walked down to the river. He could see some of the women doing the washing using the rocks as washing boards. As he walked amongst them they all started giggling and laughing. "And how are you all today?" he said,

"We are fine Mr Tony, you can see we are doing our washing,

we are good wives, we are looking after our families."

"Tell me," said Tony, "Has anyone seen any strangers down by the river in the last few days?"

"No not for the last few days but someone was here last week. Come we will show you where we saw him."

Tony followed two of the women away from the river, "There," one of them said as she pointed to some bushes, "He was there in those bushes, we saw him twice in two days, he was watching us. Normally we will come down to the river by ourselves to either bath or to do our washing, but now we only come to the river in a group. This man is no good we don't like him, but when our men came to chase him away he was gone, and we have never seen him again."

Tony bent down to look at the footprints, nearly all of his workers wore either plain soled plimsolls or they went barefoot. The footprints were very clear; they were thick treads, possibly boots. As Tony followed the tracks, it soon became clear that who ever had left the tracks had also spent time in the close vicinity, as the grass was well worn and there were various scraps of food and small bones scattered around what had been a small fire. It looked completely flattened as if whoever made them had slept in the area as well. The grass was well worn and there were various scraps of food and some bones scattered around the remains of a very small fire. Tony walked around looking for any other signs that may give him a clue, but after a few minutes it was obvious to him that whoever had been there was now gone. The freshest of the tracks led down to the river. Obviously whoever had been there was making every effort to cover his latest tracks, and using the river to wipe out his footprints. Tony decided to call it a day and to return to the farm.

When the day came for the Bright Lights to be relieved, Tony felt rather sad as he had built up a good relationship with the two of them. They were two switched on guys and it had been a pleasure to have them on his farm. Tony was now in a dilemma, he had to take these two men into Bindura and then collect the two new men. To do this it meant leaving Joyce and Benji alone on the farm and this Tony was not very happy about, but there was no alternative. He phone Mike at the Police Station, "What time are you expecting the next lot of Bright Lights to arrive this afternoon?" he asked,

"About fourteen hundred hours." replied Mike,

"Do me a favour," asked Tony, "I may be a bit late."

"If I am can you hold them up for a few minutes until I get there, and then I will have to get straight back to the farm."

"No time even for a beer?" asked Mike,

"Not even time for a quick one," replied Tony, "It will be a case of drop off and pick up and off again."

"It shouldn't be a problem." laughed Mike "What's the matter Tony are you on a promise from Joyce or something?"

Tony laughed, "Chance would be a fine thing, see you about fourteen hundred." he said.

Chapter Twenty-Seven

The next few days were uneventful, after showing Bob and Dave around the farm, the two new Bright Lights seemed to settle in. Tony briefed them about the recent events and of the situation in the area over the last few months. "Don't get alarmed," he said, "But keep focused at all times, don't let your guard drop." Bob the eldest of the two new men had his own Safari business and gave Tony the impression that he knew everything there was to be known about the farming way of life. He openly said that the present situation had been blown out of all proportion and who in their right mind would be afraid of a bunch of kaffirs. Bob claimed that the two weeks that he had been asked to do was going to be more of a holiday for him than anything else. Tony took an immediate dislike to him and knew that the next two weeks were going to be hard going. Dave the other reservist seemed very willing, but as it was his first time in the bush, he had very little experience but was a likeable person. Tony knew that he would have to watch him and make sure that Bob didn't give him a false sense of confidence. "Don't worry about us." said Bob, "We will be all right, if any of those so called freedom fighters come within a mile of this farm then they will have me to answer to." Tony shook his head, 'just what I need at a time like this,' he thought, "Let me tell you something my friend," he said, "Don't underestimate these terr's, some of them are really switched on, and very determined indeed. Whatever you do, don't think that all of them are just cowards who will only hit soft targets, some are very well trained, and battle hardened."

Joyce has settled back into her old routine. Most of her day was taken up looking after Benji, as well as doing the normal housework such as washing, ironing, and preparing meals. After cooking an evening meal, bathing Benji and putting him to bed, Joyce was ready to relax with a glass of wine, with Tony. For the last few weeks things had been quiet, there had been no more reports of attacks on any of the farms in any of the areas. Tony kept his thoughts to himself, he felt it was too good to be true. Somewhere out there, everyone knew that there were a total of five hundred terrs from Mozambique, and that was not counting the ones that they didn't know about who were already in the country. After massive follow up operations on the North East border the security forces had only found small groups of resistance. These had all been taken out, but as yet there was no sign of the main group.

The thought of this stranger who had been seen on his land still bothered him. He knew that Joshua had escaped in the last contact, and he was in no doubt of how determined he was to have another go at his farm. Tony placed his empty can of beer on the side table, "Another glass of wine?" he asked,

Joyce nodded, "Daft question. Are you having another beer?" as he opened the fridge door, she heard the snap as he pulled the ringpull. She shook her head, 'I should have known better to have asked that question,' she said to herself. Tony handed her the glass of wine and sat down next to her. Taking a sip of beer he put his arm around her, "It's lovely to have you back on the farm." he said, "It just wasn't home without you and Benji here. Don't worry we will weather the storm, in the end things will turn out OK."

Joyce put her head onto his shoulder, "It's not us that I worry about," she said "It's Benji, what sort of a future will he have, the last thing that I want, is for him to have to live his life like we are doing now."

"This won't go on for ever." said Tony, "There is no way this government will give in to these people. If they took over the running of the country it would be total chaos within months. Don't even think about it, it will never happen. Come on drink up, it's time we had an early night."

"I know exactly what you have in mind." replied Joyce as she emptied her glass of wine in one mouthful, "Come on then drink up." she said.

Chapter Twenty-Eight

Since his escape from the recent contact, Joshua now realised that Magumbo was either dead or had been taken prisoner. For the next two days he had moved only at night and taken cover during the daylight hours. As he lay hidden he could see the helicopters and the fixed wing aircraft overhead, he could also see the security forces as they combed the area. As they moved slowly away from his position he felt that once again he had given them the slip. On the third day, hunger and thirst made him leave his position and move into the open bush where fruit was plentiful. He spent a full day down by a river trying to catch fish but as the evening came he gave it up as a bad job. Fish would not be on his menu tonight. He knew that it was almost impossible for him to try and get across the border back into Mozambique as the whole area was now swarming with troops. So, he decided to head west, Camburo farm was still a target and he was determined to destroy it and everyone who was in it at the time.

For the last two hours he had been watching the village where the farm workers lived, knowing that to enter the village and to ask for food and for shelter would be a disaster for him. Just about every one in the village either worked on the farm or had a member of the family working on the farm. On both occasions when he had gone down to the river, he had been seen. On the second time he was seen, the men from the village came rushing down to the river edge looking for him armed with pangas. Even though Joshua knew that they were no match for him and his AK47 he decide to move quickly and avoid being seen again, so he crossed the river and made his way upstream heading for Camburo farm.

The two new Bright Lights spent most of the late afternoon lounging around the pool. Joshua now had a very good idea of their movements. After having breakfast they spent about half an hour each morning talking to the farmer, then as the farmer left to go to work on the farm, the two men walked to the side of the farmhouse and went inside a small building. The building was about fifteen foot square with a thatched roof. Joshua smiled to himself, it was next to the outhouse that had been destroyed when he had last attacked the farm with Magumbo. The two men then spent all of the morning inside the building. Most likely asleep thought Joshua. Then at about two thirty they reappeared and one at a time they went into the farmhouse to get showered. After a light lunch both men then changed into swimming trunks and walked towards the swimming pool. Joshua noticed that during the daylight hours at no time did either of the two men carry their weapons, either very confident, very poorly trained, or stupid he thought to himself.

As dusk fell, Joshua watched as Tony returned to the farm. The two men met him at the main gate and as he drove through the two men locked it behind him. This was something that Joshua had not been aware of, the last time he had been on the farm there had been just open land around the farmhouse but now there was this high security fence to contend with. The two men were now in uniform and were armed. They sat on the veranda talking to the farmer. The door opened and a woman with a small child in her arms spoke to them and everyone went inside, closing the door behind them. Soon the evening sky pulled its dark curtain over the farmhouse, Joshua smiled to himself as he crawled back into the thick bush, 'tomorrow,' he said, 'tomorrow.'

Joshua was awake well before dawn broke. It had been a very cold night, he had curled himself into a ball to try and keep warm, his body was aching from head to foot. Sitting with his back against a tree, he gently rubbed his arms and legs with his numb hands trying to get the circulation going. He looked up at the sky, willing the sun to appear to warm his body. Slowly he stretched his aching limbs and moved into a kneeling position. He could see the first signs of life as the two figures in uniform moved away from the veranda, slowly they made their way along the garden towards the perimeter fence. As they walked side by side with their rifles held across their chests it looked as if they were checking the fence, possibly looking for any signs of entry. Joshua watched as they made their way towards his hiding place, carefully he lowered himself into the undergrowth. The two men had now stopped and were now no more that ten foot away from his position. His heart pounding in his chest as he brought his AK47 assault rifle into the firing position and flicked the safety catch from safe and into the first position of automatic. If they came any closer then it was a good chance that he would be seen. "Hell, I'm tired." one of the men said, "It's been a bloody cold night."

"Yeah." replied the other man, "Cold and bloody boring, I'm ready for a good sleep. Come on let's get back to the warmth of the farmhouse and a hot cup of coffee."

As the two men turned and started to walk away Joshua let out a quiet sigh of relief. He flicked the safety catch back on and watched the two men as they walked onto the veranda and sat down. They then laid their weapons on the ground and sat back in their chairs with their feet up on the small table. Within minutes they were joined by Tony, who came out carrying a tray of cups and some toast. The three men sat talking as they devoured the toast and drank the coffee. Again the door opened and through it came a woman carrying the young child in her arms. The two men stood up and said something to the woman, both men then pointed to the side of the farmhouse and walked towards their sleeping quarters. Joshua watched the two men as they entered the small building and closed the door behind them. Tony then stood up kissed the woman on the lips, patted the young child on the head and walked away from the farmhouse, got into his Land Rover and drove off. Joshua felt more confident than ever, he now knew that the two men definitely slept in the outhouse, and that the farmer left the farm early to go out into the farmland. For the next few hours Joshua sat with the sun beating down on his aching body. Slowly the stiffness eased away. By noon apart from the hunger pangs he felt like a new man ready to take the world on. With his assault rifle in his hand he slowly crawled towards the fence, looking for the best place to make his entry. To his left it was too open. He moved slowly to his right, at the end of the fence he could make out some tennis courts. At the side of the court was a small changing room, just like a lean-to with a few seats and a table. 'Perfect,' he said to himself, if he climbed the fence at this point then the lean-to would give him the cover that he needed, it was a blind spot from the farmhouse.

As Bob and Dave slept, Joyce played with Benji on the front lawn, totally unaware that just outside the security fence a pair of eyes were watching their every move. Everytime Joshua was about to go over the fence and make a dash towards the farmhouse, either the phone rang, or he heard the sound of a vehicle approaching. Twice that day Tony returned to the farm, stayed about twenty minutes then left again. Frustrated as he was, Joshua decided to attempt the assault on the farm the following day. As soon as the farmer left, and when he felt confident that the two strangers were asleep, then he would make his move.

Tony sensed a happier mood with the workforce, they seemed more relaxed and every one of them gave the impression that they didn't have a care in the world. "I heard you all singing last night." he said,

"Yes Mr Tony, everyone is happy now." replied Crispen, "Everyone is happy now that you have chased the stranger away from our village. No one is now afraid to go down to the river to fetch water, or to do the washing, or to bathe." Tony could see the young girls giggling as he walked towards them, "Morning," he said to them,

"Morning Mr Tony," they replied in unison, as they held their hands up to their faces to hide the giggles.

Tony looked at Crispen, "What are they all laughing at?" he asked, Crispen looked down at the ground, and then looked up at the girls who all started laughing and giggling again, "Come on" said Tony, with a puzzled smile on his face, "What's going on?"

Crispen looked at Tony then at the girls, and started to laugh, "They didn't expect to see you for a while, as your lovely wife has just returned to the farm. They all said that you would not get out of bed for at least a week."

Tony laughed, "You must be joking." he said, "I don't even get a full night's sleep with little Benji in the house."

Everyone went quiet, Tony turned and walked out into the open air, behind him he could hear the roars of laughter coming from the workforce.

As he said goodbye to the last of the workers, Tony locked everything up and got into his Land Rover and headed home. As he drove through the gates he saw another Land Rover parked at the side of the farmhouse. With a frown on his face he walked around to the front garden and onto the veranda, "Now then," he said with a big smile, "And how the hell are you? I didn't know that you were in the area."

"Just passing through." said Mike. As they shook hands Tony said, "Has Joyce offered you a beer yet?"

"I've just this minute arrived and your good lady has just gone inside to get me one."

"Make that two love." he called through the door, "In fact you had better make it four he said" as he saw Dave and Bob walking over the garden towards the house. "So what brings you out to this neck of the woods?" asked Tony, "Normally you give us a ring to let us know that you are on your way." Before Mike could answer, Tony said, "You will be staying for dinner I hope."

"If you insist." said Mike,

As he put down his empty can of beer, Tony picked up the empty can, "I've got a better idea, why don't you stay the night."

"Well that would be very well appreciated." said Mike, "As tomorrow I still have some business to see to in the area. What I intend doing is to get around the farms, and have a talk with as many of the farmers as possible. I need to find out what their concerns are and to see if there is anything that I can do to help. I've been to three farms today, two tomorrow, then I'm off to Shamva to speak to the farmers there."

"Hell I'm sorry." said Tony, "Please excuse my ignorance have you three met, Mike this is Bob, and this is Dave."

Mike held out his hand, "Pleased to meet you, I'm the Chief Inspector in charge at Bindura, I'm sure that we will have met when you arrived at the start of your stint. Anyway how are you both doing, is it your first time, or are you both old hands at it?"

"It's my first time." said Dave, "I've never been on a farm before."

"And how do you find it?" asked Mike,

"I love it." Dave said, "I really could get used to the lifestyle, in the open air all of the time, but not with the security situation as it is. I take my hat off to the farmers, you're looking over your shoulder all of the time, it's no life at all."

"And how about you Bob?" asked Mike,

"I'm fine, I don't mind it at all. I've spent most of my life in the bush and these bloody so-called freedom fighters, they certainly don't frighten me. They are nothing but a bunch of cowards who use darkness as a weapon and run into the night as soon as any one fights back."

"Well all I can say is this," said Mike, "Cowards they may be, I agree with you on that, but just remember one thing, even a lucky shot will kill you, so don't get too complacent. What's your opinion on the new security fence then Tony?" asked Mike,

"It makes a great difference, it's another obstacle that the terrs have to overcome to get to us. It's our first line of defence really, but only time will tell. One thing is certain, it won't stop them putting a rocket over the top that's for sure."

"Come on you lot, dinner is ready." Joyce shouted, Everyone moved inside, and sat in silence as they ate their dinner. Mike was the first to finish, he placed his knife and fork neatly on the plate and gently pushed it away from him. "I must say Joyce that was beautiful, what a lovely meal. It certainly beats cooking for yourself." he said as he loosened his belt,

"You will have to find yourself a good woman." she replied,

Mike looked at Tony, "I think all of the good ones are taken what do you say mate."

"No comment." replied Tony with a smile and a wink at Joyce,

"Be careful she said, "Or you will be doing the washing up tonight."

As Joyce started to clear the table, the four men went back outside and sat on the veranda. "Whatever happened about the five hundred terrs that went unaccounted for from that camp in Mozambique?" asked Tony,

Mike frowned, "Very little news at the moment." he said, "Despite intensive troop movement in the area, observation posts being set up, it looks as if they have just gone to ground, unless they have moved further down the border. Reports coming in indicate that possibly a new front is opening up along the Eastern Border and on the South Eastern Border. At the moment no one is sure if the insurgents belong to the same group that were reported to have been in Mozambique. "Early reports that have started to come in indicate that there are six small groups operating in those areas. Until we know all of the facts we should still be on our guard as they may well be in the North East of the area. I can give you some more information that I know will cheer you up Tony, and that is the Selous Scouts are now well inside Zambia. They have returned to Mozambique as have the S.A.S. so it's now just a matter of waiting for them to relay information back to base, and then for J.O.C. to put a plan into action."

"Well it's time for us to get ready for duty." said Dave as he looked at his watch, both men got up and walked around to the side of the farmhouse.

"What do you think?" asked Tony,

"What do I think about the two Bright Lights?" asked Mike,

"Yes what is your opinion of them."

"Well I think that the young one, David, he seems like a decent bloke, obviously a bit nervous but then that's to be expected really isn't it. But I think if the shit hit the fan he would be all right. The other one, Bob well I'm not too sure of him. He seems to think that he knows it all, and as you know that can be very dangerous indeed. He gives me the impression that there is nothing to worry about and it is just a holiday out here. His attitude towards the blacks, well he seems to think that every last one of them is no good at all. I'm surprised that he doesn't take the terrorist threat seriously at all. I would say keep an eye on him, and don't let him try and brain wash the young lad."

As the two men returned, Mike and Tony changed the conversation, "So how do you feel being out here all night?" Mike asked,

"It gets bloody cold." Dave said, "And the more that you concentrate the more your eyes start to play tricks on you. The shadows seem to move when you look at them, the bushes move I'm certain of that, and there are all sorts of queer sounds. Things that I have never heard before, it can get real spooky. But the worst thing is the cold, you can't move around for obvious reasons, I would say from about two o'clock onwards is the worst time."

"It's second nature to me." said Bob, "I'm used to it, nothing frightens me anymore, and as for the so called terrs that is the least of my worries."

"Well I think it is time for us to go inside and let these two get on with their work for the night." said Tony, "If you need us just give us a call." he said as he closed the front door. Once inside Mike smiled, "What an arsehole he is, have you ever heard anyone talk so much rubbish." he said, "When I get back to my office I will make sure that he never comes out to this area again. The man is a danger to everyone around him. He has no regard for his own safety never mind anyone else. One thing is for sure, I wouldn't have him in the bush with me."

"Well you know my feelings." said Tony, "I would sooner

have no one on the farm than an idiot like that. The biggest problem we have is getting anyone at all, there are not that many people who want to swap the comfort of their homes to come out to the sharp end. So really we have to take whatever we can get, but I must say this one really does take the cake."

Joyce came into the living room carrying a tray, "There you are, two brandies for you two, and two cups of coffee for the two men outside."

"Here, I will take them out." said Tony, He switched off the living room lights, opened the door and went outside with the two cups of coffee. It was well into the early hours when Tony and Mike called it a night, Tony went into the bedroom and found Joyce was sound asleep. As soon as his head hit the pillow he joined her, oblivious to Mike as he bumped into the furniture in the next room. Tony was woken by Joyce shaking him, "What's the problem?" he asked,

"What is the problem." she replied, "Have you seen the time, I've called you twice, I've knocked on Mikes room, but there is no answer."

Tony looked at his watch "Shit, it's nine o'clock." He jumped out of bed and got dressed, "And don't make a noise." Joyce said, "Or you will wake up Benji."

Tony pulled the living room curtain back and looked out of the window, no sign of Bob or Dave, 'more than likely in bed' he thought to himself. He went into the kitchen and switched on the electric kettle, 'a good mug of black coffee should do the trick' he thought, "Make it two mugs." a voice said, Tony turned and saw Mike standing at the kitchen door, "You look like shit." he said,

"Look in the mirror." replied Mike, "You're not such a pretty sight either."

Joshua had been watching the farmhouse since first light, first the two farm guards left the veranda and walked slowly down the garden as if inspecting the perimeter fence. As they approached his position, he sank lower into the undergrowth. They then stopped about six or seven feet away. Joshua held his breath, 'had they seen him, no' he said to himself as they turned to their left and started to walk slowly towards the tennis courts. They had taken no more that ten paces when they suddenly stopped, turned around and started to walk back the way that they had just come. "Shit" said Joshua, slowly he brought his assault rifle into the firing position and flicked the safety catch from safe to the first firing position of automatic. As the two men approached, Joshua held his breath again. Soon he was looking at their backs as they made their way back to the farmhouse. He watched them as they walked onto the veranda, rested their weapons against the wall and sat down in the chairs. Both men, obviously more secure now that daylight was with them, appeared to be sitting with their eyes closed. 'No problem with you two' said Joshua, they would be no threat at all to his plans. For the next half an hour the two men sat in silence. When it was obvious that no one was going to bring them their coffee and toast, they left the veranda and made their way towards their sleeping quarters.

Time passed excruciatingly slowly for Joshua. There was no other notable activity around the farmhouse. He could see the Land Rover parked at the side of the house, but no sign of either the driver or the farmer. Joshua looked up at the sky and judged that the time must be between nine or ten o'clock. Once again he had spent an uncomfortable night, it had been bitterly cold and damp, his body ached all over, but most of all he was now starving. He was getting hunger pains in his stomach, and he was almost out of water. Joshua knew that in the farmhouse there would be all the food that he could possibly wish for but the problem was getting to it. As the minutes dragged by Joshua mentally checked over the details of his plan attack. Once the men were out of the farmhouse, he could begin. Having scaled the security fence he would gain access to the farmhouse. He did not consider the disposal of the woman and child, as they were of no consequence. There would be plenty of time to ease his thirst and hunger whilst waiting for the man to walk into his trap. Or there again he could always spend a little time amusing himself with the woman... Suddenly the front door opened, and out came a man in uniform, followed by the farmer. They stood talking for a while then the man in the uniform walked to the Land Rover, got in, started the engine and drove towards the main gates. As the farmer closed the gates behind him the Land Rover headed away from the farm.

With a deep sense of satisfaction, Joshua watched the farmer climb into his Land Rover and drive off in a cloud of dust. He waited patiently as the dust settled.

Moving stealthily out of his hiding place he made his way along the fence towards the tennis courts It was either a place that they weren't bothered about, or they just had not given it a second thought. One thing was for sure they never seemed to take an interest in it. As he reached the end of the fence he could see the tennis court. At the side of the court were a table and three chairs, near to them was a small open changing room, more like a lean-to. 'Perfect' he thought to himself, he now looked up at the fence. It was made of thick pig wire in a diamond mesh. Slipping the strap of his assault rifle over his shoulder, he reached up and grabbed a hold of the wire with his right hand then with his left foot he placed his toe into the diamond hole in the mesh. Pulling himself up, he then reached up with his left hand and took a firm grip of the wire, and with his right foot in the mesh he pulled with his hands and at the same time pushed with his legs. He was now at the top of the twelve foot high fence. Quickly looking around he gently hung himself over the top of the fence, swaying as he moved his feet, he raised one leg over the top then with his left hand he grasped the other side of the fence. Slowly he moved his body weight over the fence, he was now on the other side of the fence. Quickly he lowered himself down onto the ground; he slipped the assault rifle off his shoulder and made his way to the end of the lean-to. It had been much harder than he had expected as the fence swayed to and fro the higher he got. Peering around the corner of the lean-to he had a perfect view of the front garden, the veranda, and of the outhouse where the two men were staying. Things just couldn't be better, his only problem was that there was no cover between him and the veranda. Once he made his move there would be no going back. Joshua lifted his assault rifle in his right hand, and with his left hand he felt in his waistband for his bayonet. Pulling it of its sheath he clipped it onto the end of the barrel of his rifle. Just as he was about to make his dash across the garden the front door opened and out stepped the woman. She stood looking down the garden towards the swimming pool, 'she is never going to go for a swim' Joshua muttered with an obscene oath. As if she had heard his thoughts she sat down on one of the chairs, picked up a magazine and started to flick through the pages. Slowly Joshua moved back behind the lean-to and watched her through one of the cracks in the woodwork. 'Shaking with impotent rage Joshua glared with hatred at the woman, mentally willing her to move. The minutes dragged by as she sat reading a magazine... Just as she put it down, the young boy came out onto the veranda. Joshua sighed with frustration as she started to play with the boy. With the hunger and thirst cramping his stomach, Joshua was now getting very impatient. Just as he decided to make a move, the farmer appeared and sat down beside the woman. The woman got up and went inside the house and when she came back out she was carrying a tray of sandwiches and a jug of water. This was torture to Joshua he sat with his back to the lean-to and every few minutes he gave them a quick glance to see if they were finished and if the farmer had gone back to work.

"You have no one to blame but yourself." Joyce said, "No one forced you to drink all the brandy, so don't expect any sympathy from me, and as for Mike, well he should know better. You two are like little kids when you get together." she said, "You always try and outdo each other, so don't bother with that little boy lost look because it just won't work."

Tony knew that he was going to get no sympathy today and that by the sound of it he would probably be in the dog house for a couple of days. So he picked up a handful of sandwiches and said "I must be getting back to work, see you when I get back tonight."

Joshua could feel the excitement building as the woman got up from her chair, took the boy by the hand and started to make her way back into the farmhouse. With the tension rippling through his quivering body Joshua inched his way to the edge of the lean to. Just as he was about to leave his cover he caught a movement out of the corner of his eye. The eldest of the two men had just appeared at the side of the farmhouse. He called to the woman, raised his hand in a wave, stopped briefly to speak to the small child then turned and made his way towards the swimming pool. She stood for a few minutes looking down the garden then went inside and closed the door. Here was this man who was a farm guard, walking about in broad daylight with no firearm. Joshua just could not believe his luck. As the man reached the swimming pool he dropped his towel onto the ground and dipped his toe into the water, hesitated for a moment then he dived into the pool. Joshua could hear the splashing of the water and could just make out the top of the man's head. Should he make a dash to the pool, take out the man then go on to the farmhouse? At that moment the man pulled himself out of the water, spread out his towel and lay down on his stomach facing away from the pool. Joshua gave him a few minutes then made his move, he quickly looked over at the farmhouse, and at the outhouse, no one in sight. Bent almost double he ran towards the pool, he slowed down when he was about six feet from the sleeping figure. Just as he was in striking distance the man moved, maybe second sense told him that something was wrong. As he turned, and was about to sit up Joshua's bayonet sliced through the soft skin at the man's throat. The startled look in the man's eyes meant nothing to Joshua as he lunged again, this time the bayonet cut deep into the man's chest. In one movement Joshua pulled the bayonet out of the man's body and with his foot pushed him into the swimming pool. Just a slight splash met Joshua's ears; he quickly looked again towards the farmhouse then back to the body in the pool. Legs together arms outstretched the body floated face down in the water that was rapidly turning a dark red.

Joshua ran quickly over the freshly cut grass towards the farmhouse, as he approached the veranda he stopped and turned towards the outhouse. It would be easier to take out the youngest of the two men as he slept he thought to himself. He move slowly and quietly towards the doorway. Pushing it inwards he could feel the cool air as the fan blades pushed a breeze towards him. There lying on a single bed at the far side of the small room was the youngest of the two men. With his assault rifle held in front of him Joshua moved towards the bed, with one sudden lunge the bayonet once again sliced through skin and muscle. The whole body lifted off the bed as the body arched its back; he pulled the bayonet out and struck again, this time he could feel the blade glance off a bone as it cut deep into the body. Joshua pulled the bayonet from the body he could feel the muscles gripping the blade, he pulled harder and the bayonet came free. Blood spurted out of the wound, and then air gushed out pushing a spray of froth and blood over the white sheets.

Silently Joshua turned and made his way out of the room and back into the daylight. Moving quickly up the veranda steps, he stood against the front door, his chest was heaving as he sucked in lungfuls of air. He reached down and slowly turned the door handle, listening for any sound inside, he hesitated for a moment straining to hear, then carefully opened the door and went inside. The room was cool and airy; there was a settee and two easy chairs in the room. In one corner there was a television, and an open drinks cabinet. In front of the fire there was a large coffee table, scattered on the table there were a number of magazines. Moving as quietly as he could he crept through the living room and into the dining room. The room was dark as the closed curtains kept out most of the sunlight. In the centre of the room stood a large wooden set of table and chairs, through the doorway he could hear the sound of someone talking. As he approached the doorway the sounds coming from the room made him realise that it must be the kitchen. He could hear the sound of running water and pots and pans, and plates being washed. Joshua stood listening to the conversation, it was the woman talking to a young child. He peered into the room to see her standing at the kitchen sink on the floor by her feet was the young boy. Silently Joshua slid into the kitchen. Like a long black tentacle his arm reached out to grasp her. Joyce chattering happily to Benji suddenly felt the hairs on the back of her neck begin to prickle. Fearfully she turned to face the evilly grinning Joshua. With a deep stab of fear, Joyce moved with a protective gesture in front of Benji. She could now smell his breath as he breathed heavily in her direction, his lips curled back to reveal two sets of rotting buck teeth, she could see the blood lust in his eyes as he stared at her, beads of sweat standing out on his face. He brought up his assault rifle and Joyce could see the blood on the bayonet, her blood then ran cold, had he killed Tony? Then she thought about the two Bright Lights, were they dead also? Her eyes flickered to the draining board and to the large meat cleaver that she had been using to prepare the evening meal. She could now feel Benji clinging to her leg, she wanted to bend down and to pick him up but she didn't want to take her eyes off the animal in front of her. As Joshua moved towards her Joyce knew that she would have to do something quickly, as he raised his assault rifle with the bayonet pointing towards her the silence was shattered by rifle fire. As Joshua turned to see where the shots had come from Joyce grabbed the meat cleaver and struck him a violent blow across the right arm shoulder. Joshua screamed in agony. As he stumbled back Joyce struck him again, this time across his back. He fell to the floor but managed to get back to his feet and staggered from the room. As he dragged his bleeding body from the kitchen, through the dining room and out through the front door, he stopped briefly and looked at the figure of the young farm guard lying on the veranda. He was spreadeagled on the floor with his rifle still in his hands, a trail of blood led back to the room where Joshua had last seen him.

As the bayonet sliced into his flesh for the second time, David felt his lifeblood slowly draining from his body. Realising the danger that Joyce and the young boy were in, he desperately managed to pull his body off the bed and onto the floor. Sliding his body over the stone floor he reached his rifle. As he got to his feet he realised how badly he had been injured. Blood was now pouring from his body, but still he made his way to the veranda and up the steps. Knowing that he did not have the strength to go any further, David pulled the trigger and fired five shots into the air knowing that Tony would hear the sound and hopefully rush to the farmhouse.

As the shots echoed through the air, Tony stopped what he was doing, grabbed his shotgun, and jumped into his Land Rover. Gunning the engine he raced back to the farmhouse. Skidded to a halt he vaulted out of his vehicle and ran. The first thing that he saw was the floating body in the swimming pool. Standing at the poolside he could see that the figure was Bob, realising that the amount of blood in the pool meant only one thing, he turned and ran towards the veranda. It was then that he saw the second body lying in a large pool of blood; he looked down at the body and saw the rifle.

"Joyce!" he screamed "Joyce where are you?"

"I'm in here," sobbed Joyce.

Running through the house Tony crashed into the kitchen and saw her sitting in the corner of the room cradling a hysterically sobbing Benji.

"What the hell happened?" he asked,

"He was here." she said through her tears,

"Who was here? Where is he?"

"He ran out when someone fired those shots."

"Who was it?" he asked,

"It was a tall African, he was armed with an AK47."

"Right said Tony, "Take my pistol and get yourself into the bathroom with Benji, lock yourself in and don't open the door unless I tell you. I will check the house and then get help."

"But Tony," she said,

"No buts." he replied "Just get into the bathroom and stay there."

Tony quickly checked every room then moved quickly outside again. He bent down and looked at young David, he shook his head, then he looked at the blood on the veranda floor. It led away into the garden, he went back into the house and knocked on the bathroom door, "Joyce it's me Tony, was this African hurt at all?"

"Yes" she replied "I hit him with a meat cleaver and I'm sure that I cut him bad, he was bleeding all over the place, why?" she asked,

"Don't worry love you did a good job." he said reassuringly.

Tony ran into the living room and hit the Agric Alert, 'come on' he said to himself, 'come someone answer it.'

"This is Bindura Police Station," a voice said, "What is your problem Camburo? I repeat what is your problem."

"We have been attacked, two Farm Guards killed, the terr is wounded but has made his escape over."

"OK Camburo I have your message and help is on it's way over."

Tony ran back outside, he stopped when he saw the body of David. He looked down once again, 'I owe you so much my friend, I owe you so much, thank you.'

Moving as quick as he could, Tony followed the trail of blood across the garden, the drops of blood were leading along the perimeter fence, and towards the tennis courts. 'How the hell did anyone get past the fence?' he asked himself. As he moved past the swimming pool he took a quick look at the lifeless body floating in the water. He looked around the edge of the pool area, 'a towel' he said to himself, then he shook his head, 'no fuckin' rifle, the stupid bastard, I knew that he was a danger to himself, and to everyone else. He moved forward towards the tennis courts, the blood was much thicker on the grass now. As he approached the tennis courts he knew that whoever he was looking for was badly injured but could well be waiting to ambush him. He knelt beside a small rockery that he had just started to build, picked up a handful of stones he threw them all at the wooden lean-to. Surely if anyone was hiding behind it then they would automatically think that they had been spotted and open fire. He waited but nothing happened, slowly he inched his way forward, his finger on the trigger, hoping, just hoping and praying that at some point whoever it was that had attacked his house would make his move. As he approached the lean-to he held his breath straining to hear the sound of someone breathing. He slowly peered around the wooden support that the roof was fastened to, nothing. He looked along the ground and saw more blood, he moved forward and followed the trail of blood that led to the fence. Keeping as low to the ground as possible he moved to the fence, he could now see that there was blood all over the fence, 'the bastard has gone over it' he said to himself.

A sudden sound made Tony look up quickly. Screaming into view he could now see two Alouette helicopters as they flew over his front garden, they did a full circle of the farmhouse and then they dropped quickly to about five feet from the ground. Five fully-armed figures debussed and took up defensive positions. Immediately the men were on the ground the helicopter roared in to full power and took off again. Tony could see the gunner as he sat in the side of the helicopter moving his machine gun from side to side, looking for potential targets.

Tony shouted to the men who had just landed, they saw him, and beckoned for him to approach their position. Tony pointed to the body in the swimming pool, "A Bright Light" he yelled, "There is another one on the veranda." he said as he pointed again, this time towards the farmhouse.

"Anyone else killed or injured?" one of the Police Officers asked,

"No just the two of them, but my wife and son are in the house."

"OK go to them." the Officer said, "But keep them inside, it's not a pretty sight out here."

Tony checked on Joyce and Benji, then came back out., "They are all right." he said, "If you can leave some men at the farm, I will show you where the terr got over the fence. He is bleeding pretty badly so we should have no problems in following his trail."

"I would think it would be better if you stayed back here with your family, don't you worry we will get him for you" the police officer advised.

"No chance of that." said Tony, "I know this land better than anyone, just do as I ask, and leave a couple of your men here, it's my farm and my family that this bastard has attacked and it's going to be me that slots him."

Tony led the seven men out of the farm and along the outside of the perimeter fence. When he came to the spot where he had seen all the blood he first pointed to the fence and then he pointed down at the ground, "There," he said "Blood and plenty of it."

Overhead he could hear the sound of the helicopters as the rotors sliced through the air, hopefully they would either slow the terr down or spot him. Tony had taken up the position of lead scout and was pushing on through the thick bush, his heart was beating with excitement. This time everything was on his side, plenty of daylight left, the terr was wounded and would be moving slower. But like a wounded animal the threat of an ambush was now greater than ever. Behind him he heard a radio crackle, "Oscar Bravo this is Cyclone One do you read me over."

"Cyclone One this is Oscar Bravo I read loud and clear over."

"We have a sighting, I repeat we have a sighting. One African male with a weapon moving towards the thick wooded area just North of your position and about two hundred yards ahead of your position over."

"Read you Cyclone One over."

Tony changed direction slightly and headed north. He knew exactly where the thick wooded area was, he also knew that just past the wooded area there was a river, on the other side of which was almost impregnable bush. One thing was for sure he had to stop the terr from crossing the river. Increasing his pace to a trot he crashed through the bush, his legs were stinging from the scratches and cuts from the thorns and the branches of the bushes. As he looked down he could see that his legs were covered in blood, and small insects. The sweat on his body had now attracted hosts of the dreaded mopani flies, 'no time to try and brush them off' he thought as he pushed deeper into the thick bush.

Again the radio broke the silence "Oscar Bravo this is Cyclone One over. We have just seen the terr again and it looks as if he is heading for the river over, and is at present about three hundred yards from the river, do you want us to take him out when we see him again over?" Tony grabbed the handset, "Cyclone One, Cyclone One, do not make contact with the terr I repeat do not make contact over." Whatever happened, Tony knew that as from today there would be no more threats to his family, or farm from this man. He quickly looked to either side of him and saw the men running alongside of him, some of the faces seemed familiar but he just couldn't put a name to anyone of them. The Officer in charge of this unit seemed very focussed, and Tony felt confident that when push came to shove he would be able to rely on this one.

Tony held up his hand and stopped. He could hear the sounds of someone ahead of his position, suddenly the sound of gunfire, three shots and coming his way. Everyone hit the ground, again the sound of someone ahead of them but this time it was the sound of someone crashing through the bush. Again Tony was up and running, nothing else was in his mind except catching up with this terr. Suddenly the bush started to thin out and there ahead of him was the running figure about twenty feet from the river. It all seemed as if it was in slow motion, Tony's legs now felt as if they were made of lead, the figure in front of him was now in the water and wading in deeper and deeper. Suddenly as if he realised that he had no hope of escape, he stopped and turned. Tony was now no more than six feet away from him, both men stood there with their chests heaving as they drew in deep lungfuls of breath. Tony could now see the tall skinny frame, the thin-rimmed glasses, and the protruding front teeth. "Joshua," he shouted, "Camburo farm-does that mean anything to you?" Joshua made no answer, "Do you know who I am?" Tony shouted, "I'm the man who killed your friend Ticky."

Tony could see the hatred in Joshua's eyes, the front of his shirt was now covered in blood, 'nice one Joyce.' thought Tony, 'nice one.' Joshua raised his AK47 assault rifle, but before he could squeeze the trigger Tony gave him three shots of Triple A buck shot. Joshua's body was lifted out of the water and almost thrown onto the far side of the river. Tony waded into the river, the red water swirling around his legs. He reached down and grabbed Joshua's right arm and saw the long scar running down from his elbow to his wrist, he dragged the body out of the water and dropped onto his knees with exhaustion.

"Bloody hell you are one determined son of a bitch." a voice said, Tony smiled, "I've waited a long time for this moment." he said "And no one was going to take it from me."

Once the body had been put aboard one of the helicopters, the men decided to walk back to the farm rather than wait for the other helicopter Tony, who just wanted to get back to his family, thanked each man for his help and got on board.

Back at the farm the pool had been drained, and the bodies of the two Bright Lights had been airlifted back to Bindura. As Tony jumped down off the helicopter, he walked quickly towards the farmhouse. Standing on the veranda he could see the familiar faces not only of Joyce and his son Benji, but of Colin, Alex, Buz, and Ken all in full battle dress. "You lot are a bit late." he said with a smile as he put his arms around Joyce,

"We only heard about it half an hour ago and were told that everything was under control. When we heard that it was all over we decided to come to the farm and take care of your family until you returned." said Buz

Tony shook hands with his men, "Thanks" he said, "I really appreciate your support" He bent down and picked up his son and put his arm around Joyce's waist, "One thing is for sure Joshua won't be bothering us ever again."

Chapter Twenty-Nine

For the next two weeks Tony and Joyce tried to get their lives back to normal again. Tony cleaned the swimming pool out, but doubted if it would ever be used again. The topic of conversation was mainly about what might or might not have happened. Their thoughts often dwelled on David and his bravery in trying to save them whilst suffering from horrific injuries. With deep regret Tony voiced his opinion that if Bob had only taken his rifle, then maybe, just maybe the Bright Lights would still be with them.

It was now six weeks since the event, and both Tony and Joyce wanted to say a big thank you to everyone who had been involved that day. So they arranged to have a braai on Sunday of next week. Once planned, the invitations went out the only person who couldn't make it was Mike, but it all went ahead anyway. As usual the first to arrive was Buz, Colin, and their families, followed by Ken and Alex, wives and children. It was a very emotional time meeting the men who had gone with Tony that day, but soon the memories were temporarily forgotten as the drinks flowed and everyone got stuck into the meal. In a companionable silence the women contemplated the magnificence of the setting sun. Meanwhile the men, putting the horrors of the previous weeks temporarily out of their minds, laughed uproariously at somebody's joke. Eventually with surreptitious glances at watches the party began to break up. Couples gathering their children, heading for home before full dark.

As the last couple said goodbye, and their tail light disappeared, Tony locked the main gates and sat down on the veranda. His two new Bright Lights had done five stints before this one, and seemed really switched on. Tony pulled no punches about what had happened and why, but after a few days he felt that they were two men that he could rely on. "Do you remember the last party that we had?" Joyce asked,

"How can I forget it," said Tony, "Alan and Karen were murdered that night, it only seems as if it was such a short time ago" he said,

"Let's hope that it doesn't happen again tonight." she said,

"No chance," said Tony "They have the security fencing and the farm guards, and now everyone is on the alert. Don't worry about it." he said, reassuringly.

"The farm guards and the security fence didn't stop Joshua." she replied,

"You're just being paranoid," said Tony, "Here let me get you another drink."

"Make it a double." she said with a nervous smile.

Tony came back into the room and put her glass of brandy on the coffee table, "I've filled it up with ice." he said,

She picked it up and took a sip, "Hell Tony that's a strong one."

"You need a strong one so get it down your neck and stop worrying." He went to the window and moved the curtains slightly, to observe the two Bright Lights sitting on the veranda in the shadows. "Just relax love everything is OK." He lifted his glass and took a mouthful of brandy, he had just put the glass down when the phone rang. Both he and Joyce looked at each other, "Who can that be?" she said "At this time of night."

"We will soon find out." he said as he got out of his chair and picked up the phone, "Hi Tony here." he said, "You missed a great party Mike. But anyway what can I do for you, it must be important for you to call at this time of the night."

"Well I've been in Salisbury all day with the Commissioner and just as I was about to leave to return to Bindura he got a phone call saying that a large number of terrorists had been spotted in the Mount Darwin area. Troops were sent out immediately and fierce fighting has been reported in the surrounding areas. It looks as if the five hundred terrs who disappeared from the Mozambique terrorist camp a few weeks ago may have surfaced. On my return to the office I rang the Commissioner and reports are now coming in that Mount Darwin has been overrun and the Police Station is on fire. No contact can be made with Centenary at all, neither by telephone nor by radio, and Umvukwes has also come under heavy attack. I am afraid that this may be the big push the terrorists have been talking about for a long time. Can you do me a favour Tony?"

"Of course I can all you have to do is ask…

"Hello Mike, are you there? Mike can you hear me? Mike!" Tony pulled the phone away from his ear as a huge explosion almost burst his eardrum. He slowly put the phone back to his ear, "Hello Mike are you there? Mike, Mike." Tony moved the phone from his ear and just looked at it, the line had gone dead.

GLOSSARY OF
RHODESIAN MILITARY TERMS

BRIGHTLIGHTS	Police Reserve
CALLSIGN	Radio Identification Number or Letter
CASAVAC	Casualty Evacuation
CLICK	Unit of measurement – distance – one kilometre
CYCLONE	Air force
CRUSADER	Army
FLOT	Forward Line of Troops
FN	7.62 caliber, long cartridge, semi or automatic rifle
J.O.C	Joint Operational Command
K-CAR	Alouette helicopter armed with 20mm cannon – Kill Car
LZ	Landing Zone
MANZI	Water
OP	Observation Post
P.A.T.U.	Police Anti Terrorist Unit
POUND THE AREA	Drop bombs
RAT PACK	Government issue Ration Pack

RPG	Rocket Propelled Grenade
S.A.S	Elite 'behind the scenes' Special Air Service' troops
2IC	2nd In Command
SELOUS SCOUTS	*Government troops who dress and look like Terr(s)
Sit. Rep	Situation Report
SLOT	To Shoot
STICK	A patrol unit
TAKE THEM OUT	Kill them
TERR(s)	General word for terrorist(s)

Note:
*Selous Scouts were the ultimate in bush-warfare special forces. Operating during the Rhodesian war in the 1970's they were responsible for 68% of all enemy casualties